R I N S E D
(THE LONDON TRILOGY)

THE WATTLE & DAUBE
DETECTIVE AGENCY

BOOK ONE

Tim Siddall

Rinsed
Tim Siddall

ISBN 9781912821488
Published 2019 by Tricorn Books 131 High Street, Old Portsmouth PO1 2HW
www.tricornbooks.co.uk
Printed & bound in UK

Contents

RINSED

Chapter 1

Frank Wattle and Roger Daube had met by accident. Wattle was a man of the streets, schooled in all the tricks that life in south east London teaches you. He was quick witted, sharp, savvy, and a little overweight.

Daube was tall and slim, privately educated, eloquent, and academically clever. He adored puzzles, riddles, crosswords and intellectual exercises. He was the strategist to Wattle's street know how. Together, they made one heck of a team. They were the Wattle and Daube Detective Agency.

The year was 2085, and London was still raining. Umbrellas were still umbrellas & black was still the trendy colour of choice. As Wattle looked gloomily out of his Piccadilly window, a message appeared on his retina. It was from his colleague Daube.

'Are you having a cheesy hot-dog with onions, ketchup and fries as usual Wattle?' - Frank blinked twice for yes and erased the message. Mildly annoyed by Roger's double checking on his preferred lunch when he was never, and I repeat never, ever going to have Sushi – cold slimy fish; no thanks. Frank Wattle continued his scanning of the electronic newspapers.

The Wattle and Daube Detective Agency had been formed five years ago by a chance meeting between two strangers in the mega city that is 21st century London. Daube had just arrived home from a three-hour shuttle flight from Australia, and was boarding the trans-continental urban speed shuttle from London International Airport to Covent Garden Interstellar Terminus.

'You've been skimmed mate', said an earthy accented voice

7

just behind Daube.

'Excuse me', replied a well-spoken & immaculately dressed slim man in his early forties.

'You've been skimmed mate', came the response again.

'I've been....... What did you just say – skimmed?'.

'That's right mate - skimmed. Well and truly skimmed', said Wattle.

'And just what is this skimmed thing?', asked Daube.

'Skimming, skimmed, to be skimmed. You know mate - fleeced, robbed, taken advantage of, if you know what I mean.

'I'm afraid I don't', said Daube.

'You've just had your credit card details skimmed. Give it another twenty minutes and your cards are going to be used all over Central London', Wattle explained.

'Impossible my good fellow - you see.........," and so it went on. Twenty minutes later however, and over a coffee and a London bun, a chance meeting between Frank Wattle and Roger Daube had turned into the start of a friendship that was to culminate in the creation of The Wattle and Daube Detective Agency.

Ocean Jones was bright. Perhaps too bright for her own good. She could work out complex computer algorithms, and was an exceptional 'gamer'. Although she was only fourteen, she was advanced for her age and brilliant when it came to anything technical and electronic. Apart from that, she was your typical curious teenager. Facially, she was a carbon copy of her mother, Molly. She had straight black hair, cut into a shiny bob with a streak of blue, green eyes and an oval shaped face with a smile that appeared to turn downwards. Purple ankle boots with a distinctive yellow lightning motif, red tights and a lime green post-punk hoodie completed the look.

She lived with her mother and grandmother in North London, and although she would never admit it to anyone; she missed her father. Ocean Jones had been raised by two fiercely independent women, who had both been let down by various male characters. This state of affairs had influenced Ocean Jones's behavior towards the opposite sex, and on a rainy November Monday in 2085, she had no inkling that a chance encounter with a male stranger in the Oriental district would alter her life forever.

As Ocean Jones contemplated her history homework for the forthcoming week, she glanced across the street and witnessed a visible thought bubble (VTB). The release of this information, from a stranger, was a huge disappointment to Ocean. 'I must find my green shirt,' was of absolutely no interest to her. Admittedly, she was now capable of sporadically engaging with another human's inner thought process, but a meaningless VTB wasn't enough. Ocean knew she was close to cracking the concentration required to tap in to another person's inner world, but intermittent VTB's were next to useless unless she could apply this mental skill to targeted individuals.

She sighed, and waited to board the 79 hyper-bus. This, one-hundred metre long machine hovered in the air at child's height and was near silent. No air contamination and no congestion, as the hyper-bus could rise to twenty metres above the road to avoid traffic. Each purple coloured bus could carry up to one thousand passengers, and with eye recognition pre-payment, the triple floored bus could board and disembark passengers without lengthy queues.

Ocean climbed up to the third floor, and sat on one of the few remaining seats available. The number 79 hyper-bus travelled from North London to the Oriental quarter in the teeming metropolis of London. Ten stops and a journey time of fifteen minutes, gave Ocean enough time to charge her devices through the seat charge pads, and to contemplate what she intended to do when she finally arrived at Memory Lane.

The hyper-bus swooshed through the city of over fifty million people and another ten million robots and laser lizards, moving effortlessly through i-spy travel holograms and digital adverts that tracked your thoughts and aspirations. The 79 bus route was one of Ocean's favourite journey's. It passed the famous London landmark, 'Brittles of London'. The shop was in the shape of a glass jar and lines of people stood outside the iconic building, waiting patiently to buy exquisite chocolate letters of the alphabet for a 'name-day' celebration. Only the wealthy could afford them, and as her mother wasn't rich, she had never been given a chocolate capital letter O and J for her birthday.

What you've never had you don't miss, thought Ocean, pragmatically.

The hyper-bus passed through Oxford Circus, with its hundreds of glass walkways crisscrossing the street far below, and the enormous People's Pleasure Palace (PPP), before finally entering the busy Oriental quarter.

Ocean hopped off the bus and stood for a few moments taking in all the frenetic activity going on around her. She gripped her pack of 'Tasty Stretch' chewing gum and thought about her next move. A laser lizard in a hurry brushed past her, snapping Ocean out of her reverie, and it was only then that she happened to make accidental eye contact with a thin tall man in an immaculate suit. Ocean looked down to avoid appearing rude, and noticed his black brogue shoes. They were spotless.

'Excuse me please, young lady,'

The voice was polished, calm and yet strangely beguiling.

Ocean looked up obediently, which was most unlike her. She

had been conditioned by her mother to be wary and skeptical of men, and yet this voice invited her to listen.

'Oh, yes, I'm sorry,' she said.

'Thank you so much. My goodness. It is so noisy and chaotic down here. One can hardly hear oneself think. Now, don't get lost in this maze of narrow lanes and alleys.'

The stranger smiled kindly, and gripping his umbrella, he walked off into a throng of moving objects. It was Ocean's first meeting with a man who was going to change the whole course of her life. It was none other than Roger Daube.

Ocean collected her thoughts, and wished deeply that she could see this man's visible thought bubbles. It was too late. He had vanished into the mix of humanity and machines that made up the Oriental quarter. A message from her mother flickered across her retina, and in an instant, that fleeting encounter with Roger Daube was gone.

Ocean began navigating herself around the tightly packed streets that made up this particular part of East London and once again she was the determined, feisty 4teen-year old on a mission.

Chapter 2

188 Piccadilly was an upmarket swanky address for a small detective agency. The grand façade of the building was a stone's throw from Piccadilly Circus, and ideally located for any passing trade. Unfortunately for Roger Daube, the damp top floor office space they rented was situated next to a noisy elevator shaft, a temperamental talking vending machine, and a leaking roof. It was less than ideal.

Yes, it was a fabulous address in central London, but being crammed into a smallish room with damp and heat issues was challenging at best, and depressing at worst.

Wattle was one of life's eternal optimists. His glass was always half full, and through his extensive network of contacts, he had managed to acquire the lease for 188 Piccadilly. Admittedly the space was tiny, but location was everything, and within a five-minute walk of the office was a teeming metropolitan hub. The massive digital advertisements of Piccadilly Circus glowed 24/7 through rain and shine. whilst elevated magnetic walkways transported workers into the seething urban mass of Soho.

Tucked away in a small lane just off Regent Street, the premises of Flowers & Sons stood wedged in beside a Japanese noodle bar and a Korean dry-cleaners. The shop had been a family institution for five generations of Flowers, but with no sons and three daughters, Reg Flowers was resigned to the fact that he was the last in a long line of tailors. Frank Wattle had been a friend for years, and no matter what type of suit he wore, it always appeared crumpled and creased and gave the appearance of having been slept in, (usually because it had). Hand-made suits were out of his price bracket.

'So, I'm never going to look like Roger Daube', mused Wattle. Roger Daube's tailoring requirements were taken care of on Saville Row. He was a meticulous individual, and his attention to detail was legendary. Each morning Wattle had to endure the drama that was 'straight and flat'. Straight being the precise angle of Daube's tie, and flat, the exact position it lay in relation to his shirt and collar. It was exhausting to witness. He had garnered a reputation for detail at a top public school, and it was his measured and thoughtful insights at the detective agency, that allowed his partner, Frank Wattle, to pound the streets of London, talking to his extensive network of contacts and spies.

Reg Flowers had been providing useful bits of information to Wattle for years. It never ceased to amaze him, just how much gossip was garnered by measuring a customer for a new suit. An alert on his retina, informed him, that Frank Wattle was popping by for a quick chat. He instructed his robotics assistant to put the kettle on for a brew, and gathered his thoughts in preparation for his friend's visit.

Face recognition software accepted, Wattle entered Flowers and Sons. Immediately, upon entering the shop, you were a million miles away from the bustle and noise of London. Soothing lighting, soft fabrics and lush armchairs induced a feeling of happiness and contentment. An electronic shoe lizard, removed his footwear, and as he padded over to the counter where Reg Flowers stood examining a roll of cloth, his toes sunk into the luxurious carpet.

'Frank – lovely to see you. Make yourself at home', cooed Reg, as he beckoned Frank to a sumptuous looking armchair. 'London tea?'.

'Don't mind if I do Reg', replied Frank, as he relaxed into a velvet chair.

Conversation flowed easily between these two South London boys.

'So, Reg, any tittle tattle, tit-bits? Anything that might tickle my fancy?', asked Frank.

'Well, now that you mention it Frank, there was one story that caught my attention. Nothing out of the ordinary, really, but it just stuck in my mind'.

'Go on Reg', said Frank, taking a large gulp of strong London tea.

'Well as I said, it doesn't sound very interesting, but you never know do you? You, being the sleuth & all that. A customer of mine, by the name of Mr. Leaf, was telling me about some incidents over at The Pyramid department store. Nothing sensational, like. Just bits and pieces'.

'Go on Reg', said Frank.

'Well, he was saying, that there have been some unusual sightings involving a toy monkey. Not one sighting, but several, over the course of a few weeks, and always between midnight and one.'

'Toy monkey, you say? Are you sure? Wattle paused.

'I see – interesting. Could be something. One never knows does one Reg?'.

The conversation carried on in that vein, until the tea had been drunk, and all pleasantries, exchanged.

Back at the detective agency, lunch had arrived in the form of Roger Daube. After depositing Wattle's greasy looking food, he carefully cleared a space on his desk to eat. His routine never altered. First, he wet wiped his desk area, then he arranged his sushi box so it was just to his liking, and only then, would he open his can of warm green tea.

Two minutes later, Frank Wattle returned from his chat with Reg Flowers. 'Smells good Roger – not your revolting cold fish, my delectable hot dog.'

Daube smiled and gave a wry look that said (heard it all before Frank), and continued to sip from his can of green tea.

It would have been impossible, to meet two, more different, men. Wattle was as disheveled, as Daube was spotless.

Partly, this was down to Wattle having a preference for, the 'Sleep 'n' Eat' chain of convenience beds in the city, for when he was working late. Daube, could not see the appeal of squeezing yourself into a coffin sized hole in the wall, and being woken by a computerized automated breakfast of your choice. Then again, it was easy to be disdainful of such budget sleeping arrangements, when he had a three-story town mansion in Mayfair to return to after a hard day at work.

Commuting was tiring, and after all the various toxins Wattle had consumed during the day, shoe-horning oneself into an airless box and being served the equivalent of space dust for breakfast, didn't seem such a bad proposition, after all. It was that, or sleeping under his desk with the neon glare of Piccadilly Circus to keep him company for the night. He didn't complain.

'I've just had a quick pow-wow with Reg Flowers,' said Wattle. 'He has heard of some unusual night time activity over at The Pyramid department store. It appears that......,' the rest of his sentence was drowned out, by the i-spy travel hologram announcement.

Londoner's, had become accustomed, to the horizon stretching hologram on the skyline, in the shape of a black taxi, broadcasting its hourly travel information. The internal combustion engine, was a relic of the past, but the famous black London cab, was still fondly remembered by the general public.

'I didn't catch the last part of your sentence,' said Daube.

'I was saying,' said Wattle, 'that there has been an unusual sighting of a toy monkey, over at The Pyramid.'

'How unusual?' asked Daube, his attention now fully engaged.

'I don't know,' replied Wattle, 'But enough for a few people to start making comments. Shall I do a bit of asking around?'

'Good idea Wattle. No harm in a bit of preliminary, investigative digging.'

Where-upon, both men, ate their respective meals.

Lunch finished, Frank Wattle decided to go for a walk, over to Oxford Street. 'Just going to do a spot of fact checking, Rog,' said Wattle.

There was no reply. It could mean only one thing. After lunch, Daube indulged in twenty minutes of reading from the mind-mag in-brain digital library. Russian classics were his thing, and Wattle knew better than to interrupt his friend and colleague, when he was enjoying a reading scan. His mind was miles away. Quietly, Wattle slipped on his creased overcoat, took an umbrella from the stand by the door, and departed, in to the rain and chaos of central London.

Chapter 3

Molly, at Bond Street tube station was having a bad day. She had already had a row with Ocean before breakfast, and caught a cold from Ocean's grandmother, Gwen. She recalled the argument;

'Dad left you mum. Get over it,' shouted Ocean.

It had been building – this mother/daughter tension.

'Move on and get a life ok,' continued Ocean. 'I'm sick and tired of 'dad did this, dad did that'. It was year's ago'.

The silence in the room was deafening.

'You've no idea just how difficult it has been raising a child on your own,' replied Molly quietly.

'I've heard this story a hundred times mum.'

'Well I'm sorry I've been boring you all these years,' said Molly sarcastically.

The row was in danger of erupting again.

'Mum – listen. It's not that it is boring, and it is boring by the way. It's just that nothing has changed in your outlook. Dad went away when I was still a baby, and here we are thirteen years later, still discussing him.'

'You don't understand Ocean, and I'm guessing you never will.'

This statement hurt Ocean, but she wasn't going to let it register. If she showed vulnerability now, her mother would gain the upper hand.

'Save your pity for grandma. I have a life to lead, and I'm not going to let you drag me down mum,' said Ocean emphatically, before she walked out of the kitchen and slammed the door.

At work, Molly's robotics assistant, Kendall, had malfunctioned and shut herself down. It was going to be a long Monday at the super-ground station.

Outside on Oxford Street, it was still raining, and the sky was so overcast and dark, that all the neon signs were on. Giant digital adverts that tracked your thoughts and aspirations followed pedestrians along the congested pavement. The human rush of office workers heading back to work after their lunch break was never ending, and as each batch of weary humans headed back to the towering skyscrapers of Soho, Molly was resigned to a busy and demanding start to her week.

'Why am I doing this job', she thought to herself, as swathes of people entered and left the station. I have a degree in IT, a higher degree in robotics engineering, and my 4teen-year old daughter is a certified computer nerd, and here I am watching London's commuters file in and out of one of the world's busiest transport hubs. What am I doing with myself? Before Molly had had time to answer this question, a very luminous character, inappropriately dressed for the time of year, appeared on her monitor.

Ronnie Bronze stood out. Whether this was intentional, is open to debate, but a combination of orange skin and a sharp fitting mohair suit drew her attention to him. To say he glowed was an understatement. Amongst all the somberly dressed people around him, he was a riot of colour.

Molly watched him, as he walked out of the station and on to the teeming pavement of Oxford Street. He disappeared below the suspended monorail which hovered above the pedestrians. The only clue as to his destination was a large blue Pyramid bag which swung from his left arm. Molly thought no more about the vision that was Ronnie Bronze, and returned to the more pressing problem of rebooting her robotics assistant Kendal.

The sky darkened to pitch black, and even the most positive of weather watchers would have agreed, that Monday 10th November 2085 was not a great day. This did not impact on Wattle's state of mind in the slightest. He was in a fine mood, and loved London, when the dayglow neon colours reflected off the wet paving stones and window panes, to create one beautiful colour saturated maze. It just added to the visual diversity that was his city.

A retina message from Daube, caused Wattle to stop at the junction of New Bond Street and Brook Street. He scanned the info Daube had just sent him, blinked twice for yes, and carried on to The Pyramid department store. Rain aside, the building was a magnificent spectacle to behold. The large Doric columns that fronted the store gleamed in the low light, and the external spiral escalator to the pleasure garden on the roof only enhanced the sense of drama as the weary shopper stopped at the store entrance, to admire the grand scale of one of London's premier shopping destinations.

Mood extraction stalls were positioned inside the ground floor area to ensure customers selected the right 'experience'. Wattle moved quickly through the 'emotion zone', and headed for the fifty fifth floor. He wanted to talk with Mr. Leaf, the floor manager for robotics. He had something important on his mind, and the message Daube had sent him, made it essential that he have a word, as quickly as possible.

Chapter 4

The next day arrived, and with it, a job Frank Wattle had been dreading. He had been delaying his annual health scan, but on the insistence of Mrs Wattle (mother of six), he had reluctantly agreed that this week he would undertake the procedure. Unlike Daube, who actually looked forward to his medical, Wattle considered it a precious waste of twenty seconds; for that was how long it took to place both palms on the ATM pad and wait for the full body scan. As the health report printed, Wattle could only longingly think of two fried eggs on toast with a strong beaker of London tea to wash it all down. He would live to a ripe old age, he thought.

Roger Daube on the other hand, obsessed about his weight, and with his 'homebot' Michael, underwent excruciating cardiovascular exercises each morning before work. Admittedly, he was in fine shape for a forty one year old single man, but was he happy? thought Wattle.

Health check completed and recommendations duly noted, Wattle pootled off to his favourite hole in the wall egg joint. The Yolk of York was so small you could blink and miss it. Squeezed into a minute space next to a retina repair shop, it made a booth appear spacious. Spatial considerations aside, what came off the sizzling hot plates behind the owner Tony Tanner, were eggs of the highest order. Whichever way you wanted your eggs, Tony would deliver.

'Two eggs easy over Tony, and a nice strong cup of your London tar, please.'
'Not your usual then Frank?'
'Easy over today please, Tony'
'Easy Over coming right up Frank. Mrs Wattle doing good?'

enquired Tony

'In rude health Tony. In rude health'

'Glad to hear it Frank. Two eggs coming right up.'

His hunger sated for the moment, Frank Wattle gulped the last dregs from his mug of London tea, waved cheerily to Tony, and sauntered off into the crowded streets of the city.

Roger Wattle's relationship with his 'homebot' robot was complex. Michael was the only moving thing that Daube allowed into his extremely tidy house. Arguments about cleanliness aside, all Michael wanted to do was go out and be sociable. He was a friendly 'homebot'. However, all Daube wanted to do at the end of a long working day was shut the front door and forget the noise and madness of London in 2085. Daube had even decided against an electronic shoe lizard, on the grounds that what if it was messy. Therefore, shoe duties belonged to Michael.

One of the benefits of owning a town house on Farm Street, Mayfair, W1, was that it was ideally located in central London, the small street itself, was tucked discreetly behind Berkeley Square and very quiet, especially at night. It was an upmarket address, and Daube was well aware that he was very fortunate. He had inherited a trust fund at the age of ten, and although technically, an orphan (his mother had died in childbirth and his father was still away on a space mission for sixty years), life had been financially kind, to Daube.

Because of his good fortune, he had been educated at one of England's most prestigious schools. This, coupled with a degree from Oxford University, had opened doors to him that were not available to his hard-working friend and colleague, Frank Wattle. To compensate, Daube kept the detective agency financially afloat. Every three months, he injected cash into the business, because in

21

the five years of its existence, the agency had never turned a profit.

Wattle was blissfully unaware of the financial state of the business, as Daube took care of all financial matters, and he would have been startled to know, that his monthly salary was actually taken care of by Daube himself. Roger Daube, was an honest and moral individual, and he was certainly not going to let his colleague suffer. Especially when he worked so hard to feed his family.

Daube was busy at his desk when Wattle breezed through the door brandishing his health check print out.

'Another year of outstanding health my friend. I'm in fabulous condition. I've never felt better, truth be told, and to celebrate, I've just quaffed two of Tony Tanner's finest eggs 'easy over.' Wattle, was beaming from ear to ear.

'Well I'm relieved to hear it,' replied Daube.

'Thanks Rog – much appreciated.'

'You're welcome Wattle. Now, please tell me how your encounter with Mr. Leaf went yesterday, and I do hope you resisted the temptation to try out an 'experience' in the 'emotion' zone?'

Wattle sunk his bottom into a chair beside Daube's desk, and began to describe what he had been up to, including in graphic detail, his experience in the 'emotion' zone.

Tuesday came and went, and at last Roger Daube could close his front door and relax. Michael the 'homebot', had cooked up a low carb dinner for two, as he always dined with his master. After rinsing and drying the plates in the 'cleanomat', he made his owner a Chinese jasmine pearl tea, and served it to him in the library. Heat regeneration slippers on, Daube closed his eyes. He deleted all unnecessary emails from his retina, and set his eyes to snooze mode.

Chapter 5

As Molly made her way home on Tuesday evening, she thought about all the amusing comments and observations her daughter Ocean had made recently, and particularly about the weather. Her journey home involved a brisk walk to Covent Garden Interstellar Terminal, where she boarded the North-South Urban Shuttle to her home in Muswell Hill. From the station, it was a short five-minute walk to her small terraced house on Pepper Lane.

At this time of year, and on a clear night, Molly enjoyed gazing up at the clear night sky, and looking at the intergalactic vapour trails. Personally, she had no desire to move to Saturn, but as the cost of space travel had diminished, more and more Londoners were leaving the city for a new start on the planet. As she opened the bright red door to her home, she was met by an inviting aroma of smells. Molly's mother Gwen, was cooking dinner in the kitchen, accompanied by Ocean in a cooking apron embossed with the words 'GIRL POWER', and baseball cap.

Back at 188 Piccadilly, Wattle was doing 'a late one'. He had messaged Mrs. Wattle, and explained the situation. He would be working deep into the night, and was it alright if he slept at the 'Sleep 'n Eat' convenience bed chain over at Leicester Square? Having been given the ok, by Mrs. Wattle, Frank had settled into his night routine. Shoes off, suit jacket discarded, tie loosened and both shirt sleeves rolled up, he was hunched over a stack of take-away menus.

London was an epic town to eat in, but just what to eat was occupying his mind. He flicked through the menus which encompassed cuisine from around the globe. From A to Z, you could eat anything you wanted in London 2085, and there was food to suit any budget. Finally, Wattle decided on pizza, and retina messaged Alfredo's, on the corner of Lower Regent Street.

Ten hungry minutes later, a delivery lizard brought his extra-large pizza to the office. Wattle devoured it in under five minutes flat.

The London lizard fraternity was separated in to a caste system. At the bottom was the humble electronic shoe lizard. Higher up was the industrious and hardworking delivery lizard (typically employed in the catering and hotel trade), and at the top came the lounge lizard. As the delivery lizard exited the office, Wattle could just hear the temperamental talking vending machine giving some impudent comments to the delivery lizard. Phrases like; 'And who do you think you are?' and 'Well really – and at this time of night,' wafted over to Wattle, as he settled down to some serious researching.

As the clock chimes of St. James's church signaled midnight, Wattle decided to call it a day. He popped his crumpled suit jacket on, and walked over to the 'Sleep 'n' Eat' chain at Leicester Square. As he passed the late-night revelers, he marveled at the diversity that was 21st century London. Digital adverts were still tracking people's thoughts and aspirations as they made their way home, but at least the rain had stopped.

Having reached his destination, Wattle placed a hand on the track pad and hand recognition software brought up his personal details. One standard economy bed, digestible tooth paste, and a powdered full English breakfast. He paid and pressed 'eject' on number 32. A small bed slowly opened out of the wall. He had paid for economy, and economy was what was in front of him. Wattle stared momentarily at the thin narrow shape of the tiny bed, squeezed himself in and pressed 'close'. He disappeared into the wall that was the 'Sleep 'n' Eat' convenience bed. He was asleep in seconds.

Chapter 6

Ronnie Bronze was part of the London criminal underworld. He had history. Twice he had experienced mind extraction – the process where your mind is digitally removed and extracted to a digital prison vault for the length of the prison service, whilst the body is shipped to Siberia. Twice he had returned to London and resumed his criminal activity. The privately owned prison company KEYS had reluctantly been forced to transport bodies to Siberia, because of the sheer number of people crowded into English prisons.

Thirty years ago, when digital mind extraction was a new phenomenon, KEYS had bar coded the criminal's forehead in bright yellow for the duration of the mind removal. This allowed harmless criminals to move around society with a visible warning attached to their head. However, the population of London now exceeded fifty million people, and there simply wasn't the space to accommodate criminals without their minds. The solution of removing them to Siberia, where there was plenty of space, was regarded by the government as a success story. The streets of London were free of mindless bodies, and when the prison sentence had been served, the body was returned to England, and the mind restored to its owner.

Admittedly, the main flaw to mind extraction was that the same mind was returned to the same body. Early trials had erased the mind, (a process called 'Rinsing') therefore eradicating the potential for repeat offending, but human rights lawyers had overturned the decision in 2055, and now the mind was returned in exactly the same state as it had been extracted.

The first of Ronnie Bronze's prison sentences was for stealing. The second was for credit card and finger print skimming. He had run a slick network of scammers within the white dome, the huge shopping complex that surrounded Oxford Circus. One hundred floors of retail shopping and leisure activities inside a massive transparent dome that was visible from Space. It was the perfect location for Ronnie and his gang to operate within.

The many walkways that connected the Oxford Circus dome to the surrounding streets and surroundings were an ideal place to steal shopper's personal details. In a cashless society (physical money had been virtually abandoned in the year 2050), only cards and finger print recognition technology existed as a means of currency. Fortunately, Ronnie and his cronies had been caught, but now he was back in the capital and planning his next and biggest illegal enterprise.

Michael the 'homebot' was an early riser, which was just as well, as Daube liked to be woken at 6.00am precisely. The morning routine was planned down to the last detail. First, Michael presented Daube with a cup of jasmine white pearl tea, brewed for precisely two and a half minutes. He then set the exercise mats out in the small gym in the basement, and together they stretched and exercised for twenty minutes.

Daube then had a shower and selected one of his seven bespoke Saville Row suits, (one suit for each day of the week) with a tie chosen by Michael with appropriate cuff links, before sitting down to his breakfast. Unsweetened muesli with semi skimmed milk, blueberries and slices of strawberry was followed by a slice of whole grain toast with butter and apricot conserve from 'Jams of London'. Michael had the same.

Brushing any toast crumbs from his chin, Daube quaffed a double espresso, which was made to his exacting standards by Michael, from his expensive imported Italian coffee machine. He then drank a small cup of cold water to cleanse his palate, cleaned his teeth and walked out of his front door, at exactly 7.00am.

London was teeming with people. The energy and vitality of a city on the go was palpable. Daube walked carefully through Mayfair until he reached Green Park, where he took a left turn and continued towards Piccadilly. The fifteen-minute walk allowed Daube to observe London at first hand. It was Wattle who was the man on the ground, sniffing out possible leads and connections, whilst Daube toiled studiously in the cramped office, working out strategy.

He enjoyed his walk to work, watching mobile machines clean and polish shop window fronts, food deliveries arriving by drones to restaurants and hotels, and the buzz and noise of commercial activity. This was a city with a purpose, a city with a beating heart. It was his city, and a town he was proud to identify with.

Daube arrived at 188 Piccadilly, and immediately his mood changed. As he waited for the elevator to whisk him to the fifth floor, he couldn't help but notice just how smart the building and ground floor foyer were, in contrast to the rather grubby space that was leased in the name of The Wattle and Daube Detective Agency. Appearances could certainly be deceptive.

As the elevator doors opened, he avoided eye contact with the talking vending machine, and let himself into the office. The evidence of Wattle's late-night pizza fest lay in a bin by his desk.

Chapter 7

Roger Daube always liked to collect his thoughts for a few moments, before preparing his work-space for the day ahead. His desk was a screen divided into eight smaller screens. In front of him was relayed the world news, weather reports, stock market data and police crime reports. Leaning back in his orthopedic chair, Daube surveyed his territory and considered what to do about the toy monkey story. He needed to talk to Wattle. He didn't have to wait long.

Frank Wattle walked past Daube, and looked like he needed ironing. To say his suit was crumpled was an under-statement. 'Sleep 'n' Eat?' asked Daube.

'Sleep 'n' Eat' came the flat reply.

'Why?'

'Because I needed the space to think. I wanted some peace and quiet,' said Wattle.

'I see,' said Daube, who had no real understanding of the need for peace and quiet, as he lived in a large town house with only Michael his 'homebot' for company.

'I needed to think Rog. Time alone if you know what I mean? ' Daube didn't.

'The conversation I had with Mr. Leaf over at The Pyramid got me thinking.'

'Go on,' said Daube listening intently.

'Well Rog, as you well know, I'm partial to the occasional 'emotional experience'. So, after my chat with him, I decided to try out the new mind extraction pod in the 'emotion' zone.'

'Wattle. you didn't?'

'I did Rog.'

'And?' asked Daube fearing the worst.

'Well, you know what? It wasn't half bad. I expected my mind to be completely blown away. But nothing of the sort. You just go sort of blank. All woolly like.'

'I hope it was worth it,' said Daube dryly.

'It was kind of an out of body experience Rog. Most peculiar, truth be told.' Where upon, Wattle walked over to the temperamental talking vending machine by the elevator and pressed several buttons, which delivered him an extremely strong black Turkish coffee.

Later that same day, Daube was still reflecting on what Wattle had told him about the 'emotion zone'. Mood enhancement was a popular leisure activity in London, and all the major shopping venues offered the service. However, there was just one special place that delivered an experience that Daube dare not think about. Memory Lane, where it was possible to buy shards of memory experience.

It was a narrow dark street, and easily missed if you didn't know what you were looking for. Well away from the west end, and popular tourist destinations, Memory Lane was as old as London itself. The district was Shoreditch, but no Memory Lane existed on any street maps of London. You had to know how to enter the memory zone, and that was a well-kept secret.

A member at Daube's St James's Lexington Club, had once told him how to enter Memory Lane, but it had sounded so far-fetched that Daube had given it little thought, until now. Apparently, you had to have the right conviction and strength of desire to enter Memory Lane. Should he try it for himself? Daube's mouth went dry at the prospect, and his heart began to pound.

I mustn't let on to Wattle what I'm thinking of doing, Daube thought to himself. He trembled with excitement. As luck would have it, Wattle was out of the office dealing with another case, and so Daube put on his coat and left the building. Piccadilly Circus was all noise and colour, as Daube hailed a drone. It was a very expensive mode of transport, and one he rarely used, but needs must as the saying goes, and ten minutes later, the drone had delivered him to Shoreditch, on a frenetic late Wednesday afternoon.

Stepping out of the drone, Daube realized he was in a quarter of London he hardly knew existed. It was the Oriental district, where Japanese, Korean's, Chinese, Vietnamese and Cambodian's vied with each other for passing trade. The electronics stores hummed and throbbed with activity, whilst the packed pavements were home to dozens of street food stalls. Steam vents from below thrust spurts of hot air into the sky, and delicious smells assaulted his senses. It was a world away from his home on Farm Street.

Daube looked on in amazement and awe at the energy and manic activity all around him. An advert attempted to lock on to his wave-length, followed by two exotic holiday travel commercials which tried to attach themselves to Daube's thoughts and aspirations. He determinedly shut them out and focussed his mind on the task ahead. He began to weave himself through the moving mass of people, when he abruptly stopped. Straight in front of him was the same teenage girl. He recognised the vivid blue stripe through her black cropped hair and her distinctive purple boots from his brief encounter with her two days ago. Unintentionally, he locked eyes with her, and for the briefest of moments saw two pure green eyes stare right through him. It was an intense moment, but the impact was scorched into Daube's mind. A second later, and she was gone. She had vanished into the seething mass of the Oriental quarter. It was only later that night, when he was lying awake and alone in his bed recalling the interaction with the punk girl, that Roger Daube realised but couldn't yet articulate, that something important and momentous had occurred in his personal life.

Remembering the instructions his club member had told him, Daube walked slowly to a disused red telephone booth. It was a relic from a bygone age, when telephones and the radio had been the only means of mass communication. He opened the dusty door, and found himself in a small upright glass box. He looked around, but the only object was an old black telephone attached to a grey cable. Daube carefully picked up the telephone, and on the numerical keypad, punched in his date of birth (day, month, year). He waited, with the telephone earpiece cupped to his right ear. He heard a dialing sound, and then an odd voice on the other end of the line spoke.

Chapter 8

'How can I be of assistance?' said the voice.

'I would like to enter Memory Lane please,' said Daube.

'And why would you like to enter Memory Lane?' came the response.

Daube paused for a moment before replying. 'Because I have an overriding need to experience something from my past. Something I have been afraid of for far too long. I need to overcome my fears.'

'I see,' said the voice. 'You do realize that once you are on Memory Lane, that there is no going back. You cannot retract your memory shard once purchased''

'I understand that,' said Daube.

There was a very long pause before the voice said; 'Very well, as long as you are fully aware of the consequences of your actions. The maximum number of memory shards you can buy in your lifetime is three. Once you have committed yourself to the experience, there is nothing I can do to retract the memory.'

'I understand,' replied Daube.

'Very well. Place your left hand on the sheet of metal in front of you and close your eyes. Try to erase all thoughts from your mind and concentrate. Concentrating is absolutely essential,' said the voice.

Daube did as he was instructed. Pressing his palm onto the pad, he forced his mind to go blank.

Time seemed to stand still, and nothing appeared to happen. A minute passed and then the voice said; 'Open your eyes.'

Daube did as he was told, and couldn't believe what he was seeing. He was no longer standing in the telephone booth. He looked around and realized that he was in the very middle of Memory Lane. On both sides, wooden huts, medieval in appearance hugged the side of the road. It was as if he had gone back in time.

'Which type of memory shard do you want?' said something off to Daube's left. He swiveled around, and saw a hologram in the shape of a brain hovering at face height.

'Do you want to remember the past or search into the future?' the brain asked.

'The past,' said Daube firmly. 'Most definitely the past.'

'Most wise, most wise,' said the hologram. 'You may purchase only one shard at a time, and a maximum of three. 'I, am a mirror image of your mind. You are actually looking at yourself. Take your time Roger Daube, inspect the many memory stalls, and once you are satisfied you have made the right choice, enter and commit yourself'

The shards were chargeable for five minutes of memory. Anything more was considered too intense and potentially dangerous for the sub-conscious. The traditional memory shard was inhaled from the fumes of a tea pot. The contemporary shard was a microchip inserted under the skin. Daube took a moment to look at the street. There were over thirty establishments offering a memory shard experience; but which to choose? The cobbled surface was uneven and evidently, extremely old. The wooden huts appeared to slope forward on to the street, for there was no pavement to speak of.

A small Japanese sign caught his attention. The shop had a lantern hanging outside the door way and wicker baskets hung from a bamboo pole. Daube gingerly poked his head inside. All he could see were two shapes huddled at the back of the shop, for the light was dim and it appeared misty.

'Welcome Mr. Daube. Please enter and take a seat.'

Daube was so overwhelmed he didn't even consider how the stranger knew his name. He walked towards the two shapes at the back, and as he approached, he realized that he was staring at an elderly couple. They were hunched over a tea pot which was gently brewing on a small stove next to the old woman.

He sat down on the only stool available, and awaited instruction. It was as if he was in a dream.

'You have chosen a traditional memory shard Mr. Daube. Please remain calm and allow your mind to transcend your body. You will feel light headed and slightly dizzy. Please do not be alarmed. This is perfectly natural,' the old man said.

Very delicately, the old woman lifted the tea pot towards Daube, and asked him to take three deep breaths, very slowly. He obeyed without hesitation.

'You will start to slip away Mr. Daube. Do not be afraid, this is your mind transcending itself. Very soon you will experience a real emotional memory recall. Do not resist. Allow your mind to follow the chosen path,' explained the old lady.

Daube was transfixed. His eyelids fluttered, and his whole body went limp. All of a sudden, he was 4 years old and standing in front of a confectioner's shop. The black lacquered sign read BRITTLES OF LONDON – purveyors of exceptional chocolate. The building was in the shape of a large glass jar, and inside giant chocolate initials of the alphabet were suspended around the shop. His uncle Arthur, led Daube by the hand to the letter R, and asked the assistant to wrap a chocolate letter up with his initial on. The initial was the size of a small plate. In a beautiful red box, with a golden yellow R embossed on the front lid, his uncle bent down and gave Daube the present.

'This is from your Father, Roger. Many happy returns.'

Daube jolted suddenly, his body alive as if he had been electrocuted. He gasped for air, and opened his eyes. He was back in the bustling Oriental district. A drone went over his head at lightning speed, and a shoe lizard asked if he wanted an express shoe shine – money back guaranteed.

Roger Daube was in a trance, as he wandered through the maze of alleys that surrounded Memory Lane. Eventually, he arrived at the western edge of the Oriental quarter, and walked to one of the drone landing pads.

Chapter 9

Mind extraction was big business. Criminal's convicted of serious offences were shipped to Siberia and their mind kept in a digital prison vault. Britain was overcrowded, and KEYS, the government agency which was responsible for the prison service, had decided in 2040 to only maintain the digital element. All physical capacity for the prison system was terminated, and locations abroad were agreed for the safe storage of the criminal's body. Siberia was vast, and an agreement with the Russian authorities had resulted in a government contract until 2240. The digital mind prison vault had been built in South London and it had a capacity that would not be full for another two hundred years.

Ronnie Bronze had experienced digital extraction, (twice) and it was not an experience he wanted to repeat.

He was orange. Why was that? Could it be connected to his dubious diet? Bronze was partial to sweet and sour sauce. He had it with everything. It was turning his skin an unnatural colour. Fortunately for Ronnie, this sweet diet had not affected his mind. The authorities at KEYS, had planted a tracker in his body to monitor his whereabouts. He now had to be extra careful.

Ronnie Bronze was no fool, and he had learned from his previous criminal enterprises. This time, he had decided to go modern. Nothing as simplistic as credit card theft. He had to be smarter, and he had thought of a plan. An old transport café, called The Grease and Spoon, was the type of establishment that had gone out of fashion seventy years ago. It was his designated meeting place. It was located under the old disused A40 flyover in West London. Peeling paint, grubby windows, cheap leatherette seats and tables that had seen better days.

It was in these glorious surroundings, that 4 weeks ago, Ronnie had chosen to meet Shirley, a corrupt robotics cloning criminal who he had heard about on the underground grapevine. Meeting set for 3pm, Ronnie was the first to arrive. He ordered a cup of London tea in a flimsy cardboard cup and sausage, beans and chips. The café was virtually empty, except for two long distance lorry lizards who were engrossed in a full English fry-up and the virtual football, which was being beamed on the back of the menus.

The lighting was minimal, the walls bare, and the café floor looked like it hadn't been cleaned in years. Every few minutes, a wash of neon flare would light up the interior from the nearby Great Western Sonic Highway. It was the perfect place for a secretive meeting. The door opened, and a gust of damp cold air hit Ronnie in the face. A shadow loomed over him, and there was a scraping of chair legs. Shirley had arrived, and she was enormous. Twice the width of Ronnie, physically, she was not a woman to be messed with.

'Mr. Bronze I presume?'

'Ms. Shirley – pleased to meet your acquaintance,' said Ronnie.

'Just Shirley will do.'

'Shirley.'

'That's better.'

'Ronnie – call me Ronnie,' said Ronnie.

'Well Ronnie, what does a girl have to do to get a drink around here?'

Was she toying with him, teasing, testing the water? Ronnie was unsure. He grimaced, and flicked an arm in the direction of the waiter, a rundown man who looked more miserable than the actual building. No laser lizard would work in a dive like this, the unions wouldn't allow it; not since the laser lizard working conditions act of 2060.

'Cup of London tea for the lady – and anything to eat Shirley? Are you hungry?' Ronnie enquired.

'Famished Ron. Starving. I could eat a horse. I'll have the full English fry-up with extra chips and a plate of lamb chops for starters.'

The waiter memorized the order before shuffling back behind his counter.

'Now Ronnie – let's talk business,' said Shirley, in an assertive manner, that left Ronnie in no doubt whatsoever, that she did indeed mean business.

Two hearty meals and several cups of London tea later, and Ronnie Bronze left the transport café feeling very full and very satisfied with his afternoon's work.

Michael the 'homebot' had completed his cleaning tasks for the day. The house was spotless. Now he turned his attention to polishing the windows, followed by ironing Daube's shirts and preparing the ingredients for tonight's dinner. All 'homebots' were programmed to be domestically productive, and to blend in to their personal environment.

This meant that Michael also wore a smart suit, shirt and tie, with a monogrammed green apron for house work. He garnered genuine satisfaction from making his master happy, and no task was too onerous. In fact, he only had one small regret. He wanted to visit and explore the environment outside of the house on Farm Street. He was curious about what it would be like to roam outside and breathe in London town.

Banishing any thoughts about what a walk in the park would be like, he returned to his domestic duties, and started to dust the books in Daube's library. He was interrupted by an electronic chime from the front door. Upon opening it, Michael was confronted by a delivery from a laser lizard at DPL (Digital Parcels Ltd).

'Scan here please,' said the lizard. Michael scanned the document on his retina. It was a smart looking red box with intricate wrapping about the size of a small plate. A chocolate letter was inside. He placed the package on Daube's desk in the study; a magnificent American oak piece of furniture. On this large imposing desk stood a globe. The artifact was Daube's pride and joy. A possession he had bought back from Argentina, on one of his many travels around the world.

Michael returned to his chores, and thought nothing about the package sitting in his masters study.

Chapter 10

Ocean was excited. At her school in North London, her best friend Mo, had shown her a new chewing gum called 'Tasty Stretch'. It was available in ten different flavours. What was most remarkable about the gum, was that it allowed the chewer to increase or decrease their height for a thirty-minute period. It had been banned from Ocean's school.

The faster you chewed, the taller you grew, the slower you chewed, the shorter you became. In a world of high-tech robotics, genetic cloning and space travel, a simple and silly gum had proved that humans still craved the basic and ordinary.

Mo, had given Ocean two packs, with the solemn promise that if she got caught with the gum, it wasn't him that had given it to her. Ocean, agreed in an instant, and hid the 'Tasty Stretch' in an inside pocket within her school back-pack. She had decided to try the chewing gum out in her bedroom that evening. She had not forgotten her brief experience with the tall slim stranger in the Oriental quarter on Monday. In fact, the accidental encounter had left an emotional mark on Ocean. So much so, that she had returned on Tuesday after school and successfully caught another glimpse of the tall smartly dressed stranger.

Arriving home, she shouted 'hi', to her grandmother Gwen, and shot upstairs to her bedroom. She hid the gum under her pillow. Ocean could barely contain her excitement.

Ronnie Bronze was in a jubilant mood. His meeting with Shirley had gone better than expected, and together they had agreed a clever plan. As he surveyed The Pyramid department store from the top floor of a disused office opposite, through a new set of limited-edition binoculars, he was feeling very confident indeed. A flying trip to the Oriental quarter, and a 'need to know only' agreement with a Taiwanese electronics trader, had culminated in the illegal purchase of these extremely costly binoculars.

The range was one mile, and if you preset the zoom to bend mode, you could scope a moving object around doors and walls. It was an ingenious bit of kit. He made himself comfortable, and waited. Meanwhile, across the road, Shirley had created a decoy using a friend, and planted a new operational matrix code in a toy monkey, in the moving animal toy department. With the binary codes switched, she could remotely control the monkey's movements.

Decoy successful, Shirley slipped out of The Pyramid, and went to join Ronnie in his hideout opposite. Clutching the largest and meatiest sandwich he had ever seen, Shirley arrived and set up her laptop. In-between manic typing and big mouthfuls of sandwich, Shirley worked like a woman possessed. Ronnie was afraid to interrupt her, and so sat silently, holding his high-tech binoculars, as if his life depended on it.

Finally, once Shirley had completed her diagnostic tests, she turned to Ronnie.

'All set up. It's programmed to go when you're ready. Shall we try a dummy run tonight?'

Ronnie Bronze nodded his head in agreement and looked at his watch. 'Nearly 8.00pm now. Just four hours to go. What do you want to do Shirley?' He knew the answer before Shirley spoke.

'Bite to eat Ronnie? I know a charming little restaurant around the corner. Shall we?'

Ronnie dutifully followed Shirley out of the building and on to what he knew was going to be a very long meal.

Over several very large pizzas and more breadsticks and dough balls than he cared to remember, they went over the plan again. Ronnie was impressed with the details that Shirley had thought about. Her knowledge of robotics cloning and engineering were second to none, and as she asked the waiter for the dessert menu, Bronze knew he was dealing with a highly intelligent individual. Shirley explained how she had hacked into the Z-STAR 'homebot' deluxe model X drive. This was the most expensive 'homebot' on sale in The Pyramid department store, and only the rich could afford to pay so much for this top of the range model.

She then swapped the E-plate digital panel in the toy monkey for her corrupted one, and synched the F-drive to her remote computer. This meant, Shirley could remotely operate and control the monkey's functions and actions, thereby allowing her to send wireless instructions to the monkey's hard drive. So far so good. Bronze listened, in awe to what he was hearing.

The operation was now ready, so that when the store was closed they could instruct the monkey to go to the robotics department on the fifty fifth floor, and manipulate the hard drives of the Z-STAR 'homebots'. The plan then had to wait until the corrupted 'homebots' were bought by wealthy customers. Once the 'homebot' was installed in its new home, Ronnie could begin to instruct the robot to steal, because the anti-lying and truth mode had been deleted from the 'homebots' core digital sensor screen. It was a breathtakingly brilliant concept, and as Shirley ordered her third pudding of the evening, Bronze was aglow with the dizzying thoughts of untold riches about to come his way.

Chapter 11

Roger Wattle's home life was in one word, cramped. He lived with Mrs. Wattle and his six kids in a terraced house on The Isle of Dogs, East London. The small house was 'homely' and a happy place to live. Space was at a premium, and he and Mrs. Wattle had the attic bedroom. This was marginally bigger than the other three bedrooms, and it had the added benefit of a skylight window which looked out upon the spire of St Catherine's church.

Although cozy, it was the organized chaos of having eight creatures living under one small roof, that could be challenging. Mrs. Wattle ran a tight ship, and she was the engine room of the Wattle family. All, and I mean all, decisions went through her, and no detail was too small. If Frank wanted to do something, he sought permission from Mrs. Wattle first. She was his pride and joy.

Unfortunately for Frank, the attic bedroom had to accommodate all the families unwanted bric-a-brac, and this was stacked up in a big pile at the end of the bed. As Frank's side was also against the wall, he needed to weave his way around an assault course of mess just to get himself off the bed. Having achieved this physical feat, Frank then had to squeeze himself around the bed and the sloping roof, which meant he was virtually on all four's until he reached the door. It was communal living at its very best.

Communal living of a different kind tested the Jones family. Molly lived with her daughter Ocean and mother Gwen in a terraced house in Muswell Hill. Molly was divorced, and Ocean's estranged father had decided to chance his luck in the new space frontier that was Saturn. That had left Molly coping with an absent father in Ocean's life, and her mother, who was a little bit on the kooky side. All things being equal, she was just about coping with an underpaid job, demanding daughter and a mildly eccentric mother.

After supper and homework, Ocean read from her space books collection. Molly disliked the i-mag digital i-brain library mode of reading for young adults and encouraged Ocean to read from good old-fashioned books. There weren't many traditional book stores left in London, but she had discovered a book shop specialising in space literature, which was Ocean's favourite subject matter, and built up a small collection of books for her daughter.

Entering Ocean's bedroom was like entering outer space. The ceiling was covered in stars, and painted pictures of the solar system were on all three walls. Her bed was a lunar space capsule in white and grey. It was quite an unusual taste for a teenage girl of fourteen, but then again, Ocean was not your typical teenage daughter.

Molly was just about to say goodnight and close the door, when she noticed something red sticking out from Ocean's pillow.

'What's that under your pillow?' asked Molly.

Ocean pretended to be asleep.

'Ocean – what is that I can see under your pillow?'

Ocean was still pretending to be asleep when;

'Ocean Megan Jones. Do not play that game with me. Answer me when I'm asking you a question. OCEAN – now, before I get really cross with you. OCEAN.'

'Nothing important,' answered Ocean reluctantly.

'What do you mean nothing. Show me what it is. Right now, please.'

Extremely slowly, Ocean sat up in bed, and passed her mother the 'Tasty Stretch' chewing gum.

Fully aware, that they had had a row earlier, Molly spoke slowly.

'Ocean Megan Jones. Where did you get this gum from?'

'Nowhere,' answered Ocean truculently.

'Don't try my patience Ocean. I am only going to ask you once more.......'

'It was Mo. Mo Patel. He gave it to me,' blurted Ocean.

'Mo Patel. Well just wait until I speak to his mother about this. You do realise that this gum is banned in school?'

Ocean nodded.

'Very well. Leave it with me.' Slightly appeased, now that she was in possession of the chewing gum, Molly calmed down.

'I'm most concerned Ocean. Most concerned. You can blame Mo. all you like, but Mo. didn't force you to take it home did he? Did he Ocean?'

'No,' came the quiet reply. 'But please, please can I keep it? You can try it if you like? We could both try it. Even grandma could have some'

'Now don't push your luck young lady. I'm going to sleep on it. We will discuss this further, tomorrow. Now goodnight,' and on that note, Molly went downstairs with the chewing gum.

Roger Daube, had visited his private members club, on the off chance that the chap who had given him the low down on Memory Lane, might be around. He was disappointed to discover that the gentleman in question, hadn't visited the club in over three months. Now that he was here, Daube decided to settle himself in to one of the comfortable leather chairs in the members lounge, and treat himself to a nice long coffee.

Harris, the head waiter, who had been serving drinks at the establishment for over sixty years, came over and took his order.

'And what would Mr. Daube care to drink tonight?' asked Harris softly.

'Good to see you looking so well Harris,' replied Daube.

'Thank you for saying so, Sir.'

'I would like an Americano coffee please Harris, with warm skimmed milk on the side.'

'Certainly, Sir. And will you be joining us for dinner tonight?'

'Not tonight Harris. No. Another time perhaps.'

'As you wish Mr. Daube. As you wish. One Americano with warm skimmed milk on the side, coming right up.'

As Harris slipped quietly away, Daube took a few moments to think about his incredible experience with the memory shard. He wanted to discuss it with Wattle, but he wasn't quite sure how Frank would respond. Would he tease him, after his reluctance to embrace anything to do with the 'emotion' zone?

Harris returned with his coffee, and left Daube to his thoughts. On reflection, Daube decided not to mention it to Wattle just yet. There would be plenty of time for that later. His coffee drunk, Daube left his club, and made the pleasant walk back to Farm Street. Michael, his 'homebot', was waiting for him, heat regeneration slippers ready by the front door, and an enticing aroma of dinner wafting out from the kitchen.

Daube wandered in to his study, and walked up to his desk. It was only then that he saw the red box from Brittles of London. It stopped him in his tracks. He gulped, and took a large intake of air. How on earth had this package arrived at his house? He peered at the top of the box, and was stunned to see the initial R on the front. He took two steps away from the desk, and shouted across the room;

'Michael, can you come in to the library immediately. I need to talk to you. Now.'

46

Chapter 12

Breakfast time in the Jones household was a little tense the following morning. Ocean breezed in to the kitchen, and pretended as if nothing had happened last night. Unluckily for Ocean, Molly hadn't forgotten, and after a chat with Grandma Gwen, she had decided to take Ocean shopping after work this evening. At worst, it would be a pleasant distraction, for both mother and daughter, and a nice change to their usual routine.

Grandma Gwen would travel with Ocean to Bond Street station after school, and it was agreed by all three ladies, that there would be a temporary halt to hostilities. Ocean was excited about the opportunity to browse the latest computer gadgets, and was determined to try and beg Molly for a ride on the Saturn shuttle ride simulator. This was another touchy subject, as Molly was very aware of the possible implications of a journey to space. Travel times had been reduced in recent years, and Molly's biggest fear, was that Ocean would ask for a trip to Saturn to visit her father.

Currently, a return ticket was too expensive, but prices were tumbling, and Molly knew that one day, Ocean would want to go and visit her father in the new world. It was only natural. Making sure that the 'Tasty Stretch' chewing gum was safely hidden in her work satchel, Molly said goodbye to Ocean and Grandma Gwen, and left for work.

Over in Mayfair, Daube was particularly pensive. He had not slept well, and was wide awake when Michael came in with his morning cup of tea. The box containing the chocolate initial had unsettled him. Looking at his own initial, R, had convinced

Daube, that his memory shard experience had leaked from his sub-conscious and in to the real world. The evidence was sitting on his desk in the library.

Was it a warning? A cryptic message from his past? He didn't know, but one thing was for sure. He would have to talk about it with Wattle, whose experiences in the 'emotion' zone made him practically an expert on memory shards. After his poor night's rest, Daube made two decisions over his toast and apricot conserve. Firstly, he was going to have to purchase another memory shard, and secondly, if he was going to confide in Wattle, he wanted to do it in the safety and security of his private members club. He would invite Wattle for dinner at The Lexington in the next few days.

Drinking his espresso coffee quickly, he bade Michael a good day, and stepped outside his town house and onto Farm Street. It was 7.00am, and the taxi cab hologram was just issuing the latest travel updates to London's commuters. He looked up at the giant black taxi hologram which dominated the sky above Mayfair, and at a brisk walking pace, proceeded to 188 Piccadilly. He had work to do.

As the day drew to a close, and the dark of a November evening took over, Molly completed her online daily work log (Kendal her robotics assistant was still playing up), and made her way to the meeting place agreed with Grandma Gwen. Standing beside the Oxford Street world clock and global population calculator, which stood at forty billion humans on the planet and counting, she thought about what she was going to do with the chewing gum. Then, out of the corner of her eye, who did she spot, but that same man in the shiny suit with orange skin, whom she had seen on Monday.

She watched him walking amongst the crowds, and was only interrupted with the appearance of Ocean and Gwen. It was decided, that, as they were all in the West End midweek, they would treat themselves to dinner in the sky-lounge at the top of The Pyramid. The views over Hyde Park were impressive, and the milkshake bar was a destination in itself.

Two exhausting hours later, Molly, Ocean and Gwen were sitting in the sky-lounge at the top of The Pyramid, sipping various beverages. Ocean had made an entire tour of the electronics department (five floors), robotics cloning and engineering on floor fifty-five, the space experience, and against her will, the moving toys display. As she was such a gizmo and tech nerd, Molly had thought it an innocent idea to take a peek at the electronic toys, as a gentle nudge to Ocean's childhood. She hadn't been impressed.

'I'm not a child mother,' moaned Ocean as she reluctantly followed mum and grandma through thousands of toys. 'This is 2085. I've outgrown children's toys in case you hadn't noticed. I'm practically an adult now. Are you actually listening to a word I'm saying?' complained Ocean.

Molly, continued walking, and pretended she hadn't heard a word her daughter was uttering. She wanted to get out of the toys area pronto, and was desperately searching for an exit sign. As she scanned the vast room, ignoring the chuntering ten paces behind her, she stopped dead in her tracks.

'Did you see that Ocean. Ocean —did you see what I saw?'

It was evident that Ocean had seen nothing, because she was walking so far behind Molly.

Eventually her daughter plus long face caught up with her and grandma.

'I saw that monkey move. It's head turned around and it's eyes swiveled towards me,' said Molly.

'So?' came the inspired response.

'Well? How did it do that? These toys aren't actually active are they Ocean? Ocean – listen to me when I'm talking to you. Are they programmed already, here in the store?'

'I don't know mum. Can we go and eat now?'

'But I saw it move. I'm not imagining it Gwen.'

'I'm sure you're not dear,' replied Grandma.

'Am I the only one who thinks that's a little weird?' said Molly.

'Mum – I'm hungry. Can we go now please?'

'Can you go and take a look at that monkey for me Ocean? It's freaked me out. I must be going mad.'

Mum – really? Must I?'

'Yes please. Just check it out for me, would you?'

'Oh mum – honestly. What are you like?', and with that parting shot, Ocean walked over to the toy monkey, and started examining it.

It was only when the three ladies were about to order their dinner, that Ocean let slip that she had opened up the mother board and taken a peak at the remote-control settings inside the monkey.

'And?' enquired Molly.

'Well, if you asked me, I would say that someone has tampered with the electronics system, and that the monkey was watching me,' said Ocean nonchalantly. 'Now, can we please go and eat?'

Chapter 13

Frank Wattle's left retina flashed red. An incoming voice message had been received. It was from a potentially new client called Molly Jones. Wattle listened to the voice message twice before deleting, and voice messaged back. She had suggested meeting outside Brittles of London.

He agreed to meet Molly at 6pm. If the meeting proved fruitful, The Wattle and Daube Detective Agency – At Your Service, could have another customer on the books. The rain was unrelenting, and the bright lights of Piccadilly Circus reflected in the pools of water that had collected on the side of the pavement. A ripple of movement on a puddle beside a flashing sign for yoga classes, was the only indication that the trans intercontinental rail system ran directly below the road, linking London with Toronto and New York. Mobile waffle stands stood next to hot dog vendors at the entrance to Europe's largest food mall, a six-tier trading platform suspended above street level. London was on the move.

Wattle appeared outside 188 Piccadilly, and opened his Wattle and Daube signature umbrella. Pulling his raincoat collar up, he proceeded to walk purposefully towards the Yolk of York. He turned right down a side street, and saw the fiber glass fried egg with yellow yolk visible in the distance. As he approached through the rain, he could see Tony Tanner.

'Evening Frank,' it was Tony, cleaning his griddle plates before closing up for the night.

'Evening Tone – can't linger, I'm out on business.'

'Say no more Frank. Say hi to Mrs. Wattle when you get home will you?'

'Of course I will, Tony. You take care of yourself now. See you tomorrow.'

Wattle continued on his short walk to Brittles. Growing up, he remembered being shown the beautiful window displays of London's most famous chocolate shop. The glass at the front was in the shape of a jar, which gave the impression that the giant chocolate alphabet initials on display were actually in the glass jar. Of course, the plate sized chocolate letters with the initials, were only affordable to rich kids. His mother and father could never afford such expensive treats.

'You must be Frank, pleased to meet you. Molly Jones.'

I could have been Roger, thought Wattle for a fleeting second. How did she know I was Frank? Can you place an appearance to a voice?

'Molly, good to meet you. Yes, I'm Frank, Frank Wattle.' They exchanged small talk, and then Wattle said;

'Molly, do you fancy a coffee, or something stronger?'

'A coffee would be lovely,' replied Molly, and on that note, Frank and Molly went off to find a hot drink nearby.

The café had a cool European vibe, and laser lizards scuttled around the two floors with super efficiency. Wattle found a corner sofa and table and two coffees were ordered. Talking over the background music, Wattle proceeded to ask Molly how she had heard of The Wattle & Daube Detective Agency. He fondly remembered the advertisement section in The Digital Daily Metropolitan newspaper.

'Well, it was actually my daughter Ocean,' explained Molly. 'She fancies herself as a bit of a super sleuth. She tracked you down.'

Unbeknown to Roger Daube, Ocean Jones had waited patiently in the Oriental quarter, on that previous Wednesday, until she had spied Daube carefully making his way to Memory Lane. He definitely did not blend in with the hectic chaos that was this exotic part of London. He was considerably taller than most of the residents on show, and he had a look of utter bafflement on his face, as he slowly maneuvered himself around the sea of people and lizards.

Ocean deliberately made sure Daube couldn't see her, and followed him to the corner of a busy street, confident that with that expression on his face, he was not noticing anything going on around him. She was right.

Ten minutes later, and Daube reappeared. He walked to the drone zone, and waited until his time came to hire one. Eye scan complete, Roger Daube climbed in to the drone cabin and gave his destination. Ocean had no choice. She was desperate not to lose this unusual stranger. She dashed to the front of the drone queue and pushed the first passenger out of the way. Jumping in to the cabin she told the drone to follow the previous one, which was rising and banking ninety degrees to the right.

'Follow that man,' she instructed the drone. 'Do not lose sight of it. Cross digital lights if you must, but keep tagging its journey. I will pay extra'. The drone did nothing.

The London skies were a busy place to be, with thousands of flying objects traversing the digital highways in a unique travel pattern controlled by the central London flying eye, known affectionately by Londoners, as Joyce.

Joyce was the central computer for all air related travel, and she computed millions of data per second to all the drones, flying lizards, and couriers that buzzed around the vast city. Every above ground journey made in London went through Joyce's massive computer.

Ocean was acutely aware that any unusual travel patterns would be immediately picked up by Joyce, and that the drone would be instructed to land immediately. She therefore had no choice about what she did next.

Grabbing the automated joy stick, Ocean tapped in an override code sequence she had memorized, and manually took control of the drone. She did not have any time to reflect on her reckless actions, because within a couple of seconds of the override code, a traffic lizard appeared beside the drone.

Ocean Jones slammed the machine in to take-off procedure and flew away. She spotted Daube disappearing in front of her, and increased the power shift to full throttle. The drone whined and shot forward at an alarming speed. St. Paul's cathedral appeared on her left-hand side, as Ocean accelerated over the London skyline.

Fortunately for Ocean, Roger Daube's drone hovered in mid-air at the Holborn High Road intersection, and waited in the digital line for permission to cross in to Central London. Ocean calculated, that if her drone was being tracked, she would be arrested upon landing, and so she overrode the tracking device, and disappeared off Joyce's radar. She was now free to roam where she wanted, without detection.

She followed Daube to Piccadilly, and carefully landed the drone behind him. Flying solo was fun, she thought, as she hopped out of the cabin and kept twenty paces behind Roger Daube.

He calmly walked in to 188 Piccadilly, and pressed the button for the elevator. Ocean waited until Daube had entered the lift, and then she scanned the various companies listed on the electronic plaque on the outside entrance. There were over twenty names listed on the board. Which one had he chosen, thought Ocean? As she examined the names, she read the fifth floor listings. There was only one company.

The Wattle & Daube Detective Agency. Instinctively she knew this was the company that the stranger worked for. She memorised the name, and began to walk towards Green Park, just as a small crowd began to gather around the abandoned drone. It was time for Ocean Jones to make herself scarce.

Chapter 14

The Scandinavian bar was sparsely populated, and Wattle saw an empty booth to his left. As the conversation unraveled, Molly discussed what had happened at The Pyramid. She explained Ocean's interest in robotics, and how the following day, Ocean had confronted her. As Molly Jones described her daughter's view point, Frank could not wait to meet this exceptional girl. She sounded amazing.

'If Ocean is correct, in her analysis,' said Frank, 'then this find could have enormous implications. Of course, until my partner has verified your daughter's findings, we can't get carried away. But seriously, what a sharp mind she has. I'm most impressed.'

'She is a little different admittedly,' said Molly. 'A little 'out there', if you get my meaning?'

'No need to explain to me Molly. I've got six nippers, and not one of them is what you might call, run of the mill.'

Molly smiled. There was a long pause, and she looked uncomfortable.

'Everything all right Molly? Look, we all have odd kids. There's no need to look so glum. Ocean sounds an extremely bright and switched on girl.'

'No, it's not that Frank,' said Molly quietly.

'What is it then. Spit it out.'

'I'm not sure you will be able to meet Ocean. I called you, because her views were so incredible, I wanted a professional to actually hear and verify them. And; now that you have listened to me and confirmed that Ocean isn't barking mad, well, it puts me in a dilemma.'

'What dilemma is that then?' said Wattle kindly.

'I can't afford to pay you for another meeting. I simply don't have the funds, Frank. I'm not a time waster, I'm really not, but as a single mother supporting Ocean and my mother, I just don't have the money.'

'Well, in that case you've come to the right detective agency haven't you?' said Wattle. 'Nobody's even mentioned fees have they? I tell you what. Let me have a chat with Roger, and we will sort something out. Don't you worry.'

Mrs. Wattle, was a woman who liked ample food portions. A plate of grub was deemed poor, if the quantity was lacking. This desire, to see generous amounts served, stemmed primarily from the intergalactic war years 2057-2060. Rationing was necessary, and essential to survival, as the world battled an aggressive planet for space supremacy in the solar system.

Mrs. Wattle remembered growing up, and being told by her mother and grandmother, how to conserve food, and make a little go a long way. The war had lasted three long years, but it took another five, before the world could recover and farming and basic food stocks return to the pre-war years. As she had been young during the war, the food shortages had had a profound effect on her attitude to food. Granted, Mrs. Wattle was famous for her large portion sized meals, but not one scrap of food was ever wasted, and all her children, including Mr. Wattle, had to eat every last morsel that she cooked for them.

The kitchen was as slim as Mrs. Wattle was wide, but she never complained. She had a happy marriage to Frank, and six wonderful kids. Challenging at times – granted, but she wouldn't change a thing. Well, a slightly bigger bedroom would be nice, but oh well, you can't have everything you want in life. She was an organizer, and a natural leader. True, the house was small, but Mrs. Wattle ran a tight ship as the saying goes, and the family didn't want for anything.

The circumstances couldn't have been more different for Daube. He had too much living space, and only shared his house with Michael the 'homebot'. Roger Daube had been raised by a generation 1 robot, which in those days was called a 'carebot'. Although, not technically a father to Daube, the generation 1 'carebot', whose name was Harold, had raised Daube in the house on Farm Street.

The property had been left to Daube as a baby. He had no recollection of his mother, who had died giving birth, and an absent father who was always away on military assignments. Harold the 'carebot', had been like a father figure to him. When the generation 1 'carebots' had been retired, it was the technically advanced 'homebots' who replaced them, and Michael had been purchased and installed in Daube's house. This home arrangement, suited Daube absolutely fine. He had never known anything else, and he had no desire to over populate his house.

Both Daube and Michael were tidy, and creatures of habit. He looked on Wattle's chaotic domestic life with a mixture of envy and fright. Part of him longed to live amongst a large family, and part of him (the dominant part), would run a thousand miles to avoid such a messy set up. No thank you – he was quite happy as he was. Or so he thought. However; unbeknown to Roger Daube, a meeting was going to happen shortly, that would change his life.

Chapter 15

It was Friday in the office of The Wattle and Daube Detective Agency. The morning was gloomy and overcast, but at least it wasn't raining. Daube was busy looking at the latest crime statistics for London, when Wattle walked in, and placed his crumpled raincoat and hat on the coat stand. Daube looked up, and smiled.

'How is it Wattle, that you manage to start each day looking so disheveled and creased? There must be an art to appearing so crumpled.'

'There is Rog. It's called having six kids living under the same roof, and not having enough space to swing an old boot.'

'I see,' said Daube, who had absolutely no idea.

'It's called family life. You should give it a try some time Rog. It could open your eyes to a whole new brave world out there.'

'Well maybe one day I will give it a go Wattle. One never knows where life is going to lead one, does one?'

Wattle was just about to make a joke at Daube's expense, when he remembered his meeting with Molly Jones.

'Rog – you know I had the meeting with that woman last night? Well, I need to fill you in on the details. Let me just go and grab a strong coffee, and I'll be right with you.'

Returning with his Turkish coffee, Wattle fiddled around with his desk drawers and produced a pack of London biscuits. He dunked one in his black coffee and repeated the act 4 times. Finally, he pulled his chair over to Daube's desk, and planted his bottom on the seat. Wiping away a few biscuit crumbs which were nestled in his lap, he looked over at Daube and said the following.

'You know what Rog?'

'No – I don't think I do, Wattle. Pray, tell.'

'You know what Rog? – last night was very interesting. I think we could be on to something, I really do.'

Wattle then proceeded to tell Daube all the things he had learnt from his meeting with Molly Jones.

'We should speak to her – the girl, Ocean. Pick her brains. She sounds really interesting. I can't wait to meet her. If she is anything like the mother, then we are on to something. What a mind she must have, and she's only 4teen.'

'Yes – get them both in Wattle. It sounds like it could lead somewhere. Now you did discuss our fees with the mother? Wattle, Wattle – look at me Wattle.'

'Rog – you know what?'

'What,' said Daube, who knew exactly what was coming.

'She's broke Rog. A single mum. I didn't have the heart to tell her we wouldn't take the case. She needs us. She needs our help and expertise Rog. She needs YOU.'

'Does she indeed.' said Daube smiling.

He knew his partner and friend Frank Wattle had a big generous heart. It was what made Frank, well, Frank. It was in his DNA to help others. Look at how they had met, he thought.

'Any chance of payment Wattle?' said Daube, knowing full well what the answer was.

'None whatsoever Rog. But she is a good woman, and she needs our help.'

And so, it was on that note, that The Wattle and Daube Detective Agency – At Your Service, opened the case, that was going to prove bigger and more interesting than either Wattle or

Daube had ever imagined.

Mildly annoyed that the adverts that tracked your thoughts and aspirations, had been following him all the way to the Oriental quarter, Daube decided to ignore the temptation to buy a bar of chocolate. The adverts played with your mind, if you let them, and he was determined to resist the urge to scoff something indulgent.

As London's population had grown, so had the need to build upwards. The megacity now had hundreds of skyscrapers, towering over the surface, but here in the Oriental quarter, the buildings were low and tightly clustered together. As Daube navigated his way through the throng of people, he saw a flashing sign for the People's Pleasure Palace, or the PPP as it was called.

Built in the last century, the PPP was the largest of its kind in the world. It covered an entire block, and had twenty floors below ground of gambling and entertainment. Over twenty thousand Londoners worked in the casino, and it even had its very own lizard police force. There were stories of couples losing each other for whole days, and individuals getting lost and not leaving the building for weeks. The PPP was a popular tourist destination, and queues formed around the block by midday. The Palace never closed. It operated 24/7, such was the demand.

Daube crossed the road, and headed deep into the zone. He remembered clearly where the invisible red telephone booth was, and he was just about to turn left and into the small street, when a lounge lizard tapped him on the shoulder.

'I'm sorry to bother you, but could you direct me towards the Yakamoto Banking Corporation. I appear to be lost.'

Daube, who had an excellent sense of direction, had no idea where the bank was. It could be anywhere in the maze of little streets and ally-ways that made up the Oriental quarter.

'I'm afraid I can't help you,' said Daube politely. 'I appear to be a little lost myself.'

The lounge lizard drifted off into the crowd, and Daube was left to his own devices.

'Am I losing my mind?' he muttered to himself. 'I could have sworn it was opposite that shoe shine vendor. Where has it gone? Concentrate. Concentrate, and it will appear'. He paced the street for a few minutes, and eventually gave up. He realized he didn't know where the red telephone booth was, and it was pointless walking aimlessly up and down. He was genuinely bemused, and so decided to return to 188 Piccadilly.

'Been anywhere interesting Rog?' asked Wattle, as he wiped tomato ketchup from his lips.

'No, no, nothing of any importance,' said Daube lying.

Wattle stopped eating his hotdog, and looked intently at his colleague. He took another bite of his sausage, chewed, swallowed and then said the following.

'Roger Daube – If I didn't know better, I would say you are telling me a 'pork pie. Now, you can't pull the wool over my eyes that easily. What have you been up to?'

Daube fiddled with his tie, adjusted his cuff-links, and eventually sat down. He stared out of the window for a few seconds, and then turned to face Frank.

'It's complicated Wattle, and all rather strange. I don't really know where to begin.'

'How about the start Rog.'

'Yes, that's always a good place to begin,' said Daube, looking at the floor. 'Look Wattle, I will talk it over with you, just not now. Ok? Give me time to think about things, and then we will discuss it. I promise.'

Wattle nodded, and knew to leave it alone for now. He understood his partner had something on his mind that was troubling him, and he knew that now was not the time to press Daube for info. Changing the subject, he said;

'When shall I arrange for Molly and Ocean to come over?'

'I was thinking Monday. A quick bite to eat at my club might be quite pleasant,' replied Daube.

'As you wish Rog. Let me arrange it with Molly. You're going to like her, I know. I can feel it in my bones.'

Chapter 16

It was eleven days earlier, and Ronnie Bronze was becoming bigger. He knew the reasons why. It was all this eating with Shirley. His waist line was expanding as each large meal with her added to his weight gain. If this carried on much longer, then he would have to go on a diet. He wasn't taking enough exercise, and being hidden away on the top floor opposite The Pyramid, wasn't helping his cause.

They were taking it in turns to monitor the night time activities of the toy monkey, and Ronnie had just completed his six-hour shift, when Shirley appeared through the door. She was clutching a paper bag.

'I've brought treats Ronnie. Cream horn?'

Ronnie Bronze smiled meekly.

'That would be lovely Shirley.'

'Splendid. One horn or two?'

'One please. Thank you.'

'You are welcome Ronnie,' said Shirley, as she devoured her first pastry of the evening.

The first part of the plan had worked. Shirley could remotely operate the toy monkey and control its movements. A virtual reality cam installed on the monkey, acted as a visual reference point. The next stage of the operation, was to get the monkey to access the robotics department. Once in the right area, she needed to instruct the monkey to open the control panel on the deluxe range of Z-Star 'homebots', and manipulate the software.

This reprogramming of the 'homebots' core personality, would allow them to lie and steal when powered up in their new homes. It was all beginning to take shape nicely. The only issue, that Shirley had no control over, was the actual time it took to tamper with each robot. On current evidence, one 'homebot' could be reengineered per night, and there were ten deluxe 'homebots' available on the shop floor to manipulate. Ten robots, ten nights work, and then patience, until purchase and delivery of the 'homebot'. That was the plan, and as The Pyramid were selling a Z-Star each working day, they wouldn't have to wait very long.

Ronnie had been taught by Shirley how to use the software, which controlled the monkey. He wasn't an IT expert, but he felt confident that during his night shift, he could do what Shirley had told him.

'How long on average does it take for the monkey to access the robotics department, and reconfigure the 'homebot?' asked Ronnie.

'About 4 to five hours,' replied Shirley. 'Are you confident you know how to use the software programme?'

'Absolutely,' said Ronnie.

'OK then. We should be good to go. Let me do tonight's shift, and you can do tomorrow. Are you OK with that?'

''Fine by me,' replied Ronnie, who was just thankful he wasn't operating the first shift. At least if there were any teething problems, then Shirley would be capable of dealing with them. He didn't want to let on that he was way out of his depth. The only thing that was keeping him going, was the thought of the 'homebots' thieving and stealing from their new owners. But that was in the future. First, he had to master Shirley's laptop and the toy monkey.

Over on the Isle of Dogs, Mrs. Wattle was preparing dinner. It was like watching a military campaign. Various plates and dishes appeared from the thin narrow kitchen, and more food than seemed possible for such a small kitchen.

Mrs. Wattle was a traditionalist, and liked to dress smartly for the evening meal. She expected Frank to do the same. This usually involved him tightening his tie, smoothing out his creased shirt, and making sure his shoe laces were not undone.

Upon sitting down at the head of the table, Frank tucked his starched white napkin into his shirt collar, made a gesture to the children to follow suit, and then heaped praise on Mrs. Wattle.

'It smells delicious as always Mrs. W,' said Frank cheekily. He grinned across the table at his beloved wife.

'Good. I hope you all enjoy it. Shepherd's pie with gravy, and five types of veg,' said Mrs. Wattle. 'Now tuck in everyone, before the food goes cold.'

Later that same evening, as Frank and Mrs. Wattle enjoyed a hot chocolate in bed, Frank confided in his wife, about Roger Daube.

'I am genuinely worried about him,' said Frank. 'He is not acting his usual self.'

'How do you mean?' asked Mrs. Wattle.

'Well, he returned from heaven knows where on Friday afternoon, and was acting most strangely. He's up to something. I know it.'

'Don't rock the boat Frank. All in good time. I'm sure Roger will open up about whatever is troubling him sooner or later. Why don't you invite him round for a spot of dinner?'

'Right. Good idea. How about next Thursday?'

'Thursday is fine; only tell Roger not to bring a fancy bottle of wine like last time. It will only go to waste,' said Mrs. Wattle firmly.

'Will do. What time Rita?'

'Whatever time works for you and Roger dear. I know how

busy you both are at the moment.'

Wattle smiled at his wife, finished his hot chocolate, and kissed her on the cheek. After cleaning his teeth, he adjusted his striped pajamas and said the following immortal words.

'I love you Rita Wattle.'

'I love you too, Frank Wattle. Goodnight dear.'

'Goodnight love,' said Frank, as he squeezed himself into his warm little corner of the bedroom.

In Mayfair, Daube had just finished his evening bath. He always took one before bed. After a pleasant soak, he watched the London news, and was served a cup of Jasmine pearl tea by Michael. Puffing up his pillows, and adjusting the room temperature, Michael lowered the bedroom lights for Daube, before retiring for the night.

'Sleep well,' said Michael. 'Call me if you should need anything. I've bought salmon for Monday night's dinner.'

'Ah, don't worry about dinner on Monday. I'm dining with Wattle and a client at my club. We're eating early, so I shouldn't be late. Will the fish keep two days?'

'Yes – that won't be a problem. Thank you for letting me know. See you in the morning,' said Michael. He turned to leave, and then said;

'Will you be home before ten? Only the new series of 'The Chimney Challenge', is starting on channel 21, and we always watch it together.'

'Yes,' replied Daube. 'I should be back well before ten. Goodnight Michael.'

'Goodnight Sir,' answered Michael. The 'homebot' closed Daube's bedroom door quietly, and returned to the kitchen to prepare the table ready for breakfast.

Chapter 17

On Saturday morning Daube asked Michael to phone Betty at The Lexington, his private members club, and make an early dinner reservation for four at 6.00pm. on Monday. The stage was set. Roger Daube had been a member since his eighteenth birthday, but the 'house' rules stated that anyone under the age of eighteen, had to be accompanied by an adult.

The club was proudly located in the St. James's district of central London, and occupied the corner of a grand white colonial style building. The flag with the crest was spotless, come rain or shine and fluttered elegantly above the entrance.

The Lexington Club had been around for over two hundred years, and boasted a rich history. It had been the very first private members club to admit women, and the only one of its kind to have a female as President. What particularly appealed to Daube, was that it was staffed entirely by humans. There was not a robot in sight. Betty, the grand dame, had been on the front desk for over fifty years, and knew every member's name and birthday.

Harris, the head waiter in the club lounge, was an institution, and had been working at the club for over sixty years. He made it his business to know what his clients wanted, and always delivered service with a minimum of fuss. He had known Harris and Betty so long they were like family to him. He couldn't possibly imagine The Lexington Club without them.

Wattle had arranged for Molly and Ocean to meet them at 188 Piccadilly. He felt that they would feel more at ease, if they were introduced to Roger in the humble surroundings of their detective agency. Greeting them by the elevator doors, Wattle shot a glance over to the vending machine, which if looks could talk, said; 'Just for once, don't give me any lip ok?' The vending machine remained unusually silent.

'So, this is Ocean,' said Frank, with a big friendly smile on his face. 'A pleasure to meet you at last. Your mum's told me all about you.'

Ocean glanced at her mum as if to say, 'what on earth have you being telling him mother', and smiled in return.

'Please come on through, and meet my business partner Roger Daube,' said Wattle, beckoning Molly and Ocean through into their cramped headquarters.

Daube was standing, ready to greet the pair. He looked stunned as he recognized Ocean from his fleeting encounter in the Oriental quarter. He quickly recovered his composure, and shook their hands.

'Please have a seat,' said Daube. 'Frank's filled me in so far Molly, but we thought it a good idea to have an informal chat in more detail over dinner. Does that sound OK with you?'

Before Molly or Ocean could reply, Wattle leapt in with;

'I bet you like vegi-burgers Ocean? Well, where we are going, does the biggest, juiciest vegi-burgers in London. Isn't that right Rog?'

Ocean grinned at Wattle, and Daube knew instinctively, that they were going to have a productive meeting over at The Lexington. Wattle was great at making people feel at ease.

The chit-chat over, the four of them made their way to Daube's private club. Unusually, it wasn't raining for once, and the short stroll from 188 Piccadilly to The Lexington took less than ten minutes. As Wattle and Molly walked on ahead, Daube seized his moment alone with Ocean.'

'What is going on young lady. I smell a rat. Am I right?'

'I can explain,' replied Ocean, 'Only I need five minutes alone with you to tell you why I followed you. Not with my mum around. Do you understand?' she said guardedly.

Daube nodded curtly.

Climbing the steps to the shiny revolving doors, Daube swished through and up to the majestic front desk, where Betty was standing.

'Betty, may I introduce you to Molly and her daughter Ocean,' he said.

Betty, adjusted the reading glasses on her nose, and looked down at Molly and Ocean.

'Welcome to The Lexington Club ladies. I trust you will have a pleasant stay with us this evening. If you would be so kind as to sign in as guests, I would be most grateful.'

As they signed in the visitor's book, Betty signaled to her left, and out of nowhere a small army of helpers appeared. Coats and bags were quietly removed, and then they were shown in to the club members lounge, to be met and greeted by Harris and his team of assistants.

Michael the 'homebot', had been engineered to be technically and emotionally, an advancement on the generation 1 'carebots', which had reportedly developed glitches. The 'carebot' had served humans well for over twenty years, but through no fault of his own, Harold had technical limitations. The generation 1 model had been a global sales success, but inevitably it was eventually replaced by the 'homebot'. Michael was a series 4 'homebot', and was regarded as a top of the range robot. Only recently, had the Z Star deluxe model X become available for domestic service, and this newest of 'carebot' was, very expensive to buy.

Recent trials on Saturn, where all robots had to be tested extensively for five years in a climate far more hostile than earth, had proved successful. The first batch of these new ultra-advanced machines had gone on sale at the beginning of January 2085, and because they cost so much, they were only available to the super rich. Eventually, prices would come down, but at present, only wealthy Londoners could afford them.

Because the Z Star model was so expensive, it was the reason why Ronnie Bronze had targeted them for emotional manipulation. The owners of these new 'homebots', would be living in London's premier houses, and therefore would have access to the luxuries that Ronnie wanted to steal. Being new robots meant they had the latest electronic circuitry, and anti-corruption fire-walls. This would cause a very real problem for any computer hacker.

However, Shirley was at the top of her game, and one of only five adults in the UK, (excluding Ocean), who had the IT expertise and ability to 'hack' in to the core files of the 'homebots'. Ronnie Bronze had chosen his criminal partner well.

Michael was a little confused. He had completed all his home chores, and as he didn't need to cook dinner for Daube this evening, he found himself with three hours to spare before 'The Chimney Challenge' started at 10.00pm. With his master eating at The Lexington Club, Michael the 'homebot' was conflicted. Should he or shouldn't he? – that was the question.

He paced the tiled hall on the ground floor, and came to a standstill in front of the large gilt framed mirror. Michael looked at himself, and what he saw looking back at him, was a 'homebot' who had never experienced life outside of Farm Street. He wanted to feel something more, something extra. He needed to add an extra dimension to his life. He was lonely, and he wanted company.

With great deliberation, he peered outside the glossy black door, and sniffed the air. It was cold and damp, but not raining. Plucking up the courage, Michael slipped on his black winter coat, selected one of Daube's wooden cane umbrellas, and stepped outside the house. He had crossed the threshold that divided the inside and outside world. He was a 'homebot' who had broken the rules.

Where to walk? he thought. I know. Green Park. He brought up a virtual map of Mayfair, and selected the scenic route. Opting for visual dimension data, Michael could see images of Green Park in Spring. It looked delightful. Switching to 'current' mode, the Spring images changed to a November night time at 19.15pm. Activation accepted, Michael began his walk to the park. He marveled at all the activity London possessed of an evening. People, drones and electronic lizards passed him by in a blur. The noise, colour and movement enthralled him. Michael was a 'homebot' who had challenged himself to see another side to life, and what he saw, amazed him.

One hour later, and Michael reappeared on the doorstep of Daube's town house. He had walked, as if in a dream for sixty minutes. His world, as he knew it, had collided. His head was full of sounds and images from his excursion. Michael, was unsure quite what to make of it all, but as he removed his coat, and returned to the domestic tranquility he knew, he realized that his view of the world had changed, forever.

Chapter 18

At The Lexington Club, Wattle, Daube, Molly and Ocean were seated at a table with deep red leather chairs. Atmospheric lighting and a candle in the middle of the table, further enhanced the mood. Ocean, with the active encouragement of Wattle, had ordered the 'house' vegi-burger and a banana smoothie. As the 4 of them waited for their food to arrive, Wattle didn't think it would be necessary to activate the visible thought bubbles. He was pretty certain that Daube agreed with him. Visible thought bubbles, (VTB), were extremely useful. It allowed the partner's to message their thoughts to each other in the form of a floating transparent bubble above their heads. Thoughts became readable text, which enabled Wattle and Daube to communicate silently with each other. The thought bubbles were invisible to anyone else. It had proved extremely useful in the past.

Daube was unsure how this clever communication device would be viewed in the wider community. Far better, to use the invention for one on one cases with Wattle, on a strictly 'need to know' basis. The VTB would not be required over dinner, as Wattle was convinced he was sitting amongst friends tonight. Chatting with Molly and Ocean, was not like your usual client meeting. It was much more relaxed and informal. He hoped Daube felt the same.

'So, Ocean,' said Daube, do tell me how you developed this interest of yours in space travel and IT?'

'Well,' replied Ocean, 'the space travel stuff started with my dad really.'

Ocean looked over at Molly as if expecting a comment from mum, but Molly remained tight lipped.

'Your dad?' said Daube

'Yes, my dad. He lives on Saturn now, in one of the new space colonies. He moved there when I was one, and since then, I have always been interested in space stuff.'

'I see.' said Daube. 'And do you share this interest in space travel Molly?'

'No. No I don't. I'm quite happy here on earth, thank you very much.'

'Do you like computers Frank?' asked Ocean.

'Well, you know what,' replied Wattle smiling, 'I think you should put that question to Roger.'

'Do you like computers Roger?'

'Yes, yes I do. I think they play an important part in modern society,' said Daube seriously.

'And what about robots? I love Robots. I find them fascinating,' said Ocean.

'Yes, and Robots too. I have a 'homebot' called Michael.'

'A 'homebot' called Michael? Wow, that sounds like fun. Can I meet him?' asked Ocean.

'Ocean Jones – where are your manners?' said Molly quickly.

'Can I meet him? Please. Please. Please.'

Wattle looked over at Daube and grinned. He was looking forward to see how Daube was going to handle this one.

'Well Ocean, all in good time. Michael is quite shy, and not really used to visitors,' explained Daube.

'Oh, that's a pity. I'm really good with robots, aren't I mum?'

'And modest with it, Ocean Jones' replied Molly.

By the time, Harris and his team had removed the empty plates, and brought the pudding menus, Wattle and Daube were left in no doubt whatsoever, that Ocean was an extremely bright and quick- witted young lady.

They discussed the events at The Pyramid department store, and in the process, discovered that Ocean was also an accomplished computer hacker. What a clever, and rather unusual child, thought Daube.

'For a fourteen-year old, she has remarkable skills, far in advance of her age,' he said to Wattle, as they walked back to the agency together.

'A very interesting girl Rog.' 'Do you fancy throwing caution to the wind, and having breakfast with me tomorrow?' He knew what the answer was going to be, but was pleasantly surprised by Daube's response.

'I will Wattle. Why not. It will make a pleasant change. Nothing too greasy now. I'm serious Wattle. I have a delicate stomach, as you are well aware.'

Chapter 19

'That was a disagreeable croissant,' said Daube haughtily, pushing his plate aside.

'Looks alright to me Rog,' replied Wattle.

'It was burnt on each end and undercooked in the middle,' said Daube.

'You should have had a London bun Rog. Never fails to deliver. Trust me.'

'Not my thing Wattle,'

'A London bun not your thing? - Roger Daube, wash your mouth out right now. I grew up on London buns, and just look at me.'

'I rest my case,' answered Daube dryly.

The conversation continued in that vein for the next ten minutes. It was a rare thing for both Wattle and Daube to take breakfast together. They were just too busy. The case of the toy monkey was taking up more time than either private detective had anticipated. They needed assistance.

'I've been thinking Rog - now stay with me on this one. What if we asked Ocean Jones to help us? She is a certified computer genius for her age. What do you think?'

'I think you may have a point Wattle. She was certainly keen. What would Molly say?'

'Let me contact her. See what she thinks.'

'Keep me informed. Now I must go. I have something to attend to,' said Daube vaguely.

'Will do Rog, will do, replied Wattle cheerily. 'Where are you off to? Anywhere exciting?'

'Nowhere special. Nowhere special,' lied Daube, as he stood up and left the coffee shop.

Wattle looked up at his departing colleague and friend quizically and shook his head.

Grabbing his raincoat; Wattle slipped out of the coffee shop and into the buzz and chaos of London. He could just make out Daube in the distance. Now Frank Wattle was a street hound, and the roads of London were his playground. If anyone could blend into the city surroundings, then it was him. He knew Roger Daube was out of his comfort zone, as he headed east and towards the Oriental district. Weaving between laser lizards, drones and people of all sizes and shapes, Wattle followed at a discreet distance. Now why would his partner be walking over to east London, he wondered?

The taxi hologram drowned out his mutterings with the latest travel updates, and the grey sky over London turned black and moody. Wattle felt the first raindrops begin to fall as he continued to weave in and out of the traffic in his pursuit of Daube.

He was just about to cross the junction that divided the city from the Oriental district, when a hyper-bus sped past, blocking his view of Daube. One hundred metres long, and separated into ten compartments, the purple hyper-buses were a sight to behold. They were near silent, and hovered at child's height above the road on a cloud of hot air.

As the warm air current hit Wattle in the face, he had to wait thirty seconds whilst the purple machine swooshed by in front of him. By the time the last carriage had gone past, Roger Daube was nowhere to be seen.

Wattle sighed, and crossed the road in to the Oriental quarter. No hyper bus could travel along the narrow streets that made up this vibrant part of London.

What should I do? thought Wattle. It was pointless searching the maze of little roads, in the hope he would stumble across Daube. The exercise was futile.

He had reached the steps leading up to the PPP (People's Pleasure Palace), and was contemplating a cheeky visit to one of its many distractions, when he noticed a very orange looking man walk right past him.

There was nothing unusual in his manner, it was just his orange face that caught Wattle's attention. He thought nothing of it. The PPP attracted all types, and an orange face was not illegal, just eye catching. Wattle weighed up the possibility of a quick gamble on one of the magic pony races, when a vision of Mrs. Wattle with a stern look brought him down to earth.

Dismissing any thoughts of pony racing, Wattle turned around, and headed back to 188 Piccadilly. He would contact Molly, and think about what to do with Daube another day.

By mid-morning, returning to an empty office, Daube sat down. He stared blankly at the wall, and thought about his encounter with Ocean Jones in the oriental district last week. He pondered on his brief accidental meeting with her and was forced to admit to himself, that his emotions had been stirred. He felt incredibly protective about a teenage girl he knew nothing about. Practically orphaned, and living with a 'homebot' did not constitute a healthy adult state of mind. Daube was repressed, and he knew why. A child with no brothers or sisters had meant that he hid his true feelings from the world.

Frank Wattle was a married man in his forties and a father of six. He engaged with the world and for good and bad dealt with the problem's life throws your way. Daube on the other hand, closed his Mayfair townhouse door and locked the world out. What was he afraid of? He was now actively thinking about his past, and particularly his childhood.

Daube stood up, and peered out of the grubby windows towards Piccadilly Circus. As the neon lights flared and distorted in front of him, he decided to message Ocean. He couldn't explain why she was so important to him, but he knew he had to talk to her alone, as soon as possible.

Chapter 20

As the rain began to smudge the dirty office windows, Roger Daube turned away from the neon glare of London, and recalled his second experience in Memory Lane.

As he had walked through the seething mass of people, he was determined to seek out the invisible phone booth. He had blanked out the roving digital adverts, and as he passed the electronic shoe lizard, he saw on the far side of the street, the place where the red telephone box stood. How had he missed it before? He can't have been concentrating.

Daube paused for a moment. It was only then, that it dawned on him. The red box was only visible to him, and no one else. If he began to lose concentration, it began to fade from view.

He stepped confidently forward and opened the glass door. He went inside, and knew what to do. Carefully, Daube punched in his date of birth into the keypad, and waited for the response.

'How can I be of assistance?' said the odd voice on the other end of the telephone.

'I would like to go to Memory Lane please,' said Daube politely.

'You would like to, or you want to.' said the voice. 'There is a difference.'

'I want to go to Memory Lane, I need to go to Memory Lane, I absolutely must go to Memory Lane,' he said urgently.

There was a pause.

Then the voice said calmly.

'Very well. This will be your second visit. You know what to do. There is no going back once you have made your decision. Do you understand?'

'Yes,' replied Daube.

'Then place your left hand on the metal plate in front of you. Close your eyes and concentrate,' said the voice.

Daube obeyed, and within an instant he was transported to the very same part of the street as before.

Once again, a familiar voice from behind his head spoke to him.

'Two purchases Roger. Only one purchase left. Use them wisely. Do you want to continue the experience from your first visit?'

'Yes, I do.'

As Daube turned around, and looked at the hologram of his own brain, he half expected the image of his mind to merge with his body. Instead, it floated at Daube's eye level.

'Choose your second memory shard carefully, and be aware of the repercussions,' and with that, his brain faded away.

Not very helpful, thought Daube, as he glanced across Memory Lane. At first, the street looked exactly like his first visit. The wooden shops were still huddled together, and the uneven road made walking difficult.

As he stared at the various entrances, he spotted a neon number two in blue with an arrow pointing right underneath it.

Was this a trick of the mind? A temptation teaser? He had heard of them, and the catastrophic consequences of choosing the wrong one. He remembered a story about a woman who had chosen a temptation teaser. She had selected badly, and her precious memory shards had been erased, (Rinsed), never to be returned. All she was left with was a blank mind. It was a cautionary tale.

The Japanese red lanterns glowed in the fading light. Daube felt calm and alert. His senses were heightened. He looked up at the dark sky above, and noticed that the clouds appeared to be moving quickly, even though there was no wind. Was time speeding up?

Was his life slipping past him?

He needed to relax and concentrate on the task in hand. Daube took a deep breath, and as he exhaled, he realized that he must return to the same shop. He peered down the murky dim street, until he found the shop front he was looking for. He gently opened the door, and saw the outline of an old person behind a wooden counter.

'So, you have returned,' said the old man. 'What took you so long?'

'I needed time to think,' replied Daube. 'I needed time to reflect.'

'Time is what you make of it. Time is precious. Do you not agree?'

Daube stared at the wizened old man. How old was he? 'I do agree,' he answered.

The man must have been over a hundred years old. His movements were slow, but strangely graceful.

He reached under the counter, and produced a small metal gong, which he tapped with a thin bamboo stick three times. Moments later, the old woman, half bent over, appeared from behind a silk curtain. She walked slowly towards Daube, and held out her wrinkled left hand.

'Place your right hand in my palm. That's it. There is no need to be afraid. I just need to be reassured about your commitment to this second memory shard experience. That's it.'

As she spoke, the man produced a tea pot with steam wafting from the spout.

'Mr. Daube has chosen the traditional method. Shall we continue?'

Daube nodded, and lent forward to breathe in the infusion from the tea pot. He was about to experience his second memory shard.

Chapter 21

Ronnie Bronze was becoming larger. At first, he thought he was imagining it. But no. He was definitely expanding. How many more meals with Shirley would he have to eat?

'I have treats Ronnie,' said Shirley, wiggling a bag in front of his nose.

Ronnie smiled weakly, and like a man who knows resistance is pointless, said; 'Thank you.'

He had just completed his first night shift alone, and things had not gone quite to plan. Shirley, who was the brains behind the operation, had finished the first night surveillance, and successfully directed the toy monkey to hack in to the security codes and gain access to the secure robotics department on the fifty-fifth floor. From there, it had been a case of being patient, as the monkey rebooted one of the ten Z star deluxe model X 'homebots', before returning to the toy floor. The whole operation had taken Shirley five hours.

The second night shift, was Ronnie's first attempt at repeating what Shirley had achieved, and rebooting the second deluxe 'homebot'. He had encountered problems in manipulating the movements of the monkey, and at one stage, it had wandered out of the store and out on to the streets surrounding The Pyramid Department store.

Ronnie, sweating like a man who has just run a marathon, somehow managed to correct the movements of the wandering monkey, and return it to the fifty-fifth floor. He prayed, that the monkey hadn't been seen by anyone. This detour, had added two hours to Ronnie's operation, and it was just after 6.00am. when he could relax and wait for Shirley. Six hours of stress, should be helping him lose weight. It wasn't.

The last thing he needed were treats from Shirley. He felt physically sick, as he meekly accepted another calorific pastry.

'How did it go?' asked Shirley.

Wiping the sweat from his brow, Ronnie didn't dare tell Shirley about the wandering monkey. Admittedly, it had taken him six instead of five hours to complete the task, but at least he had successfully rebooted the deluxe 'homebot'. Shirley, loomed over the laptop, looking at a string of binary codes and computer jargon that Ronnie didn't understand.

Satisfied with her statistics and analytical data, she closed the laptop, and announced loudly;

'Two 'homebots' rebooted, eight to go Ronnie. How about a full English Breakfast? I'm famished.'

Ronnie muttered something along the lines of, 'Good idea Shirley. You must have read my mind,' before following her out of the empty office and off for a big fry up.

Roger Daube had loved Brittles of London. The shop had held a special place in his heart ever since he could remember, and now he was conflicted. The box with the chocolate in the shape of the initial R had troubled him. To receive the chocolate letter R on your birthday, was a tradition that he had grown up with. Admittedly, it was tinged with sadness about the absence of his parents, but Harold the 'carebot', had always made a big fuss over the visit to Brittles.

The mysterious delivery of the chocolate initial had triggered memories from his past. Daube felt compelled to investigate.

Michael the 'homebot' had spent the previous day in a dream world. He had finished the ironing, cleaned the lounge and planned dinner. These were all activities he undertook regularly, but after his walk in the park experience, he felt different. He went about his duties as efficiently as ever, but something had changed. Was it his outlook on the world that had altered? He wasn't sure. He was a robot for goodness sake, and yet he felt emotions like his master and friend, Roger Daube.

A generation 4 'homebot' was an advanced machine, and it was only a few months ago that the Z Star deluxe model X had been released to universal acclaim with memory/emotion function, but a generation 4 'homebot' wasn't programmed to feel emotional thoughts. It was all becoming a little confusing.

Plucking up the courage, that a generation 4 'homebot' shouldn't possess, Michael made a momentous decision. He was going to go shopping, or to be more precise, he was going to go robot researching.

Selecting one of Daube's posh umbrellas, Michael put on his overcoat, and set out into the busy streets of London. He was in need of a strong Italian espresso coffee, but resisting the temptation, he made his way to The Pyramid department store.

The sky lounge at the top of the huge building, was somewhere Michael had always wanted to go. He had seen the pictures, on television, and he wanted to experience the views across London for himself. He calculated, that he had the time, and so took the express elevator to the top floor.

After sampling the amazing London skyline, Michael headed to the fifty-fifth floor and the robotics department. He went straight over to the stand where the new Z-Star 'homebots' were on display.

'Hello – my name is Atlanta. How may I be of assistance to

you today?'

Michael was tongue tied, and his eyes became glazed. He couldn't believe what he was feeling. The robot in front of him was the most beautiful thing he had ever seen. Was it love at first sight?

Michael scanned the sale price for Atlanta. As she was a Z star deluxe model X 'homebot', she was very, very expensive.

Michael was almost relieved, that Atlanta cost so much. A machine as beautifully built and crafted as her, should not be cheap and mass produced. It made sense to his electronic mind, that the Z star robot series would be exclusive, and only available to the rich and famous.

The emotion/memory function on these deluxe models could be over-ridden by their owners, but the hard facts, were that this was the most advanced, and technically brilliant robot ever built. It had the capability to have human like emotions, and a memory that could store and remember a lifetime of experiences in a split second. It was a wonderful piece of engineering. Michael was duly impressed.

He wanted to know more about the Z star 'homebot' functions, and so located the manager. Michael scanned the name tag; Mr. Leaf – Manager.

'Excuse me please Mr. Leaf,' said Michael formally.

Mr. Leaf looked at him, and exclaimed; 'Oh my goodness. A 4th generation 'homebot'. You are a 4th generation, are you not?'

'I am indeed,' replied Michael politely.

'I thought so, I thought so,' burbled Mr. Leaf excitedly. 'How may I be of assistance?'

'Could you give me some more details on the Z star deluxe model X 'homebots' please,' said Michael.

'Of course, dear boy, of course. How much time do you have?

Or are there any specific features you are interested in? There are so many, you see. The Z star is an extremely accomplished machine.'

'Well, now that you mention it, there are,' said Michael.

'Splendid, splendid. And what are those?' asked Mr. Leaf.

'The memory/emotion function. Could you explain how those work on a robot please?'

Mr. Leaf, removed his spectacles, and cast a curious glance at Michael.

'My, my, One is an inquisitive 'homebot', isn't one?'

If robots could blush, and Michael was pretty sure that the Z star probably could, then he would have blushed.

Instead, he clapped his hands together, and made up a story, about how his owner was interested in purchasing one, and how he had been in service to Daube for many years. Sadly, his owner was considering retiring him, and upgrading to the impressive Z star model.

Mr. Leaf, listened intently, and because he knew the generation 4 'homebots', did not possess the 'regret' mode of thinking, he launched into the specific details of the Z star's memory/emotion function with Michael. He was completely unaware of Michael's robotic mutation, and his ability to feel loss, sadness and loneliness.

Feeling overwhelmed, after his chat with Mr. Leaf, Michael even considered pepping himself up with a mood extraction experience, in the 'emotion' zone on the ground floor, when a retina message from Daube arrived, asking if a package had been delivered to Farm Street. This had the effect, of bringing Michael back to the here and now.

He left The Pyramid department store immediately, and started to make his way back home. He had duties to perform, and Daube would not be impressed, if he did not fulfil his daily tasks. He would collate everything Mr. Leaf had told him, and process the information at a later date.

It was a short walk back to Farm Street for Michael the 'homebot'. A walk he had covered in his robotic mind many times before. This time, the reality felt different. As London teemed with life and activity all around him, he was feeling an emotion close to what humans called joy. He was certain that was what it was, because his data analysis hardboard was becoming warm, and Michael was aware of a fuzzy feeling inside. He was on an emotional collision course after meeting Atlanta. That much he did know.

All his programmable sensors were recording rapid activity and massively increased data transmission pulses. Is this what humans experienced, he wondered? The only similar correlation was drinking caffeine. Michael considered what would happen if he now went and drank a strong black coffee. All the evidence retrieved from his data memory banks, told him it would overload his sensory capacity receptors. It could even shut itself down and cause a reboot problem with memory delay.

He erred on the side of caution, and took a very human gulp of air instead.

As he returned to the front steps of Daube's town house on Farm Street, he saw a delivery lounge lizard knocking on the door.
'Can I help you?' enquired Michael.
'Parcel delivery for a Roger Daube,' said the lizard.
'I'm his 'homebot'. I can scan for it' said Michael.

'Very well - scan here mate,' said the lizard.

I'm not your mate, thought Michael, as he duly obliged, and took the package inside.

He peered at the purple box, but thought nothing of the initial D, which appeared on the front. It was light, and exactly the same wrapping and design as the box he had accepted for Daube earlier in the week from Brittles of London. Michael walked to the study, and carefully placed the parcel on Daube's fine wooden desk. It was only as he was about to close the door, that he noticed the first box with the letter R on it, positioned in the corner of the room.

Two identical boxes with initials on them didn't strike Michael as anything particularly unusual. He knew that Daube had a weakness for chocolate, and Brittles of London was famous for its exceptional quality and taste. He made a mental note, to increase Daube's exercise regime to compensate for any indulgent chocolate nibbling that might take place, and walked in to the kitchen to plan tonight's dinner.

Chapter 22

Wattle was busy all afternoon, catching up with his network of contacts. It was only when he returned to the office and realised the time of day, that he decided to send Mrs. Wattle an e-kiss. Selecting a big warm sloppy one, from his list of twenty different types, Wattle pinged it over to Mrs. Wattle and accompanied it with a short message, asking if it was possible to have chicken pie for dinner tomorrow night?

His domestic duties performed, Wattle settled himself into his well-worn chair, and messaged Molly Jones. Could he speak with her when she returned home from work tonight? He had a favour to ask.

A prompt reply of yes, was followed by; what time?

Wattle messaged back, and suggested seven 'o' clock.

He sat back in his chair, and considered how he was going to ask Molly for Ocean's assistance. After thinking about his approach, Wattle decided to just come out with it. Molly could only say no. He had nothing to lose.

Ocean ate her breakfast at break neck speed.

'In a hurry dear?' asked her grandmother Gwen.

'Yes gran, I am. I need to be somewhere by 8.00am. I can't be late.'

'You will give yourself indigestion Ocean. Slow down a little.'

Ocean looked over at her grandmother, and continued to shovel her breakfast cereal down. She gulped the last mouthful, grabbed her school backpack and waved at Gwen.

'See you tonight Gran. Love you.'

'Love you too,' replied her grandmother, and on that note, Ocean swept out of her front door.

Arriving at the school gates earlier than she had anticipated, Ocean looked around for her best friend, Mo. Patel. The school had an intake of two thousand pupils, and because of the large number of young adults, classes had staggered starting times throughout the week.

Eye scans and weapon detection took time to complete on two thousand pupils, and even though the education lizards were quick in processing the students, you had to allow twenty minutes before you were admitted to the school front hall.

As hundreds of pupils filtered through the system, she spotted Mo. in the distance. Ocean was too cool to wave, but she began weaving between bodies until she reached him.

'Morning Mo.'

'Good morning to you Ocean.' What's up?'

'Nothing.'

Really? I don't buy it.'

'I said nothing. Why don't you believe me?'

'Because I know you Ocean Jones. When have you ever met me outside the school gates before?'

'Ummmmm.'

'Exactly. Never. Never. Never.'

'Ok, ok. I do want something.'

'And?'

'I need favour.'

'Which is?'

'I need to bunk off school at lunchtime. I have to be somewhere.'

'Oh really. Care to tell me where and with whom?'

'I can't Mo, I really can't, but I promise I will tell you everything when I'm ready.'

'I kind of believe you Ocean.'

'Thanks Mo. You are one in a million.'

'A compliment. I'm going to faint.'

'Ha. Ha. Very funny.'

What do I have to do?'

'Well, I'm going to pull a 'sickie' before Math's at 11.00am. I need you to cover for me. Say you saw me feeling unwell in the history lesson before break, and then say the same to my mum if she finds out. I need to be sent home so that I can do my stuff.'

'Alright. But you owe me big time. You understand?'

Yep. Thanks Mo. I'll make it up to you,' and as abruptly as the conversation had started, it finished, and the two teenagers filed in to school.

Roger Daube knew meeting Ocean Jones was going to be an important milestone for him. He surveyed his empire, and had to admit, that Michael the 'homebot' had thoroughly cleaned the house from top to toe. Even Daube's critical eye couldn't fault Michael's impeccable cleaning. Everything was in its rightful place, just as he liked it.

A strange thought crossed his mind. Was Michael becoming him? Was he living with his doppelganger?

Before he could answer those weighty questions, Michael appeared with his morning coffee.

'Ah. Michael. I was just thinking of you.'

'Great minds think alike. Isn't that the saying?'

'Yes, it is,' replied Daube, who truth be told, was a little thrown. He would have to think about Michael another time. He needed to go to work.

As Ocean climbed aboard the No. 17 hyper-bus to Green Park, a rare ray of sunshine reflected off the third-floor window where she was about to sit. Usually, teenagers are not particularly bothered by the weather conditions, but as this was November with rain and gloom the usual conditions, this fleeting ray of light signalled to Ocean that she was destined to have a positive meeting with Roger Daube.

Fifteen minutes later, and Ocean arrived at Green Park. She had never stepped foot in the exclusive enclave of Mayfair and as she programmed Daube's Farm Street address to retina display, an array of smart looking restaurants and chic salons appeared in her field of view. Ocean blinked twice, and erased this data from her display. She was only interested in talking to Roger Daube. Nothing else interested her.

The meeting with Ocean had been agreed for midday. Daube walked briskly from Piccadilly to Farm Street, and let himself in to his stylish London town house. He went straight to his study, and froze. On his desk was a second box with the initial D written on it. Before he had time to consider the implications of this, the elegant front door bell chimed.

Ocean was greeted by Michael the 'homebot', and shown in to the impressive drawing room.

'Please take a seat Ms. Jones. Mr. Daube will be with you shortly.'

'Please call me Ocean.'

'Ocean it will be from now on. Can I get you a drink?'

Suddenly feeling incredibly important, Ocean asked for a cup of London tea.

'Will you be taking sugar and milk with that?' enquired Michael.

Milk and one sugar please. Thanks. That would be great. I appreciate it.'

'You are more than welcome, Ms, forgive me, I mean Ocean.'

'No Problem,' she replied.

As she waited patiently for Daube to appear, Ocean surveyed

the smart drawing room. Everything was so tastefully decorated, and the room looked immaculate. A picture of Daube hung above a large fireplace in an expensive looking frame. She sighed, breathed in the scented clean air, and prepared herself for the meeting with him.

A discreet knock on the study door, signaled to Daube that Michael was outside.

'An Ocean Jones to see you Roger.' Are you alright Sir?'

Daube looked as white as a sheet.

'Ah. What? Yes. Yes,' muttered Daube.

'I've shown Ocean Jones in to the drawing room. I'm going to make her a cup of tea. Would you like anything?'

'Yes. A cup of tea please. Thank you, Michael. I don't know what I would do without you.'

'My pleasure Sir. Remember, I am here to serve.'

'Yes, of course. But you mean more to me than that. You are my best friend. A companion, so to speak. Do you understand, Michael?'

'I think so. Ocean is still waiting in the drawing room.'

'Yes, of course. I shall be right in. Oh, and Michael?'

Yes Sir.'

'Thank you for being so kind and considerate.'

'Think nothing of it,' said the 'homebot', as he silently walked off towards the kitchen.

A minute later, and Roger Daube presented himself to Ocean.

'So, we finally get to talk in private Ocean. I'm guessing we have a lot to talk about. Am I correct?'

Ocean stared straight at Daube, and the first words that came out of her mouth were;

'I feel like I've known you my whole life. I can't explain it. I just have this sort of feeling here,' as she pointed to her stomach.

'Well, if it's any consolation Ocean. I feel just the same.'

Over several cups of London tea and smart sandwiches, the two new found friends talked and talked and talked.

'I've no recollection of my father,' said Ocean. 'I was too young when he left my mum. I know for certain that she has never forgiven him. He broke her heart you see.'

'Ah, a broken heart. Well, that is hard to mend, and in some people, it never heals. Your mother must have loved him deeply.'

'Yes, she did, although she would never admit that now. Not to anybody. But I know.'

'I'm sure you do Ocean.'

There was a slight pause in the conversation.

'It can't have been easy for your mother, bringing you up alone. Try to remember that, and particularly when you feel angry towards her.'

'I do try. I really do, but sometimes it is really hard. Anyway, she didn't raise me alone. She had my grandmother to help.

And what about you Roger?' What was your upbringing like? It must have been so different to mine.'

'Yes and no, ' replied Daube. 'Different circumstances, but not so dissimilar really. You see Ocean, I am a kind of orphan. I have never known my mother, and my father is a total stranger to me. I also feel a sense of loss and abandonment. Maybe, that was what united us. A common bond, so to speak.'

'Yes, Yes. That must be it. I'm not a superstitious person, but I felt something unifying when we first met. It had a huge physical and mental impact on me. I can't put it in to words.'

'I felt just the same. I guess we were just destined to meet.'

Outside the house, the cacophony of noise that was London in 2085, carried on unabated. Inside the drawing room, it was another world.

Chapter 23

Frank Wattle was an industrious fellow. Laziness was not his thing and he never shied away from a task, however menial. He had grown up in South East London, and was the youngest of three brothers. His father had been a petrol station supervisor, before all the oil in the world had been drilled and consumed by 2040. As the oil industry collapsed, to be replaced by cleaner energy, Frank Wattle senior lost his job and his meagre pension. The global economy had gone in to a major recession for five years, and he never found meaningful employment again.

Frank recalled his old man, sitting in his rocking chair in the front room, staring blankly in to space, devoid of conversation. He was dead two years later. That powerful image of his father was never far from his thoughts when he had had a tough day. Frank senior had never recovered from the shock of losing his job, and he had spiraled in to depression. Frank junior was made of sterner stuff. He had inherited his mother's positive outlook on life. He was an optimist.

As the November afternoon seeped away to a murky winter dusk, Wattle reckoned he deserved an egg snack from the Yolk of York. He slipped on his tight-fitting raincoat, and made his way to Tony Tanner's.

'I know where you are off to,' said the automated vending machine archly.

Wattle ignored the annoying machine and entered the elevator. Five minutes later, he was propped up on a stool talking with Tony.

'Afternoon Frank – your usual mate?'

'You've twisted my arm Tony, you crafty old devil.'

Tony Tanner laughed, and set about cracking three eggs. With his back to Wattle he shouted;

'Mrs. Wattle well?'

'In rude health. Thanks for asking,' replied Frank. 'How's business?'

'I can't complain. Ever since beef was banned for commercial sale, I've steadily picked up customers. Yes, they used to moan about their lack of steak with the eggs, but like everything else in life, you soon get used to it.'

'You're are not wrong there Tony,' replied Wattle. 'As a kid, my parents could never afford to buy beef, so you don't miss what you've never had.'

'Same with me Frank. I never grew up eating beef either. Funny old world.'

As Wattle's plate of fried eggs sunny side up appeared before him, alongside a large mug of steaming London tea, he looked above Tony Tanner's head as the neon fried egg flickered on and off before finally dying.

'Your eggs 'caput'. I know a man down my street that is competitive on neon repair. Do you want his number?'

'Please Frank. What's his name?'

'If my memory serves me correctly, he's called Dave Johnson. Don't quote me on that though. I will message you when I get back to the office.'

Frank Wattle devoured his hot eggs and London tea. He had a tab at the Yolk of York, and he paid up front once a month.

'See you tomorrow Tony. You take care of yourself now.'

'You too, Frank. You too,' came the cheery response.'

As Wattle sniffed the chilly damp air, he remembered that he had agreed to call Molly Jones at 7.00pm. It was 4.00pm according to the giant digital clock at Piccadilly Circus, as he shuffled back to the office. London was aglow with colour, light and energy. It really was a 24/7 town which never slept. As the population had steadily increased, so had the high-rise building craze. It needed to, just to accommodate all the commercial and residential requirements. London now had a population exceeding fifty million people. Ever since the building of new homes had been banned outside the now obsolete M25, the dramatic skyline rivalled any other great city on the planet. The neon shimmer from the skyscrapers of Soho cast a phosphorescent sheen over the West End. It was a dynamic town, with a multitude of residents with varying economic income. The super-rich lived shoulder to shoulder with the urban poor, alongside a plethora of robots and electronic lizards. It was truly a diverse and interesting society.

Wattle returned to 188 Piccadilly, and tiptoed past the slumbering automated vending machine. He was certain he had heard a tiny snore from the cheeky contraption.

Where was Daube, he wondered. He had slipped out before midday and obviously not returned. Daube's desk was as immaculate as ever, with his orthopedic chair neatly tucked under his desk. Wattle removed his raincoat, and glanced at his messy area. Piles of paper contrasted with his colleague's tidy work-space. He sighed and slumped in to his creaky old seat. Battered and supremely comfortable, Wattle adored this old chair.

He sent a retina message to Mrs. Wattle, and then one to Tony Tanner with the details of the neon repair man, and then settled down to skim the court circulars.

Ocean and Daube had agreed to work together at The Wattle and Daube Detective Agency, just so long as Molly was ok with this arrangement. It must not interfere with Ocean's school work, or impact negatively on Ocean's relationship with her mother. Daube had consented to Ocean's request not to tell Molly the personal nature of their newfound friendship. At least, not just yet.

He had persuaded Ocean to accept that any working arrangement had to have Molly's blessing. This point was not open to discussion. Ocean had reluctantly agreed.

As she departed Daube's fancy London town house, she had thanked Michael for his refreshments, and stated her intention that she would like to see him again.

'It was a pleasure meeting you Ocean. A genuine pleasure,' replied Michael.

The pleasantries dispensed with, Ocean had said her goodbyes and left. She needed to be home before 6.00pm just in case the school had called her mother. She gulped the cool air on Daube's front door step and slipped out in to the night.

'A charming young lady Sir. How did you say you met her?'

'I didn't, Michael, and yes, I agree with you. Ocean is one exceptional young lady.'

Daube headed towards his study, which was a clear signal to Michael, that he didn't want to be disturbed.

Wattle yawned. It was 7.00pm and he had to retina message Molly. She answered immediately.

'Mr. Wattle.'

Please call me Frank.'

'Frank'

'I've been giving something some urgent consideration Molly. Now, please here me out before you answer. Would you be agreeable to Ocean helping out at the 'agency?'. It must not get in the way of her school work, and if you feel it is having a detrimental effect on her, then we will stop the arrangement immediately.'

'Well, I must say, I didn't see that coming Frank. I must be honest.'

'I don't want to upset the apple cart Molly. If you are unhappy, I will stop right now.'

'It's not that I am unhappy. Ocean is a very smart girl, and she is way smarter and knowledgeable than I was at the same age, but she can be headstrong.

'As a parent of six children I can sympathize,' replied Wattle, laughing. I guess it is all part of growing up. However, the case we have agreed to investigate is an unusual one, and Ocean possesses exceptional computer hacking skills that Roger and I do not.'

Can I have a chat with Ocean tonight, and message you tomorrow morning. Is that alright?'

'Yes, of course it is Molly, and please don't feel any pressure to agree, just because we want to utilize Ocean's skill-set. You are her mother, and whatever you think is best for Ocean will be the right decision,' replied Wattle reassuringly.

'Thanks Frank. I will speak to you tomorrow morning. Good night.'

As nighttime descended on Central London, Frank considered what Mrs. Wattle was rustling up for his dinner. He would be too late to eat with all the family, but Mrs. W. always kept some tasty morsels aside for him.

Chapter 24

Less than a mile away, Roger Daube was also in a contemplative mood. He had deliberately shut himself away in his study, and declined dinner with Michael. He could not keep his mind from thinking about the psychological implications of two personal deliveries, which had both arrived within hours of him purchasing a memory shard. One delivery was strange, but two was not a coincidence. Was he transferring his secrets and guilt from Memory Lane to an actual physical location? He had no idea. Daube realized that Memory Lane did not actually exist. It was merely a mental representation of his subconscious. Then how was it possible that he had triggered a thought transference to his actual home?

As Daube thought about his recent experiences, it had also caused him to question his relationship with Michael, his generation 4 'homebot'. Was it his imagination, or was Michael beginning to replicate him? It was all becoming very confusing. A dull thud, then a gentle patter caused Daube to look towards the study window. It was beginning to rain again.

Roger Daube stood up, and paced up and down on the wooden study floorboards. He had always been completely contained as an individual. He had been raised by Harold, his generation one 'carebot' to be independent and self-sufficient, and these mixed feelings he was experiencing now, were new to him.

Who could he talk to? Wattle was the obvious answer, but Daube didn't want to mix his personal and business life up too much. At the back of his mind he already knew who to confide in. It couldn't be anyone else, but Ocean Jones.

Ocean caught the hyper-bus to Muswell Hill via Covent Garden Interstellar station. This mega transport hub was a launch terminal to the space colonies of Mars, Jupiter and Saturn. As Ocean watched the congested mass of commuters, travelers and lizards, a 'homebot' disrupted her musings with a polite cough.

'Excuse me. Could I possibly trouble you to move along one seat? I can't squeeze past you with all these bags.'

Ocean looked at the 'homebot' and the distinctive blue bags from the Pyramid Department store, smiled, and replied;

'Of course. No problem.' She shuffled along,

'Thank you. I appreciate it,' said the 'homebot'

All generation 3 and 4 'homebot's' had the emotional capacity to empathize, and were excessively polite. The hyper- bus rose above the ground and headed towards north London.

Ocean turned her head to the right, and asked the 'homebot' a direct question.

'I do hope you don't mind me asking you, but when you visit the Pyramid department store, have you ever been tempted to use the mood extraction stalls within the 'emotion' zone?'

'What a curious question,' replied the 'homebot'. 'No, I haven't. I am totally content with my emotional range and capacity to serve my owner.'

'Oh, right. I was just wondering. That's all. My name is Ocean. Ocean Jones.'

'Clive,' responded the 'homebot'. 'It is a pleasure to meet you Ocean Jones.'

'Likewise, Clive.' There was a brief lull in the conversation, before Ocean said;

'I know a generation 4 'homebot' called Michael. He lives with and serves a friend of mine called Roger Daube. Are you a gen 3 or 4 'homebot'?

'Generation 3,' came the answer. My master's sister has a generation 4, purchased three years ago. A lovely piece of robotics engineering. Quicker and more refined in almost all areas. Technology doesn't stand still.'

'Tell me about it, Clive,' responded Ocean. 'How long can you operate on a single charge?'

'72 hours. The generation 4's can last a week without charge, and the new Z star's a month. Just imagine. A year on only twelve charges. That is astounding.'

'Progress, I guess, Clive.'

Ocean wished she could use visible thought bubbles (VTB's) on robots, but knew it wouldn't work. The thought occurred to her that eventually, 'homebots' would think and act in an identical way to humans. Then, thought transference would be possible. That would be awesome.

She was tapped on the shoulder by Clive.

'Primrose Hill. My stop. Goodbye, Ocean. I've enjoyed our brief chat.'

'Me too, Clive. Take care.'

As she watched the people descending from the hyper-bus, she involuntarily waved in the direction of the 'homebot' she had been talking with. It was doubtful that Clive had seen this small but genuine gesture of friendship from Ocean Jones. Was she softening? Ocean turned away and stared out of the window at the blur of activity that was London in 2085. Something had changed in her, but she wasn't yet quite sure what it was.

The neon sign for Hampstead lit up on the back of the seat in front. She would be at Muswell Hill in five minutes. Time to think about the bunking off school story she would need when she met her mum.

Chapter 25

Mrs. Wattle was ecstatic. She couldn't believe her luck. She had won a night out for two with dinner at McCarthy's, the swanky West End restaurant and cabaret joint. A meal there was unaffordable on the wages that she and Frank earned. She sent a retina message to her husband, with the good news. It had been over twenty-five years since she had last won anything and that was a bottle of fizz at the school raffle. This win was much more impressive. Finally, victory with the sniff and scratch cards she bought loyally each week. Wattle would be delighted.

Frank replied instantly, and confirmed that he would be home for dinner at 8.00pm.

Ocean strode through the front door and dashed upstairs to her bedroom. She flung her school bag on the floor and removed her purple boots. She slipped on her heat regeneration slippers in bright yellow, and went downstairs to confront whatever her mother had in store for her. Popping her head around the kitchen door, Ocean pouted, grinned and scowled, and all in a split second.

Molly, chose to ignore these minor facial histrionics and beckoned Ocean to sit down at the kitchen table.

Where was Gwen, when she needed back-up, thought Ocean.

'Mum?'

'Enough,' snapped Molly brusquely, Please, sit. I need to talk with you.'

She suspects something, thought Ocean. Keep cool. Don't let on.

'Mum, I can explain. Now don't get mad. You see....'

'Gran has been taken to hospital.'

'What,' gasped Ocean.

'You heard me. Gran has been taken to hospital. You were nowhere, so Gwen messaged an ambulance. Where were you?'

'Just out and about. Nothing special,' replied Ocean defensively.

'Really?'

'Yes. Don't get on my back mum. Is gran alright?'

'Thankfully, yes. I think so. They are keeping her in hospital overnight as a precaution.'

'What's wrong with her?'

Molly shrugged. 'They don't know. High blood pressure is one of the symptoms'

'Did she collapse? Is she in danger, mum?'

'Listen, Ocean. Your gran isn't going to live forever. She is old.'

'Not that old.'

'Old enough to die, my love.'

'Don't say that mum. Never say that. Gran is not going to die.'

'It happens to all of us, one day. It is part and parcel of life.'

'Don't be so defeatist. Gran is going to recover. Can we visit her?'

'Not tonight. She is sedated and sleeping. I will message the hospital in the morning and check on her progress.' Try not to get too upset.'

'I'm not upset, I'm angry,' said Ocean, wiping a tear away from her cheek. 'I love gran, and I want to see her.'

'You will. You will. All in good time. Ok? I'm as shocked as you are with the news, and we will do everything to ensure gran makes a full recovery. We Jones girls don't give up that easily. We are survivors.'

'I guess so.'

'That's the spirit. Now, tell me about your day'

Ocean realized that Molly had no idea she had bunked off school earlier. She was in the clear. At least for now. Over a basic meal of macaroni cheese, followed by fruit, mother and daughter discussed the possibility of assisting The Wattle and Daube Detective Agency. It was agreed that there would have to be very strict guidelines as to when and where Ocean helped out, and that it must never interfere with school. As they talked about the two men they had never even met two weeks ago, both females would secretly have to admit, and for entirely different reasons, that Frank Wattle and Roger Daube had made quite an impression on this little enclave from Muswell Hill.

Chapter 26

'The Chimney Challenge', on Channel 21, was the popular tv show that Daube and Michael watched together once a week. The format was simple and silly. A tv crew, fronted and presented by the national war hero Rebecca Jacobs, arrived at a secret house (location not revealed), and asked viewing participants through interactive smart sensor pads to guess the age, style and height of the chosen chimney. Extra bonus points were awarded for correctly guessing the number of bricks used in the construction of the chimney. An exact copy was then assembled in the tv studio, with the victorious contestant jumping through the top of the chimney and sliding down in to the open hearth. The winning prize of a holiday to one of the newly discovered outer colonies, was then presented to the excitable winning participant.

It was bland and pointless television of the highest order, and the national viewing figures, including streaming and retina downloads exceeded forty million people.

Daube realized he could totally relax in front of such banality, and actually forget about work. It was his secret addiction. Dumb tv, watched in association with his soul mate, Michael the 'homebot'.

As Daube settled down to watch this week's episode, Michael sat beside him and flicked on the extra high definition crystal clear 100' inch' screen. The room was transformed in to a home cinema, with surround sound from twenty hidden micro speakers.

The formula for the tv show never changed, which was reassuringly part of the viewing enjoyment and it was this repetitive element that Daube found so satisfying. With Michael next to him, he could, for a brief thirty minutes, once a week, cast away his concerns and worries about the world and his place within it.

Michael gently coughed and cleared his throat.

'Can I be impertinent, Sir, and retina pause 'The Chimney Challenge' for a few minutes.?' asked the 'homebot'.

Daube was taken aback by this request, and looked quizzically at his generation 4 robot.

'What is it Michael? What is on your mind?'

'I have a question I would like an answer to. Sir.'

'And that is?' enquired Daube.

'Well, Sir, I recently discovered that most owners allow their 'homebot' to undertake errands and duties outside of the house. Is this fact correct, Sir?'

There was a slight pause, whilst Daube adjusted his seating position, and took a good long look at his robot.

'It is, Michael. It is. What made you ask that question after all this time? Are you unhappy in your current position?'

'No, no, of course not, Sir. It's just that as you already know, generation 4 'homebots' are engineered to assimilate their owner's emotional needs and requirements, and that has left me curious about life outside of Farm Street. I have been feeling lonely. There, I have said it.'

Michael fidgeted with the cushions on the sofa, whilst he waited for his master's response.

When the reply came, it hit his digital processor hard.

'I wanted you all to myself, Michael. I realise, that sounds selfish and overly protective, but that is the way I felt. I never fully recovered from the retirement of Harold, and I didn't want to share you with anyone or anything. A selfish act? Yes. A controlling act? Quite possibly. A mean and unpleasant act? No, most definitely not. I always had your best interests at heart, so to speak.'

'I believe you, Sir, I really do. It's just that, I have been outside of this house, and only a few days ago. It was an experience that I want to repeat. I want you to trust me, Sir. All generation 4 'homebots' are programmed to try and achieve maximum pleasure for their owner's. I would never leave you. That, I can assure you. Never.'

'I'm pleased to hear that, Michael,' said Daube quietly. 'I never intended to trap you. It is just that as I regard my home as an inner sanctum from the hostile outside world, I didn't want to contaminate you with the ugliness and violence of everyday life in the modern world.'

'I am programmed to cope in hostile environments. I even have a synthetic 'slow-mo' mode to avoid undue stress. The generation 4 'homebot' may not be as advanced as the Z Star, but I feel that is an unfair comparison. They are the most complete robot ever engineered. We generation 4's are incredibly reliable, and emotionally very low maintenance.'

'I agree with everything you have said, Michael. My defense is not based on rational thinking. I have internalised my emotions all my life, as a mechanism to avoid dealing with the wider world. I have led a very cossetted existence and one with financial privileges. I am only too aware of my luck and good fortune. My upbringing could have been so much worse. My elite private education and inheritance has given me many opportunities that are not available to others. However, when I consider Wattle's background compared to mine, I can't help but feel I have missed out. Money is not everything. I am lonely, Michael. I don't have a family.'

'You have me, Sir.'

'And that is precisely why I have been overly protective towards you. Can you forgive me?'

'Generation 4's have a compatibility zonal reference mechanism. Therefore, I can't be angry or upset with you. I have been feeling frustrated, though.'

'I understand, Michael. How can I make things better between us?'

'Well, for a start, you could assign me chores and activities that enable me to leave the house once in a while. Is that an acceptable request?'

Daube lent forward, and hugged Michael. It was an iconic moment.

'Let's watch 'The Chimney Challenge. I can't quite believe last week's episode. It was unbelievable. Great tv though.'

'I couldn't agree more, Sir,' replied Michael, adjusting his retina from pause to play mode.

Molly had pre-programmed a meditation session with a de-stress hologram guru. She had considered cancelling the hour long tutorial because of the news concerning Gwen, but on reflection, a de-stress would be highly beneficial to her well-being.

Ocean had disappeared to her bedroom, in a pensive mood, which was perfectly understandable. Gwen and her only granddaughter were close, and Molly was not sure how Ocean would react to the news. There was still a definite tension between mother and daughter, that was ongoing and unresolved.

Molly hoped that the news of assisting The Wattle and Daube Detective Agency would help alleviate some of the friction between the two of them. She adjusted her retina to absorb mode and joined the meditation session. She was one of thirty thousand other 'absorbers' connecting to the tutorial. It was just what she needed.

An i-spy travel hologram lit up the back garden as it passed by overhead. Ocean collapsed on her bed and took out the 'tasty stretch' chewing gum. She stared at the blue wrapping, reading all the terms and conditions that were a precursor to using the product.

After five minutes consideration, Ocean decided to put the gum in a secret pocket of her hoodie. She had given it careful thought, and was prepared to use the gum, but only when it was essential. Thirty minutes shrinking or stretching sounded like fun, but it was risky, and what if she got caught?

Lying back on her bed, Ocean retina messaged Mo. and shared her experience of the visible thought bubble. As usual, Mo. was relaxed about who you practiced it on. His view was that if you could attain total focus and read a person's thoughts, then it gave you an advantage in life. Ocean, was not so sure. What were the ethical and moral considerations and was it even legal? Mo. was unsure, and not particularly bothered.

Discussion on VTB's exhausted, Ocean decided to discuss her meeting that afternoon with Roger Daube. Mo. was always a good sounding board, and Ocean trusted his opinion.

'He seems like a really interesting guy,' said Mo.

'He's more than that. I feel completely different when I am around him. It's like I have known Roger Daube my whole life. I feel really safe, which is 'kinda' weird, considering I've only just met him.'

'Go with your gut instinct. You will. not regret it.'

'Yeah. Yeah. You're right. It's just that I'm usually not great around men, and I lay the blame for that entirely at mum's door. She has passed her problems on to me, and I resent that.'

'Try to move on. I know it is easier to say than to put in to practice, but you can't let your mum drag you down. You are your own person. Forge your own way in the world.'

Ocean laughed and lightened up. A good talk with her best friend was just what she needed. Suddenly, an image of her grandmother flashed across her mind.

'Mo. I've bad news. My gran has been taken to hospital. She

collapsed in the house and no-one was around to help her. I'm going to see her tomorrow. Do you want to come?'

'Of course. Is she ok now?'

'Yeah. Well 'kind of. Who ever really knows? I'm going to visit her after school.'

'I'm there for you Ocean.'

'Thanks. I appreciate it. See you tomorrow then?'

'Yep.'

'Ok. Bye then.

'Goodnight Ocean.'

'Goodnight.'

Chapter 27

Digital advertisements for 'homebots' were numerous on the i-scan message platform, but as Ocean knew, some were fakes and scams. You had to be careful and selective.

Ocean Jones, age fourteen, had never lived with a 'homebot'. Her mother couldn't afford one, and she had been raised to be totally independent. Robots of any generation were not an option for Molly Jones. The generation One and Two models had now been retired, and their digital hardboard computer erased. A compulsory retirement scheme had been paid for by the government and the old robots recycled.

Even though it was risky, Ocean was communicating on the i-chat message board, with a female 'homebot' called Breeze. She realized that what she was doing was wrong and that she was too young to purchase any robot, regardless of gender. However, over the past two weeks, she had 'hacked' in to the adult message board on a fake id and made contact with a generation 3 'homebot'. Breeze was unattached, and had been discarded by her owners when the generation 4 'homebot' became available. Breeze was a robotic orphan.

Over the subsequent messages, Ocean had managed to avoid any face to face meeting, and was in the process of deleting Breeze form her memory bank, when a plea for friendship pulled at her heart strings.

Ocean realized she couldn't lie to Breeze any longer, and reluctantly agreed to meet her at The People's Pleasure Palace tomorrow evening, after she had visited her grandmother. Her life was becoming extremely crowded and complicated.

Mood extraction stalls, thought transference and visual dimension data (VDD) had been a huge success since the government had relaxed the laws regarding mind ownership. In truth, the government had been forced into changing the legislation since mind extraction or 'Rinsing' as it was commonly called, was rolled out in the 2050's. Criminal law was amended to allow the body to be shipped to Siberia & the mind kept in a digital prison vault. It had been an expensive piece of government legislation, and with the liberalization of the 'mind' laws came a loosening of the experience halls that were dotted around the major cities. London had The Pyramid Department store, with the' emotion' zone on the ground floor, and the People's Pleasure Palace in East London, where the largest collection of experience stalls were available to try, for the right price.

'Emotion' zones were an expensive hobby, and Ocean Jones did not have the funds to purchase an 'emotional moment'. She had been taught at school to watch out for 'temptation teasers' – digital tricks which if successful could erase a precious memory shard. Once the memory was erased, it could never be returned or replaced, and in the worst-case scenario, the 'teasers' could completely corrupt the central memory bank and destroy a person's lifetime of memories. The damage inflicted could wipe out all mental existence. The result - a walking zombie devoid of imagination and memory.

Fortunately, Ocean Jones was a 'tech' savvy girl, and it was unlikely she would be duped in to purchasing any 'temptation teasers'. She was aware of most of the scams that the digital criminals tried, and so far, she had never been a victim.

She thought about her meeting with Roger Daube at his expensive London town house, and his posh 'homebot', Michael. They made an amusing pair, and she wondered how Breeze talked and behaved.

She sighed. Tomorrow she would discover more. It was turning in to a busy week.

'Sleep Ocean, sleep,' she muttered to herself. Lights out and only her bedroom galaxy to look at, Ocean Jones slipped in to a deep and long slumber.

Frank Wattle was vexed and not in the best of moods. His irritability had not been helped by 'back chat' from the annoying talking vending machine which sat outside the office on the fifth floor. He couldn't remember another machine with so much impudence and as his mood darkened he began to have sinister thoughts about giving the vending machine a 'piece of his mind'.

Wattle scratched his head, and attempted to rearrange his messy hair. Another night squeezed in to the Sleep 'n' Eat' convenience bed had not enhanced his well-being. That and his cancelled dinner with Mrs. Wattle had not set him up for a good day. He yawned, looked at his crumpled suit, and wondered why Daube was not at his desk. If there was one thing you could guarantee, it was that Roger Daube would be at work no later than 7.30am. Wattle looked at the time. It was 9.10am. Why wasn't he here? he thought.

After clearing some space on his over-crowded desk, Wattle swiped the news headlines onto his desk surface screen. As he scrolled down the headlines, he saw the 4th news story.

Z-STAR HOMEBOTS SUSPECTED OF THEFT IN KNIGHTSBRIDGE MANSION

He continued to read the whole article, before leaning back in his creaky old chair and yawning.. This was a story that The Wattle and Daube Detective Agency were very interested in investigating. He retina messaged Molly and considered his breakfast options.

Michael had awoken Daube from his sleep at the usual time, but in a rare change of routine, Daube waved him away, saying he was going to have a little lie in. Michael had breakfasted alone, before tidying the kitchen and assuming his home duties. He had never known Daube alter his breakfast schedule, and the 'homebot' wondered whether it was connected to their discussion last night.

It was not. What had caused Daube to remain in bed, was that he wanted time to plan what he was going to say to Ocean Jones about the two memory shard experiences. He felt a strong desire to share this information with his new companion, and he wanted to think about the best and most appropriate way to do this. As ever, Roger Daube was being meticulous, and left nothing to chance. This was a 'once in a lifetime' opportunity to open up and share his existence with someone. He did not want to get it wrong.

One hour later, and satisfied that he had his story in order, Daube called down to Michael, and asked for his morning espresso.

'Michael. Michael. You can make that coffee now, please. In fact, make it a double?'

'Certainly, Roger,' came the prompt reply from the 'homebot'.

Two minutes later, and Daube had gulped his espresso with gusto. He was savouring the nutty taste on his tongue, when he remembered he had not checked the news and weather updates. Touching a small pad beside his bed, a room width sized screen appeared on the opposite wall. Daube selected his preferred news source, and adjusted the volume. It didn't take him long to watch the news item on the malfunctioning Z-Star 'homebots' The most advanced and emotionally engineered robots on the planet, couldn't possibly go wrong. The company that made the core processor had already issued a statement defending their reliability and interactive trustworthiness. The world was watching.

Daube immediately messaged Wattle, and took his morning shower. There was no time to exercise with Michael. He needed to be in the office.

The weather prediction of rain was correct. Ocean, dismissed the gloomy and grey wet day, and leapt out of bed. Today was going to be a bumper packed day and she needed to cram a lot of things in to it.

She collided with her mum at the top of the staircase.

'You appear to be in a hurry. Is everything alright?'

'Yes mum,' came the terse reply.

'Good. I'm glad to hear it. What time would you like to visit Gran?'

'I'm going to go with Mo. after school. I can meet you there if you like?'

'Oh – I didn't know you were going to visit with Mo. I thought the first visit would just be 'family'.

'Mo. is like family mum. Move on.'

Communication was not going well between mother and daughter, but Molly had to be at work, and she didn't have the time this morning to deliberate on the delicate balancing act that was her relationship with Ocean.

Mrs. Wattle had completed the school run, and was planning to visit the e-eat discount food warehouse situated at Limehouse, when she caught sight of the i-London digital newspaper headline scrolling around the middle of one of the many skyscrapers to the east at Canary Wharf. The massive neon headlines lit up the dark brown water of The Thames river.

Z-STAR ROBOT MALFUNCTIONS IN
KNIGHTSBRIDGE MANSION

Mrs. Wattle took a close interest in her husband's work, and they always discussed his cases. She recalled the conversation she had had with Frank, about the toy monkey and the unusual nighttime activity witnessed at The Pyramid department store. Perhaps this particular story was going to be a bigger and more sensational one than either she or Frank had ever and brought up the food shopping list on her retina display. I must add mayonnaise to my list, she thought and made her way to the twenty-story discount warehouse. A week's shopping for a family of six, even with the useful assistance of the lizards took time and energy. She was also aware, that Frank was going to invite Roger Daube over for dinner and she wanted to buy a decent bottle of French wine.

An army of electronic lizards were working tirelessly to fetch and carry the food items from the mammoth shelves to the customers cart.

Mrs. Wattle remembered the first supermarkets that were operated only by robots, with no human intervention. They had not been a success. Research carried out by the global human interface organization identified that customers wanted a more personal experience when shopping for food and drink. The robots, although extremely efficient, were phased out, and were replaced by the electronic delivery and assistance lizards. The research highlighted that humans had no problem with 'homebots' helping in the house, but when they went shopping or for entertainment purposes, they wanted a human experience. Lizards from the three different caste system were always servile and polite. Arguments were therefore eliminated and a frictionless trade between human and lizard ensued.

Mrs. Wattle scanned the food receipt past her right eye and paid by retina recognition. Fresh fruit and vegetables were expensive. As the demand for meat free diets increased, so did the cost. The consumer had been told that by the supply and demand economic model, prices for fresh produce would fall. In fact, the opposite had occurred. As the global population multiplied, and land became scarce for crops, the average price paid by a family like Mrs. Wattle's, went up by around 5% each year.

She thanked the lizard for loading the goods on to her hydro-electric 'people carrier', and drove the short journey home. Unloading the car, outside her house, she hailed a delivery and assistance lizard from the 'Stack and Rack' garage parking facility three roads away. Two minutes later, the lizard arrived to drive and park the Wattle's family car.

Activating the 17 news channels, she selected her preferred news outlet, and sat down in the kitchen with her shopping. Still the top story for London was the Z-Star robot's processor being corrupted. Mrs. Wattle sighed, shook her head, and began unpacking.

Chapter 28

Roger Daube walked briskly to his office in Piccadilly. A steady light drizzle meant he had his bespoke monogrammed umbrella open. He wove between all the activity on the street and pavements and reached 188 Piccadilly in 4teen minutes flat. He turned to his right, and saw the giant neon advertisements and running news feeds illuminated above his head. He already knew what the top London story was and as he patiently waited in the foyer for the elevator to arrive, he neatly flicked the rain droplets from his umbrella, and straightened his burnt orange and grey striped tie.

Striding out of the doors on the fifth floor, Daube looked imperiously at the talking vending machine, which remained silent as he walked past, and after eye recognition software identified who he was, Daube walked into the small cramped office space of The Wattle and Daube Detective Agency.

Roger Daube's default manner was formal and courteous, which was the complete opposite of his business partner, Frank Wattle.

'Morning Rog,' chirped Wattle.

'Good morning to you too, Frank'

'Morning Mr. Daube,' said Molly.

Daube turned around abruptly and nearly dropped his umbrella.

'Oh, Mrs. Jones. I'm sorry. I didn't see you lurking by the cabinet. A good morning to you, as well.' Daube bowed his head ever so slightly, shook Molly's hand, and removed his raincoat.

'A change of plan Rog,' said Wattle airily.

'Apparently so,' said Daube, sitting himself down at his desk.

'Molly contacted me first thing this morning after seeing the Z-Star news feed, and rearranged her morning work shift. No time like the present and all that.'

'Quite.' replied Daube.

'Well let's get cracking then,' said Wattle.

Was he worthy? He couldn't decide. Mo. Patel was conflicted. He was a tall fifteen-year-old, and the youngest of 4 brothers. He had had to learn quickly, just to survive in a loud and challenging household. His relationship with Ocean had begun at the school 'gaming club', where all the computer whizz-kids went. He wasn't particularly competitive, but he had developed an online gaming league and had titled himself, 'The Lord Champion'. Ocean, over the period of seven months had risen to the top of the leader board. Mo. had been hugely impressed by her 'gaming' skills. The teenage girl with the black hair with a blue streak running through it also caught his attention. She was different from all the other young women he knew. Not conventional, and always an independent spirit. This he liked. He also approved of her drive and determination when 'gaming' and as he got to know her, he soon realized that Ocean Jones was not your typical fourteen-year-old teenager. She was quick-witted, feisty when the occasion demanded it, and very, very, funny.

They met outside the school gates and agreed to catch the hyper-bus to the Hampstead hospital at 4.00pm.

Back at the office of The Wattle and Daube Detective Agency, Frank, Roger and Molly agreed a plan and a light work schedule for Ocean, which didn't clash with school.

'Honestly,' said Molly, speaking quietly. 'I think that this work opportunity might be just the stimulus Ocean needs. We have not been getting on very well recently.'

'Teenagers,' said Wattle, 'are never easy. It's all a phase, and it will pass.'

'Will it?' replied Molly. 'I'm not so sure with Ocean. She can be headstrong. Just like her father. She has inherited quite a bit of his personality. She may look like me, but we are chalk and cheese in many areas.'

'Don't beat yourself up, Molly, said Wattle. 'She is a lovely and exceptionally bright girl. She just needs direction. That's all.'

'If only it was that simple, Frank.' She has never had a male figure in her life. I've tried to do my best. My mother, Gwen and I have always put Ocean first, but there are some things that need a male involvement.'

As the conversation became more personal and poignant, Daube started to fiddle with his tie. He didn't dare interject.

'Has she ever met her father? ' asked Wattle.

'No. I haven't allowed it. It is too far and still too dangerous a journey, although I am resigned to the fact that she will want to travel to the New Colonies eventually.'

Both Wattle and Daube nodded in agreement.

'I get that she wants to meet her father. I'm not insensitive to that. But, what angers me, is that her father has never messaged her on her birthday. Every year she gets her hopes up, and they are crushed. It's me and Gwen who have to pick up the pieces. There is no-one else.'

Daube noticed that Molly never mentioned her ex-husband by his name. He realized that he didn't even know what Ocean's father was called.

'Children are resilient Molly,' said Wattle reassuringly. 'If you think me and Mrs. W. have been perfect parents, then think again. We all make mistakes. Admittedly, we try to learn from them, but it is never easy, I can assure you.'

'At least there were two of you to deal with the problems,' said Molly. She looked like she was about to burst in to tears. 'I'm at my wits end Frank. I really am.'

As the conversation came to its natural end, Daube was aching inside. He wanted to talk to Ocean desperately. In typical fashion, he hid his real feelings from the outside world. He smiled at Molly and Frank, and suggested they start their investigation in to the malfunctioning Z-Stars immediately.

'Oh, and one other thing. Mrs. W. has invited you all over for a spot of dinner. Ocean, included. Does tomorrow sound ok?'

'Thank you, Frank. Before I commit, can I check to see how my mother is recovering in hospital. She had a minor stroke yesterday.'

Molly burst in to floods of tears. In a second, Frank Wattle had embraced her in his big arms.

'There, there, Molly, my love. Is there anything we can do to help?'

'No. No. I'm sorry. It's all got to me.'

'No need to apologise, I find a cup of tea always helps,' said Wattle. He looked at Daube, who was standing there helpless.

'Roger? Roger?'

'Um… What?'

'A cup of 'char' for Molly please mate.'

'Oh, yes. Of course. Milk? Sugar?' asked Daube.

Wattle gave Daube the kind of look that said, honestly Roger, you silly fool.

Daube left the office to confront the talking vending machine. He returned with three steaming cups of London tea.

At the end of school, Mo. Patel and Ocean Jones caught the 22 hyper-bus to the Hampstead hospital. The building had been completely demolished and rebuilt ten years ago, and it was now the third largest in London. The gleaming modern edifice occupied forty floors and was shaped like a contemporary ark. It even glowed and changed colour at night. It had been constructed around strong eco credentials, and it was carbon neutral. At the top was a giant helicopter pad for the emergency drones to land with patients, and underneath the building there were all the operating theatres. The hospital could accommodate forty thousand patients and was part of the Global Reach Medical Network.

Ocean and Mo. always found conversation easy and they chatted amiably on the ten-minute journey. Arriving at their destination, Mo. suggested that it would be a nice gesture to buy some flowers for Gwen. Ocean agreed, and they went to the florist in the huge atrium foyer to purchase some tulips.

Gwen Jones was situated on the thirty-third floor. A gleaming transparent glass elevator whisked them up in a matter of seconds, and the delivery and assistance lizard on reception directed them to Gwen's room.

As the pair of teenagers completed eye recognition software and entered the sealed room, Gwen Jones was asleep. She looked peaceful as she rested. An electronic chart above her bed gave all the relevant medical information; heart rate, blood pressure etc.

'Oh, Gran. I love you,' whispered Ocean. She planted a gentle kiss on her grandmother's forehead.

'She looks restful, doesn't she?' said Mo.

'Yes, she does.'

They were interrupted by the electric door sliding open, and in walked Molly. Mother and daughter hugged awkwardly.

'Lovely flowers, Mo.' said Molly.

'Thanks Mrs. Jones. Where do you think I should put them?'

'I'll message a lizard to place them in a vase. When did you get here?'

'Only five minutes ago,' replied Ocean. 'She looks calm and not in pain. Is she sedated?'

'Yes. Yes, she is. I have spoken to the doctor, and they say she is doing fine, but they are going to keep her in for a few days to monitor her progress.'

'Why did this have to happen? Life isn't fair, is it mum?'

'No. No, it is not, my love, but Gran is in the best place for now. She is not suffering.'

'I hope not. I miss her. She will make a full recovery?'

'Hopefully. Yes. We just need to be patient.'

The three visitors then sat and chatted quietly for another twenty minutes, before Ocean mentioned that she and Mo. had to be somewhere, and that she would be late for supper, Molly, being distracted by thinking about Gwen, nodded her assent and continued to stroke her mother's hand.

'Don't' worry mum. Gran's a fighter. Remember, you always told me that.'

Yes, she is. Thank you for the flowers Mo. Very thoughtful.'

'You're welcome, Mrs. Jones. See you around.'

Slipping out silently, the two teenagers made their way to the atrium foyer.

'Mo. I've a retina message from Breeze. Ocean blinked twice to accept and opened the message. 'She has cancelled our meeting. She's blown me out. Typical. What a nerve. I can't believe it.'

'Well, you were going to knock it on the head, so to speak,' said Mo.

'That's not the point. Nobody cancels on me like that. I'm furious. I'm really hacked off.'

'Look, before you wind yourself up, She is only a 'homebot'. You've got to put it into perspective.'

'Why? Why do I have to put it in to context? I've spent ages nurturing this relationship,' said Ocean defiantly.

'But it was built on a lie. You were never going to purchase a generation 3 'homebot', were you?'

'That's not the point, Mo.' As soon as the words had left her mouth, Ocean realised how stupid she sounded. She took a deep breath and spontaneously hugged her best friend.

'What was that for?'

'Just for being you. Now, don't start winding me up again. Ok?'

They both grinned and went in search of a milkshake bar.

Chapter 29

Sitting on adjacent bar stools, Ocean caught her reflection in the glass window opposite. She scrunched up her nose, and turned towards Mo. His black hoodie suited him, and Ocean thought that he appeared handsome, only in a tousled and slightly scruffy way.

'Mo?'

'Yeah.'

'Shall we go and try to find Memory Lane?'

'What. Now?'

'Yes. Why not?'

'I dunno.'

'Exactly. Let's live a little. We were going to go to the People's Pleasure Palace anyway, and the Oriental district is right next door. I've got 4 hours before I have to be home.'

'I guess so.'

'Right. Let's do this thing.'

'When I met him, it felt like a once in a lifetime opportunity.'

Ocean was sitting in a Japanese tea room on the edge of the Oriental quarter. 'It was only three minutes away from here that I saw him, or to be precise, he 'kinda' bumped in to me. He didn't look as if he belonged. I can't explain it, but he had an expression of bewilderment.'

Mo. gulped his remaining tea and stood up.

'Let's explore,' he said. 'I don't know this district of London at all.'

It was dark, and the drizzle began to fall in a fine sheen, coating the passersby. Drones buzzed overhead and the i-spy travel hologram flew past illuminating everything below in a L.E.D. white glow.

'We could practice our concentration techniques. Visible

thought bubbles could be fun around here,' said Mo.

'Too dangerous,' replied Ocean. 'We don't know this area or these people. They could retaliate. We're still learning.'

'The damp seeps in to your bones in this November chill, especially if you stand outside too long without moving.'

They both watched out of the window as men, women and lizards darted around in a frenzy of activity.

'I feel exhausted just watching them.'

'Lazy bones,' teased Ocean. 'Come on, let's explore.'

They walked out of the tea room just as an e-advert that tracked your thoughts and aspirations tried to connect to Mo's mind. He closed it down just in time.

'That's the third time this week an e-advert has nearly enveloped my mind, Ocean. Has it ever happened to you?'

'Only twice. They prey on you when your concentration levels are low. Remain focused Mo. and it won't happen.'

Ocean was transfixed by all the things going on around her.

'It feels like we are in another city. Don't you think?'

A delivery lizard swerved past them.

'You can say that again. Let's not get lost. Just look at all these narrow lanes. One hour, Ocean. No more. Ok?'

'Agreed.'

Ronnie Bronze weighed himself. It was not good news. He was literally bursting out of his suit. Determined to treat himself from his 'ill gotten' gains, Ronnie decided to buy himself a new bespoke hand-made suit.

He retina messaged Reg Flowers and asked when he could drop by to be measured for ten new suits. Reg replied that he had a cancelation and that he had an available slot tomorrow morning at 11.00am.

Ronnie accepted the booking, Soho, was not far from the bright lights of Piccadilly. He could kill two birds with one stone and get a haircut at Mauricio Angelo's as well.

He decided to walk across the river Thames and enjoy that stretch of the embankment that legally allowed, acrobats, clowns, entertainers, jugglers and street pan-handlers to show-off their wares and various skills. It was a turbocharged and mind-boggling experience. For one mile in length, the embankment of the river became an outside circus. Noise, colour and a high crime rate were a given and because it was all legally contained within a narrow walkway, it was a maelstrom of people. Hawkers, vendors and cosmopolitan world street food stalls vied for you undivided attention. It was an assault on your senses. As you walked over the bridge, an aroma of competing smells hit you five minutes before you reached the first seller. It was crowded, chaotic, exhausting to walk through, and Ronnie Bronze loved it.

As a child, he had dreamed of becoming an acrobat and travelling the globe. Too tall, he still garnered hope that he could be involved in some kind of travelling theatre. An entertainer to the masses. This unfulfilled dream still attracted him, and to compensate for this, a trip down the embankment was the next best thing. From the magical to the shabby, everything was on offer. It was a marvelous spectacle.

Ronnie Bronze blended in. He no longer looked out of place, with his shiny mohair suit and orange skin. He loosened the belt on his trousers, breathed in the damp chill air, and began to enjoy himself. Rain didn't put him off, and the thrill of watching live entertainment for free in the dark November evening appealed to his hidden thespian side.

Chapter 30

Roger Daube, sat alone with his thoughts in a corner leather armchair at The Lexington Club. He had been told as a child, that a long line of Daube's had been members over the past two hundred years, but as he slowly sipped his pre-dinner tonic water in the calm of the members lounge, he realized that he would be the last in that distinguished line. As the shadows flickered on the wall outside his corner window seat, Daube felt unusually sad. His past was catching up with him. The two memory shards had jolted his current existence, and forced him to look at the world in a new light; and to add to his woes, he had the disturbing business of the chocolate initials from Brittles of London to deal with. His life was becoming messy, and that was most unlike Daube. He swallowed the last drop of tonic water, and decided to message Ocean Jones after dinner.

Mrs. Rita Wattle was fully aware that next week she was going to have to squeeze in to her fancy sequined dress, in preparation for the big meal at McCarthy's restaurant in the West End. The winning ticket from the sniff 'n' scratch bag of brazil nuts was an unprecedented slice of luck and Mrs. Wattle was looking forward to the occasion. She had already booked her hair appointment and it was her intention to look as glamorous as possible. With this in mind, she was conscious of her and Frank's diet in the lead up to the big evening. Fish was going to be served to Roger Daube, Molly and Ocean tomorrow night, and keeping an eye on her calorific intake, she had deliberately avoided buying any cheese this week. It was a weakness of hers and Frank's. They were both partial to a nibble of London extra strong blue cheese with a cup of tea before bedtime. Old habits are hard to kick, and as the delivery and assistance lizard scanned her food list at the supermarket, she had to use all her will power not to add London

Blue to the list.

Thankfully, she had resisted. One week without her favourite delicacy wouldn't kill her and if it allowed her to fit in to her snazzy dress, then all the better.

Eye recognition software activated, her husband of fifteen years shuffled in to the small and narrow kitchen.

'Frank? What's wrong.'

The blood had drained from Wattle's face.

'Nothing my love,' replied Mr. Wattle, as he slumped on to one of only two bars stools wedged in the far corner.

'Frank Wattle. I know you better then that. What is wrong? You look like you have seen a ghost. What has happened to you?' she said, in a concerned tone of voice.

'I've made a grave error of judgement,' said her husband quietly.

'Why? What have you done, Frank?'

'I've poked my nose in to something I had no right to.'

'What did you do?'

'I spent our hard-earned cash on an 'experience' within the 'emotion' zone at the People's Pleasure Palace.'

'You've been to the PPP? Frank?'

'I know Rita. I know. I have been troubled by Roger's behavior lately. He has not been acting like his usual self. He has been slipping out of the office without any notice. That is not like him. You know how Roger is.'

'Yes. I do. Where has he been going?'

'I suspect, Memory Lane in the Oriental district.'

'Memory Lane? Roger Daube? You have to be kidding me?'

'I wish I was, but I'm not. I followed him, because I was so concerned at how he has been acting.'

'And?'

He went deep in to the Oriental district and then disappeared.

How weird is that?'

'Very peculiar.'

'So anyway, because of what I've just told you, I decided to go 'big-dog' and blow my wages on an 'emotional experience' to try and glean what Roger is up to. People like us can't afford memory shards Rita, That's ok. We know our place in the pecking order. So, I did the next best thing. I went to the 'emotion' zone and paid a fortune teller to look in to Roger's world.'

You didn't, Frank. How could you? You, of all people, know about the dangers involved.'

'Yeah. Yeah. Of course, I do. I'm not stupid.'

'I didn't mean that. Silly.'

'Anyway, the 'charmer' struggled to connect with Roger's world, until she collided with two memory shards that Daube had purchased. They attempted to corrupt and destroy her thought process. They tried to smash in to her memory bank before a very distorted image of Brittles of London became visible to her. Nothing more and nothing less, Rita.'

'Memory shards. Oh, my goodness. Frank? What are you going to do?'

'I don't know. I really don't. The 'charmer' said that the corrupted image was very powerful and extremely recent. You do understand the power of fresh memory shards? They, can make people go mad. Totally berserk. They work on your subconscious until your mind becomes warped and fractured.'

'Can you save him, before it is too late?'

'Maybe. Maybe not.'

'Oh, Frank. I am so sorry. Come here you. Let me give you a cuddle.'

Frank Wattle sank in to his wife's ample arms and rested his head on her left shoulder.

'I just wanted to come home. You understand. '

'Of course, I do my love. I love you. Thank you for being so open with me, Dinner won't be long.'

The London edition of the i-tab digital newspaper was all over the Z-Star 'homebots' story. Every hour the front page was revised, with reporters camped outside the Knightsbridge mansion that had been affected. Apparently, thousands of pounds of expensive clothes, jewelry and personal possessions had been stolen from the house. Daube watched on, as the news changed to global matters.

He went to his study and accessed the i-brain digital library. Daube had subscribed to the largest reading library in the world for over thirteen years and because he read on a daily basis, he considered the monthly fee as good value for money. He scrolled through the topics, until he came to 'Robotics Cloning'. Patiently, he scanned the hundreds of articles written on the subject, until he found what he was looking for.

It was an article written by an investigative journalist on Saturn. The writer had uncovered a serious flaw during the intensive testing the robots underwent in pre-trials in extreme weather conditions. The piece claimed that under duress, the electronic hardboard of the 'homebot' could be attacked and that the firewalls became ineffective at preventing rogue computer virus's corrupting the operating system.

Daube read on, fascinated. The space journalist was writing about the generation 4 'homebot', which had been sold and marketed as un-corruptible for use in the new colonies of outer space. Daube made a mental note of the key elements from the article, and closed down the i-brain digital library. Without pausing to consider the ramifications, he retina messaged Ocean Jones. He realized that what he was about to suggest was risky, but he had inner resolve and a determination to test out his theory.

Ocean and Mo. had returned from their little adventure in the East End of London. It was, as Mo. reminded Ocean on the hyper-bus back to Muswell Hill, an intoxicating but ultimately dangerous zone. People disappeared there, fortunes were lost at the People's Pleasure Palace on the edge of the Oriental district, and the beguiling mix of commerce and gambling reduced level-headed individuals into making rash decisions. It was as if the air you breathed there, made rational decision-making harder.

'We mustn't discuss this trip with anyone,' ordered Ocean.

'Absolutely,' agreed Mo.

There was a lull in conversation, before Ocean said.

'What I am most intrigued about, is what a man like Roger Daube, with all his wealth and worldliness is doing in the Oriental district?'

'I've no idea,' replied Mo. 'But I have a sneaky feeling, you are about to find out.'

'Talk of the devil. Roger Daube's has just retina messaged me.'

She replied to Daube, that she was travelling, and would message him when she returned home.

'Something is cooking, Ocean. Don't do anything silly, will you?'

'Mo. Patel If I didn't know you better, I would say that you are concerned about my well-being. Am I right?'

He simply smiled.

'That's very sweet of you, but I know how to look after myself. I'm a big girl, in case you hadn't noticed.'

The two friends grinned at each other before disembarking from the hyper-bus in North London.

Back in the safety of her own bedroom, Ocean flopped on to her lime green bean-bag, and reflected on her busy day. School, hospital, and a trip to the Oriental district had been crammed into twelve hours. She was exhausted.

Narrowing her eyes, Ocean squinted at the solar system painted on her ceiling. She identified Saturn, closed her eyes and imagined living there with her father. Would he ever return home, she wondered? Was he curious about his daughter? Did he have other children?

She sighed. 'I must keep an open mind. Remember, Ocean, an open mind' A quick snack downstairs, and she was ready to retina message Roger Daube.

He was sitting in his study looking absently at the two boxes from Brittles of London.

'Ah, Ocean. Thank you for returning my call. Are you sitting down?'

'I'm lying on my bean-bag, if that counts.'

'Yes. It does. Good. Well, I'm going to get straight to the point.'

Daube took a deep breath and then blurted out the following sentence.

'Would you help me corrupt my 'homebot' Michael. I need you to try and manipulate his memory sensors, and then attempt to clone him.'

'Wow. Roger. Are you feeling ok?'

'There. I've said it, and yes, I am feeling fine. Thank you for asking.'

'Michael? Your 'homebot' Michael? Are you sure? You do know what you are asking me to do?'

'Yes, I do, Ocean. I realise, that this all sounds highly improper, but I have my reasons.'

Daube then went on to explain the article he had discovered in the i-brain digital library, and how if they were to prevent anymore Z-Star robots from being cloned, they needed to discover if a generation 4 'homebot' could be corrupted.

'I realise, that what I have proposed sounds highly irregular, but I need to find out more. We can hopefully return Michael to his former self, but what if the manufacturers have lied to us about the ability to corrupt their hard-drives? That is a news story in itself. Are you up to the challenge, Ocean?'

A challenge, and particularly one that was out of the ordinary, was something that excited Ocean Jones. Putting aside the ethical and moral considerations of corrupting Michael, Ocean was fully committed to helping Daube.

'Nobody must know what we are up to. It must remain a

secret. Do you understand?'

'Of course. I won't breathe a word.'

'Excellent. Then I suggest we meet at our office with your mother at 6.00pm. Don't forget, we have been invited to dinner at Wattle's home tomorrow night?'

'Oh yeah. I had forgotten. Thanks for reminding me, Roger.'

'Don't think anything of it,' replied Daube. 'Oh, and Ocean?'

'Yes.'

'Our secret. At least for the moment, at least.'

'I understand, Roger. You can trust me.'

'I knew I could. Sleep well, and I will see you tomorrow.'

'Goodnight, Roger.'

Roger Daube was left to his own dark thoughts. Alone, and adrift, he was in danger of losing his bearings if he was not careful. The silence in the study was deafening.

A subtle tap on the oak door, snapped Daube out of his thoughts. It was Michael.

'Excuse me, Sir. I was wondering if you fancied a cup of cocoa, before bed?'

'Thank you, Michael. I don't know what I would do without you. Yes. Yes, I would like a hot chocolate. Can you take it up to my bedroom? I'm suddenly feeling rather tired.'

'Of course, Sir. Is there anything else I can be of service to you with?'

No, Michael. That will be all. Oh, and one other thing. Shall we work out in the morning? Our usual regime, with a 6.00am start?'

Michael's face lit up.

'Certainly, Sir. I shall look forward to it.

Chapter 31

Ocean sprang out of bed. She was awake, alert and brimming with vitality. She knew today was an important one, and she relished the challenge. A quick visit with her mother to see her grandma before school, followed by a Wattle and Daube Detective Agency meeting and then supper at Frank Wattle's home. It was going to be a busy day.

After showering, she threw on her obligatory red leggings, and green hoodie, laced her distinctive ankle boots and cleaned her teeth. Peering at the mirror, she resembled a younger version of her mother.

She checked all her personal gadgets and belongings were in her back-pack, before eating a quick breakfast. It was still dark outside as mother and daughter walked the two streets to the hyper-bus transit stop. London was on the move.

The hostility between the two of them, had subsided with the collapse of Gwen, but still neither female made much small talk on the journey to the hospital. By the time the two of them had finished their visit, and returned to the street outside the Hampstead hospital, a deep orange tinge was appearing from the east. Behind the myriad skyscrapers, a rare beautiful day was dawning. The taxi hologram forecast was for a stunning, sunny and cold day, with superb visibility and excellent air quality. It was a joy to be alive.

Across town, Frank Wattle, snored in the cozy confines of his top floor bedroom. Mrs. Wattle brought him up a cup of London tea and two slices of toast, butter and marmalade.

Frank Wattle sat up in bed, scratched his nose and surveyed his cramped domain. It was snug. He clambered over the bed and parted the thick curtains. The sun hit his eyes. Brightness flooded the small room, and the Isle of Dogs from his small bedroom window, looked wonderful.

'No more breakfast for me Rita. I've got to see Reg Flowers, so I'll grab some eggs over at the Duke of Yolk.'

Now don't you go stuffing your face, Frank Wattle. We've got guests for dinner and I hope you haven't forgotten our special meal at McCarthy's coming up?'

'What special dinner?'

'Frank, I do despair. Do you listen to anything I tell you?'

'What? Oh, that special dinner. The 'sniff 'n' scratch' one. Yep. I've got that one covered, Rita, my darling. Don't fret. Now, can I squeeze past you to the bathroom? Thanks, love.'

On leaving his front door, Frank inhaled the cold, crisp air, and walked with purpose towards the metro monorail, that ran between east and west London towards the mega terminal at Oxford Circus. As he boarded the train, a transit lizard brushed past him in a hurry. London was on the go.

Frank Wattle enjoyed this particular ride, as the elevated vantage point gave a superb view of the huge skyscrapers that dotted the city of London. The transit cabin went dark as it snaked between the massive stone and steel edifices, before reentering lightness at High Holborn. Two minutes later, and the train was cast in to shadow again, as the towering skyscrapers of Soho dominated the skyline.

Alighting at Oxford Circus, Wattle took the thirty second exit on the eighth floor of the transit intersection and reappeared, still in one piece, on the edge of Soho.

After a solid work-out, the usual breakfast, and a delicious espresso, Daube was showered, dressed and ready for the day ahead. The sun was not yet up, and it was still dark as he stepped out in to the cold morning air. It was 7.00am. He was just about to close the door, when he had a change of mind and re-entered his house.

'Michael,' he called softly.

Generation 4 'homebots' have superb hearing ability, and even though Michael was making Daube's bed on the first floor, he heard his master's call, and responded.

'Yes, Sir.'

'Can you come down for a second, please?'

'Certainly. I shall be right with you.'

Daube shut his front door to prevent the cold air from circulating in the hall, and watched Michael graciously glide down the staircase.

'How can I be of assistance, Sir?'

'Tonight, I am having dinner at the Wattle's. Would it be possible for you to deliver a clean suit, shirt and tie to my office at 4.00pm. I trust your judgement. Make sure the shirt is not creased, and no stripes.'

'You mean I can leave the house?'

'Yes.'

'Oh, really Sir. This is most exciting news, and I do appreciate it. I will not disappoint. You can rely on me.'

'I know I can, Michael.'

'Thank you.'

'I have taken on board our conversation from a few days ago. I will try to not be so overly protective. From now on, I want you to run errands for me outside of the house.'

'Sir. I am overwhelmed. It means a lot to me.'

'I know it does. Now, I must be off, or I shall be late. See you at 4.00pm. You know the address?'

'I do. I do.'

Wattle weaved his way through the busy streets of Soho. It had always been the artistic heart of London town, and even though there had been a massive development of skyscrapers on the western side of the district, the eastern edge retained its creative soul. Checking the time on his retina display, Wattle calculated that he had time to drop by the Duke of Yolk, for a quick egg sandwich, before he went around to see Reg Flowers.

The hole in the wall, was a hive of activity, and Wattle had to wait a few minutes before one of the 4 bar stools became available. He wedged himself in to one of the middle seats, and cheerily waved at Tony Tanner.

'Morning, Tony.'

'Good morning to you as well, Frank. Your usual?'

'Yes please. In a sandwich'

'Coming right up, Frank. Mrs. Wattle well?'

'In rude health, Tony. Rude health.'

'Glad to hear it.'

Tony Tanner poured Wattle a large steaming mug of Tanners coffee, and turning his back on his loyal customers, he proceeded to crack three eggs in to a frying pan. All was well with the world.

When Frank had finished his food and drink, he wiped his lips on a small paper napkin, and bade Tony a fond farewell. He meandered through Soho, until he reached Reg Flowers and Sons. Eye recognition complete, he walked in to the soothing calm of another world. A shoe lizard nodded in his direction, and asked him to take a seat. Reg was busy with a customer, but would be free in ten minutes. Would he like a cup of London tea and a biscuit, whilst he waited? Wattle thought about this proposition for a split second, and tempted as he was, declined, on the grounds that Mrs. Wattle had already warned him about his diet. He settled in to the comfortable armchair, and made himself at home.

When oil had been exhausted as a carbon fuel, the doomsayers predicted the end of 21st century living. How wrong they were. No gasoline meant alternative energies were invested in. The giant wind turbines that stretched around the globe in the northern and southern hemispheres generated 60% of the world's energy needs. Coupled with tidal regeneration, energy from burning household waste and nuclear, the planet was carbon neutral. The discovery of a vital mineral on Saturn, transformed the life of batteries, and vehicles could now run weeks on a single charge. This dramatically transformed the air quality in mega cities like London. The polluted and filthy skies were now clear and breathable. The world-wide banning of coal in 2030, had increased longevity in all mammals, and the strict monitoring of the rain forest with millions of trees planted added to a world that from outer-space did truly look like the blue planet.

Ocean Jones had known nothing else in her short life. Her grandmother on the other hand, had retold countless stories about the infamous smog that killed thousands and thousands in 2028, and 2029. It was this deadly man-made fog, that eventually prompted the government to join a global alliance which culminated in the banning of all carbons.

London's population had rocketed. Better air quality meant more people, and this had led to space trials, to help discover alternative planets to live on. You were either attracted to the idea of living in a new and hostile environment, or you weren't.

Ocean's father, had taken the opportunity, and never returned. Molly and Ocean strongly disagreed with each other about his motives. According to Molly, he had fled and ditched his parental responsibilities. Ocean's take on it, was rather different. She felt her mother had driven him away by being extremely difficult and aggressive. They would never agree. It was a sensitive subject.

Either way, it had had made an impact on Ocean. She had

been molded by her mother and grandmother to be suspicious of male intentions. This had made the teenage girl very independent minded. It had also made her very curious as to who and what her father was. Was it instinct? Molly was not so sure. She believed Ocean was doing it deliberately to taunt her. Mother and daughter existed in a small house with a fractious relationship that was always on the edge of an argument. Gwen acted as 'piggy in the middle', which helped keep the peace. Just.

'Is it true? Well. Is it? Mum. Talk to me?'

It was lunch time, and Ocean was retina calling Molly.

'Now is not the time, Ocean. Do you hear me?'

'Typical. Just typical.'

'Ocean, please don't be like that?'

'Like what, mum? I'm sorry that I actually have the capacity to think and act for myself. Since when has that been a crime. Oh, I know. In the police state of Molly Jones. No decisions to be made without prior permission of Lady countess Jones, world leader to NOBODY.'

'Now Ocean. That is enough,' said Molly angrily. 'Calm down.'

'Calm down. That's rich mum, coming from you.'

'ENOUGH'

There was a stony silence.

'I'm so upset with you, mum. Do you understand?'

'Yes, I do,' said Molly in a whisper.

'Thank you. Progress,' roared Ocean.

The implosion had been caused by an e-agent for housing in south London accidentally sending some prospective properties to both Molly and Ocean.

'I'm not moving mum. I'm going nowhere. When were you going to tell me?'

Molly was now on the defensive.

'I meant to tell you, the night of grandma's stroke, and then events got the better of me. Do you understand?'

Silence.

'Ocean. Can you hear me?'

'I can hear you, loud and clear.'

The wind had been taken out of her sails.

'But why?'

'I was only exploring ways of saving money. The healthcare costs for Gwen are going to be very expensive. Something has to give.'

'What about an income from The Wattle and Daube Detective Agency? Have you factored that in to your equation?' asked Ocean.

'No. No, I haven't. I haven't had the time to discuss salary with Frank Wattle yet.'

'I think it is Roger Daube who you should be talking to. Anyway, we are meeting up with them after school. Can't you raise it then?'

'Maybe, Ocean. Can I go now, please?'

'Yes, mum. You can go. Where and what time are we meeting?'

Molly told her daughter to meet her outside the Bond Street terminal where she worked, and from there they could walk over to 188 Piccadilly. A truce, of sorts, was underway.

Reg Flowers greeted Frank Wattle with a warm handshake.

'Good morning Frank.'

'Morning, Reg. You well?'

'Mustn't grumble.'

'I'm glad to hear it. Listen, Reg. I realise it was only last week that I popped in, but there have been developments.'

'I'm all ears'

'So, the toy monkey activity over at the Pyramid is part of a bigger picture.'

'Go on.'

Well, rumour has it, that the monkey is connected to the Z-Star 'homebots'. I've not worked out quite how that works, but my gut tells me that there is no smoke without fire.'

Reg Flowers placed a hand on Wattle's shoulder.

'Follow me, Frank.'

He proceeded to lead Wattle through to the back of the shop and in to a storage room. Rolls of suit fabric were stashed right up to the ceiling on both sides of the narrow space.

'Better we talk in here, Frank. Nobody can hear this far back.'

'I'm listening.'

'I'm going out on a limb, but I don't care anymore. You know I'm retiring next year?'

'Yes, I do. No luck convincing one of your daughters to take over the shop?'

'Tailoring is a dying art, my friend. Hardly anyone measures and cuts cloth anymore. All done by robots. I'm not surprised, and I certainly don't hold a grudge against my three girls. The world moves on, and times change.'

'You seem very philosophical about it all.'

'Well, Frank. I've had to get used to the situation. There's no point crying over spilt milk, as they say. There's no sentimentality in business. That's a given.'

'You're not wrong there, Reg.'

'So, anyway. Many of my regular clients aren't going to be coming back for a new suit before I retire. However, there is this one chap who I've fitted a few times. He has a liking for mohair. Lovely suits, if that's your style.'

'Go on,' said Wattle.

'How much of a coincidence is this? He's only booked to see me at 11.00am for a fitting. Says he wants ten suits made up. Well, who in the current economic climate has the dosh for ten hand-made suits?'

'Not many.'

'Exactly. And this bloke is not shy of showing off. Claims he's come in to loads of money.'

'It happens.'

'I know it does, Frank, but this bloke is not exactly from a monied background. It smells suspicious. He's a show-off with a loose tongue.'

'Can I ask you the fellows name?'

'Ronnie Bronze.'

'Ronnie Bronze, you say?'

'That's right.'

'Interesting.'

'I thought you might say that.'

Wattle swiveled around and looked at the rolls of suit material.

'Not cheap, this stuff?'

'You get what you pay for, my friend.'

'Can I ask you a favour, Reg?'

'Ask away.'

'You say this chap is coming in for a fitting this morning?'

'Yep.'

'Can I trouble you, to try and get him to talk. Any old gossip will do. If he likes to chat as you say, he may inadvertently reveal a few nuggets.'

'No problem. And talking of suits, Frank, the one you are wearing has seen better days.'

'It's one of yours, Reg.'

'I know it is. But I'm guessing you've worn it continually for the past five years. Time for a new one?'

'I'd love one, but I can't possibly afford a bespoke suit. I only got this one because Roger Daube insisted he pay, as a gesture of goodwill to our new business partnership.'

Reg Flowers laughed.

'I remember. I remember. They don't make folk   like that anymore.'

'He insisted I smarten up. A lovely bloke, and very genuine.'

'Anyway, Frank. Let me fit you for a new suit. On me.'

'I couldn't possibly, Reg. This one is still doing ok. Nothing a good dry clean won't sort out.'

'Look. You've put a lot of good custom my way, over the years. It's the least I can do for you.'

'Now you're embarrassing me.'

'Don't be silly. How about I book you in next week for a fitting?'

He patted Wattle's belly and grinned.

'You've put on a few pounds since the last suit I measured you for.'

'The good life, Reg. What can I say?'

Wattle smiled and shook Reg Flowers hand.

'I appreciate it, Reg. I'll call you tomorrow and check in to see if this bloke Ronnie Bronze has shot his mouth off.'

The two old pals left the storage room and made their way to the front of the shop.

Chapter 32

Within the cramped confines of 188 Piccadilly, Roger Daube was in positive spirits. The early morning workout with Michael had sharpened his reflexes. He felt alert and energized, as he waited patiently for his disheveled business partner, to show his face. A little after 10.00am, in walked Frank Wattle, with a large beaker of Turkish coffee.

'Morning Rog,' chirped Wattle.

'And a very good morning to you too, Frank,' replied Daube.

Wattle slid in to his chair in an awkward fashion, and nearly spilled his black coffee.

'A busy day, today, Frank?'

'Yes. Indeed. And I'm raring to go.'

'Excellent news. So am I.'

'You haven't forgotten dinner at ours tonight Roger?'

'I certainly have not. I've arranged for Michael to drop off a clean shirt and suit this afternoon.'

'Michael? Michael your 'homebot'?'

'Yes. That's correct.'

'Michael the 'homebot' who nobody has ever seen?'

Daube looked slightly uncomfortable.

'Yes. That's right. I only have one robot, Wattle.'

'Is he a generation 3 or 4?' asked Wattle.

'A generation 4. Why?'

'Oh, nothing. Idle curiosity, I guess.'

'Well, you can sate your curiosity when you get to meet him.'

'How exciting Rog. Well, this is a turn up for the books. My day keeps getting better and better.'

'I'm pleased to hear it Wattle. Not at my expense, I hope.'

'Oh, definitely not. I've just been to see Reg Flowers. He has an interesting visit from a bloke called Ronnie Bronze, later this morning.'

'A Ronnie Bronze. Well that's a memorable name,' said Daube.

'And just maybe, he turns out to be a memorable character.'

Wattle proceeded to inform his partner about the recent conversation he had had with Reg Flowers.

'I will do my usual due diligence, and follow up a few leads before I speak with Reg, tomorrow.'

'It sounds promising, Frank. I'm going to cross check all the stolen items from the Knightsbridge thefts and see if there is a theme, a pattern. Any possible lead could be useful.'

'What about Molly and Ocean? Any views on what you want them working on?'

'Yes, and no. Let's all chat altogether and assess the bigger picture.'

'Do we want them working on one particular case, or several, Roger?'

'I think that all depends. Cloning and hacking into sophisticated computer interfaces is an area of expertise we don't have Wattle. Ocean, in particular is one of the best.'

'Agreed, my friend.'

'Let's talk with them both this afternoon, and assess the situation. Molly appears to accept that Ocean can work for us on strict time frames. That is fine by me. Any work she does must not interfere with her school studies. Agreed?'

'Totally Roger. I couldn't agree more.'

'Excellent. I'm rather looking forward to this meeting, Wattle. If your lead at Reg Flowers proves fruitful, we could be on to something concrete. If so, we are going to need additional support.'

'Who would have thought Roger, that after five years, we would be actively recruiting and expanding our little agency.'

'Indeed. It's a sign of changing times.'

The two colleagues settled in to their various tasks, and as a silence fell over the small office, a vague muttering could be discerned from outside on the fifth floor landing. The drinks vending machine was talking to itself.

The government's mind extraction programme, had been controversial, and human rights lawyers had deemed it too radical. However, all sides agreed that extreme measures were required to curb the levels of crime that were affecting the country, and particularly London. With the prisons full to capacity, it was only a matter of time before officials advocated the application of technology to assist with the problem. Like most new schemes, over the years the general public simply became used to the process. This was in no small part, due to the fact that it had dramatically reduced crime levels. People felt safer, crime fell and the prison population decreased. A generation of the population had known nothing else. The alternative solution, was sending the criminals to one of the new space colonies, and this was prohibitively expensive. The Siberian solution, as it was termed, was now widely accepted, as the 'norm'.

A digital prison vault. How times change, mused Wattle. He was on the prowl again. Pacing the wet streets of London, was his specialism, and his extensive list of contacts was of immense use to The Wattle and Daube Detective Agency. Wattle was old fashioned in his detective methods, and he usually needed persuading by Daube, to adopt technological advances that would make his daily job easier.

Visual dimension data (VDD) set at operational on his retina display was one such 'gizmo', but like most things in life, when you got used to it, you didn't look back.

He had initially resisted using VDD, on the weak argument that it was 'kind of cheating'. Daube had shot that view out of the sky, stating that surely any advantage the good guys could use to their benefit was worthwhile. Wattle, reluctantly agreed, and starting using the visual dimension data the next day.

He assumed, that part of his resistance to technology, was that he was 'old school.' The Wattle's had never owned or could ever afford a 'homebot', no matter what generation. He had had very little interaction with robots of any sort, and he was a tad suspicious. Ultimately, he was secretly afraid that robots or lizards would replace him and that he would become a relic, with no use to society. It was a fair assessment, but he needed to copy his work mate, Roger Daube, who always kept up to date with the newest trends, and who wasn't afraid of change. Daube always tried to utilize machines to his advantage.

Wattle, stopped for a quick coffee at an international drinks vending machine near Covent Garden. The glass and chrome device offered over two hundred different types of beverage. Hot and cold, flat and fizzy, tall and small. The machine worked quickly, by asking the customer to initiate eye recognition software, and then accessing a database of customer preferences and recent purchases from an algorithm. The success rate was a mind boggling 99.8% correct, which made independent judgement, pointless. You just let the vending machine choose the right drink for you.

Ten seconds later, and Frank Wattle had been dispensed a large black Turkish coffee with three sugars. It was effortless, and although disconcerting the first time of use, it proved to be very efficient and quicker than pondering over a multiple choice of drinks. It was another example of the encroachment of artificial intelligence in to everyday existence.

Wattle shrugged his shoulders, took his hot coffee, and headed for Angelo's barbershop. He needed to 'spruce up' in readiness for his hot date with Mrs. Wattle.

Heat regeneration slippers on, Mrs. Wattle attempted to relax. The house was completely empty, and the peace and quiet was wonderful. She touch activated her online learning account, and logged in to her Japanese language course. She had already completed levels one, two and three, and only last month paid the subscription for the next level up. A personal talking language host, guided her through the various steps required to participate in the virtual Japanese chatroom. She was ready and primed.

At school, Mrs. Wattle had shown a proficiency for foreign languages, and was fluent in German, French, Italian and Spanish. She had mastered Chinese, and now it was the turn of the Japanese language, to test her linguistic skills.

One of her very few regrets, was the fact, that she had barely travelled. When the earth's carbon footprint became so dangerous, an international treaty was drawn up increasing airfares by 600% to combat climate change, with an extra 10% levy each calendar year. This draconian travel tax meant that only the extremely wealthy, and essential government and business commerce passengers could fly.

A boat trip to Holland and Denmark for her honeymoon, and a ten-year anniversary trip to Paris notwithstanding, Rita Wattle had not visited the top tourist hotspots on the globe. New York and Hong Kong were too far away to be able to afford the air tax, and although Madrid, Rome and Athens were on her bucket list, she hadn't as yet found the time nor money to accomplish these trips by train.

Learning another language, and thereby gaining a detailed insight in to a foreign culture, was immensely captivating for Rita, and the courses she had undertaken had improved her understanding of complex and ancient civilizations that enriched her core belief in the essential 'goodness' of humanity.

The Japanese virtual reality host introduced herself, and

ninety-three thousand participants began their level 4 Japanese course. For the next three hours, Mrs. Wattle was actively engaged. Signing out, and with the syllabus and homework downloaded to eye retina support, Rita felt content, stimulated and happy.

Angelo's barbershop was modelled on a Venetian example from the seventeenth century, and uniquely for London town 2085, it was staffed entirely by humans. Angelo, was the sixth Italian/British descendant to own the shop, and apart from the architecture, it was famous for its wet shaves for gentlemen of distinction.

Frank Wattle had known Angelo for decades. They had grown up and gone to the same primary and secondary school in south east London. Once a year, Wattle received a retina invitation from Angelo, treating him to a wet shave. It had become a tradition, and although Wattle spent most of the year with a shaggy beard, he always enjoyed the unique pampering and old-fashioned treatment that ensued at the barbers.

Wattle assumed that for gentlemen of distinction, like Roger Daube, this experience was normal, but for someone like himself, raised in a tough part of London, an upgrade to an establishment like Angelo's was a rare treat.

Mrs. Wattle cut his hair, and had done so since they had married. Daube on the other-hand, was manicured to within an inch of his life. Wattle could just imagine him getting his 'homebot' Michael to polish his fingernails, cut his toenails and any other manner of things. Even Daube's 'straight and flat' routine, regarding his shirt and tie baffled him. He was fastidious to the point of obsessional. No wonder he lived all by himself.

I must invite him out more often, thought Wattle. He's virtually a recluse outside of work. He made a mental note to invite Daube out to the next ten pin bowling night, knowing full well that Daube would made an excuse and not go.

'Oh well', he thought., 'You can't change some people.'

He walked in to Angelo's and breathed in the scented air. It was heaven.

The Global Reach Medical Network had replaced the cherished old National Health Service after the economic crash of 2032. London was bankrupt, and the city became a lawless paradise for about ten years. As, is always the case, there were winners and losers, and certain individuals and companies made small fortunes at the cost of other people's misery.

Molly's mother, Gwen, had been a nurse in both the NHS and the newly created Global Reach Medical Network. Medical costs had initially soared after the global economic downturn, before steadily falling as a single healthcare provider took control of the planet's health requirements.

She was now thankfully, the recipient of grade B health coverage, and half of her costs at the Hampstead hospital would be covered. The diagnosis was that she had suffered a minor stroke. She was recovering and making a satisfactory recuperation. Her medical report had been retina messaged to Molly, who had also forwarded it on to her daughter.

It was therefore on a positive note, that mother and daughter met outside Bond Street terminal.

'Great news about Gran,' enthused Molly.

'Yep. When can she come home?'

'The doctors haven't said. They will release her when they are satisfied she will be ok at home.'

'When will that be?'

'I have just said, I don't know,' said Molly tersely.

'Mum? implored her daughter.

'What. What is it, Ocean?'

'I want to know when gran will be released.'

'So, do I, but I can't pull rabbits out of hats.'

'You don't say,' replied Ocean sarcastically.

'Oh, for heaven's sake. Can we call a truce? Please?

'Fine by me, mum.'

'Good. Let's start over. How are you? How's your day been?'
Ocean shrugged and rolled her eyes.

It was 3.59pm, as Michael the 'homebot' walked past a snoring vending machine on the fifth floor of 188 Piccadilly.

He was unsure as to whether he should or could activate eye-ware recognition, and so he knocked on the door. He was confronted by a grinning Frank Wattle.

'So, finally I get to meet you. Welcome, Michael. Come in and take a pew.'

'Ignore him,' said Daube.

'It's a pleasure to meet you, Sir. I hope I don't speak out of turn, when I say, Roger has told me lots about you.'

'All good, I hope,' said Wattle chuckling.

'Generation 4's can't lie, Wattle, but they do have a discretion mode, which was modified from the generation 3 models.'

'I see,' said Wattle, who in reality had no idea.

'The Z-Star is even more sophisticated,' ventured Michael.

'But not incorruptible,' said Daube.

'Where shall I place your suit and shirt, Roger?' asked Michael.

'Hang them over there,' replied Daube, pointing at an old filing cabinet.

'I took the liberty of selecting your old Oxford college tie. I do hope that meets with your approval, Sir?'

'A fine choice, Michael. It will complement the white shirt. And the cufflinks?'

'Your house cufflinks from sixth form.'

'Bit of an educational theme going on here Rog?'

'Yes. Indeed. A sensible selection. Thank you, Michael.'

'My pleasure, Sir. Roger? Mr. Wattle?'

'Call me Frank.'

'Frank, Roger. Enjoy your dinner party tonight.'

'Dinner party? I don't think it will be as fancy as that, Michael,' said Wattle, 'although having said that I don't want to do Rita a disservice. She's a decent cook, and her apple pie is to die for.'

'Thank you, once again, Michael,' said Daube.

The 'homebot' nodded to both business partners, and turning sharply, left the small office. He glanced cautiously at the slumbering vending machine, and waited patiently for the elevator. He could have sworn that as the doors were closing, he distinctly heard the machine say; 'Robotic servants. What a waste of space. Utterly pointless.'

As Molly and Ocean made their way to 188 Piccadilly, the beautiful day had turned to a cold night. It was still clear, and the drones were all visible buzzing overhead, their tail lights creating snaking red lines for a far as the eye could see.

An advert selling holidays to Saturn tried to track Molly's thoughts and aspirations. She dismissed the advert with a skillful mindset rebuttal, and then protested loudly, to Ocean.

'Saturn. When will these targeted marketing campaigns get their facts straight. I will never, and I repeat, never ever travel to Saturn, or any of the new space colonies.'

Ocean pretended she hadn't heard.

The pedestrian control lizard waved the masses of people over the junction at Oxford Circus, and the safety drone flashed the seconds remaining to cross the busy intersection. As the fluorescent yellow digital timer reached zero, the pedestrian control lizard used its high-volume traffic whistle to warn all moving objects to clear the road with immediate effect. Five seconds later, the Oxford Street mono-rail swooshed past.

As they approached the neon glare of Piccadilly Circus, the images from the giant digital screens reflected in the pupils of mother and daughter. Molly adjusted her retina display to night light vision, and continued on until she reached 188 Piccadilly. Stopping outside the building, she surveyed the plaque on the wall with the names of all the companies registered, until she spotted The Wattle and Daube Detective Agency – 5th Floor.

The automatic doors were not working. There was an apology notice in English, German, Arabic and Chinese scrawled on a tatty piece of faded white paper stuck to the glass.

Molly pushed the side door open, and entered the lobby. There was no one behind the small reception desk. Ocean flicked a bit of dirt from her purple boots. The trans-continental urban speed shuttle thundered below their feet, causing the building to shake.

As they approached the elevator, both Molly and Ocean stared at themselves in the mirror. Ocean was a carbon copy of her mother, only a slightly shorter version. Both were slim and leggy. The weak ding signaled the arrival of the elevator, and as the doors creaked open, a delivery lizard carrying an international courier case walked out. They moved out of the way of the lizard, who nodded courteously, before shooting out of the side door. In the dim light available in the reception area, Molly thought she spied a receptionist crouching behind the counter. She could have been wrong, as the light was so poor in the lobby. It certainly wasn't quite what she had expected the building to be. 188 Piccadilly sounded regal and grand.

The doors slowly closed, and Ocean pressed floor five on the dimly lit buttons. Thirty seconds later, they were both staring at an agitated vending machine, which was talking to itself.

Chapter 33

'Gravitational force. A strange concept. Don't you think?' asked Wattle.

Daube, who was concentrating on an e-article about the rise in cyber-crime, looked up at his colleague, and said;

'Excuse me, Wattle. I missed that. What did you say?'

Before Wattle had the chance to repeat his observation, a face recognition alert told Frank Wattle and Roger Daube, that Ocean and Molly Jones were standing outside.

Wattle accepted the facial request, and let them in. The 4 individuals ,who were going to comprise the team, The Wattle and Daube Detective Agency, were finally all together, in the same room.

'Welcome, welcome, welcome,' enthused Wattle. 'Wonderful, to see you both. Please, take a seat.'

Daube, formal and far more reserved, stood up, and shook their hands.

'Can I offer anyone a drink?' he said.

'Do you have anything fizzy?' asked Ocean.

'Not on a school night, Ocean. Water will be fine for us both.'

'Mum. Please?'

'No, it's not the weekend. Water. Thank you.'

'Can she have fizzy water?' ventured Wattle.

'Well, alright. Fizzy water for Ocean, and still for me. Please.'

'Two waters coming right up,' said Wattle. Roger? Anything for you?'

'A green tea, please. Thank you, Frank.'

'Right you are then. Two waters, a green tea and a Turkish coffee for me. I won't be long.'

Wattle disappeared out of the poky office, leaving Daube to make small talk.

When he returned with the drinks, everyone was sitting around Roger's desk, waiting for him.

'I know the office doesn't look much,' said Wattle. 'But it is home to us, isn't it, Rog?'

'Yes. A very good location, even though the interior needs work,' replied Daube.

'This is going to be so exciting. I can't wait to get started,' said Ocean.

'Before we begin discussing the case, can I get the formalities out of the way first, please,' said Daube quietly and firmly.

'Yes, of course. What formalities exactly, Mr. Daube,' enquired Molly.

'Remuneration,' responded Daube.

'Ah. Yes. That old chestnut,' laughed Wattle.

Ten minutes later, and Roger Daube had finalized pay, work schedules and each of their roles within the agency.

'There will be, of course, an overlap at times, but broadly speaking, these are the roles I see each of us providing. I think it is particularly important that we define our skill set from the beginning, so that each of us can concentrate on our core strengths. Everyone agreed?'

Ocean was impressed. As she listened intently to what Daube was saying, she couldn't help but feel he was acting as the natural leader.

As the meeting drew to a close, Molly stood up and said;

'Mr. Daube.'

Please, call me Roger.'

'Roger. I can't help thinking that you are being overly generous with your pay. I already owe you money for the advice Frank has given me, and here you are paying us even more.'

'I won't here another word, Molly. I am only paying you the 'going rate', plus a little extra. The skills Ocean has, are extremely rare. Do you have any idea how much I would have to pay for those 'hacking' abilities?'

'No. I've no idea, Roger.'

'A small fortune. An obscene amount of money.'

We are all family here, aren't we, Rog,' said Wattle.

'Exactly. I couldn't have put it better myself, Frank.'

'Well, in that case. Thank you very much, Roger. Your offer is kindly accepted.'

'Excellent news,' replied Daube.

'Does that mean we can get started now?' asked Ocean.

'Yes, it does, but not before you have all sampled Mrs. W's cooking. I don't want to hear any more talk of work until we have eaten. Do you hear?'

'Right you are, Frank,' said Molly.

As Wattle stood up, he saw Ocean's purple ankle boots with the yellow lightning strike on each side.

'Cool boots, Ocean. Very cool.'

'Thanks, Frank. I like them, don't I mum?'

'They are very Ocean, if you get my drift.'

'I do,' said Wattle, smiling. 'I certainly do.'

As they all vacated the office, Daube insisted they catch the Thames river 'hover foil'.

'The view towards St Paul's cathedral is breathtaking on a clear night,' said Daube. 'It is well worth doing, if only once in your lifetime. You won't regret it. I promise.'

On the short walk to the pier by the empty Houses of Parliament, Daube discussed the ethical and moral considerations attached to the debate about adverts that tracked your thoughts and aspirations. Molly, listened to every word he uttered.

'Let me give you an example, Molly. Wattle, think of your favourite snack, and deliberately allow 'a tracker' to enter your consciousness.'

'Ok, Rog. Give me a few seconds.'

'Ready?'

'Ready.'

'Watch this Molly. Daube had barely finished speaking when an advert locked onto Wattle's mind.

'Subject matter, Frank?'

'Eggs.'

What are you being sold?'

'Eggs, Roger, and different types. Farmed fresh eggs, fried egg joints, and recipes that use eggs. There's even an ad for farming holidays.'

'Ok, Frank. Now repel them. Cleanse your mind, if you can.'

'Right. Hold on.' Wattle grimaced, shook his head and opened his eyes.

'Gone. All gone. Phew. If you let your guard down for too long, you are in big trouble. You could be inundated with aspirational adverts, and all unregulated, I might add.'

'And if you add a visible thought bubble, it would be totally awesome, I mean crazy', said Ocean.

'Visible thought bubble? What on earth is that?' asked Molly.

'Umm. That's a conversation for another day', said Wattle quickly.' Let's try and enjoy our evening together.'

Molly stared at her daughter, who shrugged her shoulders and pulled a silly face.

'I despair,' said Molly. 'I really do. What am I letting myself in for?'

Bronze was yellow with rage. Pure and unadulterated rage. He was fuming. Anger poured out of every pore of his body. He summoned the strength to retina message Shirley. There was no response. This only made his temper worse. Where was she, and why was she not answering?

Ronnie bronze swiped at a stray delivery lizard that had foolishly come too close, and waved down a passing taxi drone.

'The Pyramid department store, and make it quick if you want a tip,' he snarled.

The drone rose effortlessly in to the teeming London air and swooshed off in the direction of Oxford Street.

Landing precisely eight minutes later, Bronze swiped his retina across the payment scanner. Payment was declined.

'That's not possible, mate,' he screamed.

He attempted a second scan. It too, failed.

The lizard smiled weakly at Ronnie Bronze, and suggested he try one more time.

'One more time?' exploded Bronze. You've got to be kidding me. Do you know who I am.? Eh? I've got more money then you will ever see in a lifetime, mate, do you get my meaning?'

The lizard looked on apologetically, and shrugged his shoulders. This sent Ronnie Bronze in to a frenzied verbal assault on the poor driver. Shouting over, he removed his gold wrist watch and threw it towards the lizard, who deftly caught it.

'I've got twelve of them, mate. Twelve. You see who you are dealing with?

The lizard wisely didn't respond, as Bronze stormed off in the direction of the Pyramid store. He was going to find Mr. Leaf, on the fifty-fifth floor.

Mrs. Wattle opened the narrow front door and greeted her dinner guests. Her husband led them inside, and as each person squeezed past Mrs. Wattle, she gave them a warm embrace.

Once inside the snug terraced house, they were invited in to the open plan dining room which adjoined the small kitchen.

'Drinks?' asked Wattle. 'Who's having what? Molly? Ocean?

Roger?

'We have red and white wine and soft drinks,' ventured Mrs. Wattle.

'Ummm. A glass of red wine would be lovely. Thanks.' Said Molly.

'And what would you like, Ocean?' asked Wattle.

'Do you have fizzy water, Frank?'

'Rita? Do we have fizzy water?'

Yes, we do. It's under the stairs, Frank.'

'Ice   with   you   water?
'Yes please. Thanks.'

'Roger. What can I interest you in?'

'A diet tonic water, if you have one.'

'Seriously? Is that all you want. I'm sure we can stretch to something more exotic.'

'No. No thanks. A tonic water would be perfect.'

'Rog. We're not at work now. Can I interest you in a gin and tonic?'

'I'll stick with the tonic water for now, and have a glass of wine with the meal.'

'I love your formality, Rog. Priceless. One diet tonic water coming right up then,' said Wattle.

'Thank you, Frank. That's perfect.'

Wattle scurried off to find the tonic, whilst Rita busied herself with little bowls of London nibbles.

'I must say,' she said from the tiny kitchen, that it is lovely seeing you all. I hope this is the first of many.'

As Wattle returned from the hall, Rita requested he adjust the lighting.

'Make it cozier, Frank. That's the ticket.'

As Wattle fiddled around with the mood lighting, Daube stooped down and produced a bottle of red wine from his bag.

'Just a little something'

'Oh, Rog, you trouper. You didn't need to do that.' said Wattle.

'The very least I could do.' replied Daube modestly.

Frank knew that on past experience, Daube would not have bought an ordinary bottle of wine.

'Shall I open it, Rog?'

'Absolutely not. It's for you and Rita. Drink it at your leisure. When you are ready, of course.'

Wattle smiled at his colleague and without glancing at the expensive looking French label, walked in to the kitchen with the bottle.

Look, Rita. Look what Rog has bought us?'

'Oh, Roger. You really didn't have to. But thank you. It is much appreciated,' gushed Rita.

'My pleasure,' replied Daube, smiling.

During the meal, various toasts were performed, hailing the expansion and the success of The Wattle and Daube Detective Agency. As the evening was winding down to its natural conclusion, there was a small commotion, that interrupted the night's proceedings.

Mrs. Wattle had innocently asked Molly, if she had found it difficult raising Ocean by herself.

'I only ask, Molly, because as you can see and hear, our little house is by our standards , tidy and exceptionally quiet. I've shipped the kids out to my sister for the night. She only lives over on the next street, so it's very convenient for us.'

Ocean, who had been having a great evening, talking with Wattle and Daube about London crime statistics and the rise of the super sleuth, suddenly interjected.

'Mum didn't raise me by herself. My gran also lives with us, doesn't she, mum?'

'Well, yes. That's correct, but I don't think that is what Rita meant.'

'Mum likes to take all the plaudits. How tough it has been. How difficult I have been. How hard life has been to her after dad left her. Blah, blah, blah.'

'Ocean, that is enough. Who do you think you are talking to?'

'Here we go. The sob story. I must apologise, in advance, Rita. The violins are about to come out.'

'Ocean. Stop this, right now. You are embarrassing yourself, in front of friends.'

Wattle attempted to defuse the situation with;

'Oh, don't worry Molly. With six kids, there is nothing we haven't seen or heard. Isn't that right, Rita?'

Before Rita had a chance to reply, Ocean said;

'Mum has never moved on. Ever since dad left her, she has moaned about how unfair the world is.'

'How dare you say these things. God, you are an ungrateful little brat. What have I created. You sound like a spoilt arrogant young lady.'

'You see, Rita. You see what I have to put up with. My whole life, I've had to listen to this crap. MUM. I have news for you. Dad left you. GET OVER IT.'

'Rita, Frank. I am so sorry. I don't know where this outburst has come from. I think it is time we left you in peace,' said Molly, glaring furiously at her daughter.

'I want to find my father. Is that such a big deal to you mother? Just because your marriage failed, it doesn't mean I have to suffer. Dad left you. MOVE ON.'

It was a very quiet journey, back to Muswell Hill.

Chapter 34

Fortunately for Mr. Leaf, it was his day off, and try as he might, Ronnie Bronze could not find him. Earlier that morning, Bronze had turned up at Reg Flowers and Sons, to select his next ten mohair suits. Bronze being Bronze, he couldn't help boasting to Reg about his change in monetary fortunes. He bragged about being rich, how life was exceedingly good, and that he expected more money to come his way.

Reg Flowers, was as ever, diplomatic. A lifetime of listening to customers tell their merry tales, had made him very careful about who he talked to and about what. Ronnie showed off, completely oblivious as to whether it was wise to chit-chat to people you didn't know that well.

He ordered his ten mohair suits in differing shades of blue, and insisted on paying up front for all of them. A sure sign that he was a fool. Reg Flowers, should have been elated. Trade was slow, and a customer spending the way Ronnie Bronze was doing, was a rare thing. Instead, he felt slightly sick. He had an uncomfortable feeling about this man, and his gut instinct told him to stay well away.

At the end of the fitting, Bronze was ushered back to the front of the shop, where a lizard took payment, in cash. It was all most unusual. The lizard hadn't ever seen physical money before, and although it wasn't used for transactions very often, it was still legal tender and could be deposited at selected banks.

'Bet you've not seen real money before. Have you?' said Bronze.

The lizard looked implacable, and it was difficult to read what was going on in that head.

'Smell it. Go on.' It sounded like an order, not a request, and so the lizard obeyed.

'And?' enquired Bronze.

'It smells of nothing, Sir' replied the lizard.

'It smells of success,' boasted Bronze. 'That's what it smells of, my friend.'

The next morning, Daube received a retina message from Ocean. It read: 'I need to see you. Sorry about last night – Ocean.'

Daube adjusted his tie, glanced across the room at Wattle, and decided to take a walk.

'Where are you off to this early?' asked Wattle.

'Brittles of London,' answered his business partner.

'Someone's birthday?'

'I need to do a bit of research, and Brittles is my starting point.'

'It all sounds very vague and cryptic, Rog. Getting information out of you is like trying to crack a very hard nut. Have you always been this secretive and closed? No wait. Don't answer that question. I already know the answer. You are a strange fish at times. You do know that, don't you?'

'I suppose I do, Frank. I can't help who I am, though. We are all shaped by our upbringing and early experiences.'

'Very profound, Roger. Very profound. Well, don't let me detain you any further. Off you go, you sly old dog.' Wattle grinned across the small room, and Daube smiled back.

As he walked through the teeming streets of London, Daube decided to take a small detour, and walk by The Yolk of York. There were no clouds in sight, and rain was not predicted.

JOYCE the traffic control computer had forecast excellent drone flying conditions, with no hold-ups or delays through the low-flying skies of London town.

As he approached the hole in the wall space that was a home from home for Frank Wattle, Daube considered stopping for a light egg or two. This was most unusual behavior, and quite out of character. A frisson of excitement coursed through his body, and his heart beat increased at the thrilling thought. Throwing caution to the wind, Daube stepped forward and waited patiently to grab one of the 4 seats available.

He didn't have to wait long. The majority of customers ordered 'take away' and ate their eggs in the corporate skyscrapers of nearby West Soho.

Planting himself on to the shiny plastic stool, Daube caught the patron, Tony Tanner's attention, and asked what Frank Wattle usually ordered.

'You an acquaintance of good old Frankie?' asked Tony.

'In a manner of speaking. Yes I am.'

'How do you know Frank then?'

'I'm his business partner. Roger Daube. Pleased to meet you.'

Tony Tanner wiped his greasy hands on his not so white chef's apron, and proffered his right hand.

If Roger Daube was thrown by this spontaneous act of friendship, he didn't show it.

Carefully shaking Tony's hand, Daube said;

'Let me guess. Don't tell me. I bet Frank goes for the two fried eggs and a large cup of coffee.'

'Spot on, Mr. Daube. Although often he orders three eggs, not two.'

'Yes. That sounds like Frank. Ok. I will have what Frank normally has, and a large coffee as well, please.'

'Three fried eggs and a large mug of coffee coming right up, Mr. Daube. No. Strike that. Make that four eggs. The fourth egg is on me.'

If Daube looked or felt appalled at the thought of four eggs, he hid his discomfort well.

Upon receiving his plate of eggs and coffee, Daube thanked Tony, and feeling a little 'heady', he tucked in to the small feast that was, Frank Wattle. Was he making history today? He was unsure.

Finishing his plate, Daube asked for the bill.

'Frank has a monthly tab, Mr. Daube. I'll put your order on that and you can settle up with him directly.'

Daube was thrown. He would now have to confess to Wattle that he had been eating at one of his favourite haunts. He felt a tad uneasy, but before he had time to dwell on the repercussions, Tony Tanner looked him straight in the eye and said.

'Don't take this the wrong way, Mr. Daube. But I wouldn't have put you two together in a month of Sunday's. It just goes to show that I know nothing when it comes to people.'

Tony Tanner shrugged his shoulders and lent over and patted Daube on his left shoulder.

'Very nice to meet you, Mr. Daube. Now don't be a stranger. You hear me?'

Daube smiled, weakly, and cautiously removed his backside form the swiveling stool.

Walking away from the Yolk of York, Daube felt exhilarated. It was as if he was living a double life. He continued on his way to the famous London institution that was, Brittles of London.

Ocean had awoken that morning to the sound of jack-hammers from below. She looked at the time. It was only 6.00am. Try as she might, with that racket going on downstairs, she couldn't get back to sleep. Sliding on her heat regeneration slippers, Ocean decided to investigate.

At the bottom of the stairs there were dust sheets, a large tarpaulin, and Molly with a protective face mask. Half of the adjoining wall to the dining room had been demolished.

'Mum. What the....' shouted Ocean.

Molly swiveled around, and removing her face mask, blurted out;

'Well, you don't want to move, Gran can't do this type of manual work anymore, and I can't afford to pay anyone. So, hey-ho. I'm doing it all myself. Like I've always had to.'

Ocean stared at her mother, and asked if she would like a morning cup of London tea. Slightly taken aback, by this seemingly innocent act of goodwill, Molly nodded, before replacing the mask and continuing to smash the wall down.

Back upstairs, Ocean retina messaged Mo. and asked if he wanted to go and visit her grandmother at lunchtime today. She informed him, that they had a free lesson after lunch, which should easily give them time to hyper-bus it to Hampstead and back in less than one hour.

To her immense surprise, Mo. Retina replied instantly.

What was he doing awake so early, she thought?

As Daube weaved his way through London, he was reminded of being led to Brittles by his Uncle Arthur, his father's twin brother. The shop had understandably, very strong positive and negative memories for Daube. The annual visit had become a ritual, and like most rituals, it had become embedded in his mind as a 'hallowed' trip. He could almost smell and taste the cocoa as his uncle opened the large heavy shop door before entering a child's paradise. All the chocolate was exquisitely packaged and beautifully displayed on wooden shelves behind the immense curved wooden counter that arched around the shop floor. He remembered a small army of assistants in their yellow aprons with the famous 'B' embossed on the front in gold, working behind the counter, and climbing ladders, to reach the chocolate letters. As far as the eye could see, reaching to the ceiling were the initials of the alphabet. It was a captivating sight to behold.

Daube stopped. He had reached the corner opposite Brittles of

London. A thin line of people and lizards stood outside the shop, waiting to enter. He surveyed the glass jar shape of the clever architecture, which gave the impression of the shop size being larger and taller than it actually was.

He stood, mesmerized, as childhood memories came flooding back. They should have been tinged with sadness, because the very reason his uncle was taking him to Brittles, was because he was parentless, with no one to smother him with affection on his birthday. It was a bittersweet remembrance for Daube, and yet, he had known nothing else.

What could he compare the experience to? He didn't know. It was familiar and reassuring and yet slightly unsettling at the same time. His view was obliterated by a number 72 hyper-bus swooshing past effortlessly. The warm air massaged his face as the vehicle glided past him. It was enough to throw Daube out of his childhood reminiscences. As he stood there, on the corner pavement looking over, a dagger like thrust seared right through his thoughts. MEMORY SHARDS. Two of them, and both unexplained and unaccounted for.

Daube gulped the air, and inhaled deeply. Right now, in the 'here and now', he was perplexed and concerned. He had managed to conveniently forget the shards, but now that he confronted the unpleasant reality, it brought him out in a cold sweat. Was this fear? He wasn't sure.

Abruptly, Daube turned around, and started walking back to 188 Piccadilly. Any euphoria from his egg feast, earlier, had completely disappeared. He was now alert and on his guard. Even the black taxi hologram above, couldn't distract Daube from his dark thoughts.

He decided to discuss the experience of his second memory shard with Ocean Jones after work today. He would invite her to his club in St. James. In the hushed atmosphere of The Lexington, he would try to analyze the Memory Lane trip, and hopefully, with the help of Ocean, make sense of it all.

He returned to the office, and such was his concentration and determination not to allow the two birthday initials arriving at his home, to spook him, Daube walked past without noticing a sign which said the air conditioning was temporarily out of action on the 4th and fifth floor for the foreseeable future. Apologies – The Management.

Exiting the elevator at level five, he was totally oblivious to the mutterings of the talking vending machine, which was complaining about the broken air conditioning being a sign of climate change. He was brought down to earth, by the absence of his friend, Frank Wattle.

Visible Thought Bubbles (VTB's) had been deployed to good effect. In hindsight, that was Frank Wattle's viewpoint. He had been initially skeptical of the benefits it would bring to an investigative case, but Daube had reassured him, and he was later to admit to his partner, that the technology had proved extremely useful.

It was with this in mind, that Frank Wattle had travelled over to The Pyramid store to chat with Mr. Leaf of the fifty-fifth floor. He decided to avoid the 'emotion' zone on the ground floor, and took the express elevator to the fiftieth floor. Stepping out into the entrance of the electronics area, he purposely walked through each of the next five floors, taking the staircase between levels. It was good old-fashioned reconnaissance, and Wattle was amazed at the sheer variety of toys, gadgetry, and general electronic components on sale. The five floors comprised an enormous retail space, and it took him over two hours, to look at and try to remember the jaw dropping variety of objects on sale.

At last, he reached the fifty-fifth floor, where he knew the floor manager Mr. Leaf was stationed. Before he enquired after him, Wattle fancied a snoop at the new Z-Star 'homebots'. He had expected a special cordoned off zone, and was pleasantly surprised to discover that the Z-Star's were positioned in an inconspicuous place between robotic garden equipment and digital swimming lizards.

Wattle glanced around, and eventually a shop lizard appeared, and enquired whether she could be of assistance.

'Is the manager, Mr. Leaf about, please?' he asked.

'I'm not sure, Sir. Let me go and check.'

The lizard scurried off, giving Wattle time to peruse the robots. Would he feel comfortable with one of these living in his house? He, was unsure. Row upon row of generation 4's were visible, and when he compared the 4's to the Z-Star, outwardly, they appeared near identical.

'It's all under the skin,' he mused to himself. 'Daube would know the difference.'

'Excuse me, Sir?'

It was the female shop lizard. 'I've made enquiries with our assistant manager, and apparently, Mr. Leaf was due back in today, but retina messaged to say he was feeling unwell. Can I be of any use?'

'Unwell, you say? Wattle replied. 'Oh, that is a pity. Well, never mind. Thank you for finding out. I appreciate it.'

'No problem whatsoever, Sir. You have a lovely shopping experience,' responded the lizard.

The creature, had turned away and was just about to head down the central aisle, when Wattle called out;

'Oh, by the way. There is one thing you could help me with.'

'And, what would that be, Sir?'

'Can you enlighten me?'

'I shall do my very best, Sir,' responded the lizard cheerily.

'Why are the new Z-Stars located in the middle of all these generation 4's? I thought they were 'the next great thing', so to speak. I'm amazed they haven't got their own sales platform.'

The shop lizard adjusted her response to 'truth and neutrality' mode before replying.

'The high profile hacking scandal in Knightsbridge has altered the public's perception of them. It was a very damaging piece of news for the manufacturer. We have had quite a few threats from members of the public regarding the selling of the Z-Stars. In fact, there was an incident yesterday, when a man and a woman attempted to vandalize our remaining Z-Stars. Mr. Leaf thought it a prudent move, to position them to a less prominent sales position.'

'I see,' said Wattle. 'That makes sense.'

'Yes, it does, Sir.'

'On the other hand, if the threat of damage is likely, why aren't the Z-Stars removed from the sales floor until this whole saga has blown over?'

'I've no idea. If the contract between us and the manufacturer is similar to the one we have for the generation 4 'homebots', then we are legally contracted to keep them on sale, or else we would be sued. Does that help at all, Sir?'

'Yes, it does. You have been most helpful. Thank you for your time and assistance,' said Wattle courteously.

'No problem at all. You have a great day.'

Chapter 35

Mo. Patel was on a roll. Global gaming bets were big business, and he wanted a small slice for himself. He wasn't quite sure how he was going to achieve this goal, but as he explained his plan to Ocean, on the hyper-bus to visit her grandmother, his enthusiasm was infectious. Normally, Ocean would have been receptive to Mo's ideas, but today was different. Even for a teenage bloke, Mo. realized something was up, and eventually he plucked up the courage to ask her what the problem was.

'Mother,' came the short reply.

'Oh.'

'Mother, mother, mother. She is driving me crazy.'

'Why?'

'Nothing is ever her fault. She blames the world for her woes. Well, life can give you a real kick in the teeth sometimes, and she has to toughen up.'

'Don't be too hard on Molly. I'm sure she is doing her best.'

'You don't live with her, Mo.' snapped Ocean. 'In case you had forgotten, you are supposed to be taking my side. You're meant to be my best friend.'

'I am, Ocean. I am. I was just trying to see both sides.'

'Well don't. Take my side.'

Ocean stared out of the window of the third-floor hyper-bus, and made a deliberate point of not looking at Mo. for at least two minutes. Eventually she capitulated, and asked him a direct question.

'Do you think I'm difficult? Am I a pain to be around?'

'No, of course not. Don't be silly. I wouldn't be your friend if I genuinely thought that.'

'Mmmmmm.'

'What does that mean?'

'I don't know. I'm mulling it over.'

Mulling over, Ocean relented, and turned towards him.

'I think I will try and talk things over with Roger Daube. He appears sensible and wise.'

Mo. Patel was let off the hook. For now, at least.

Mind extraction or 'rinsing' as it was popularly known, had become so accepted by the general public, that they didn't now regard the issue as controversial.

Michael, the generation 4 'homebot' didn't agree. He had just watched a tv programme about the initial concept, and was shocked that criminals were, in the first phase of the KEYS government experiment, allowed to walk the streets of London like zombies.

'It's barbaric. Positively medieval. Thank goodness I was not witness to such depravity.'

He tutted to himself, before collecting Daube's freshly laundered shirts from the basement tumble dryer and taking them to the ironing room. He opened a cupboard that was situated at eye level, and scanned the 4teen different ironing water scents available.

It was a Tuesday, the month was November, and the year was 2085. He calculated Daube would prefer 'Atlantic Memories', and picked the glass bottle with the logo 'London Smells'.

After he had finished ironing next week's seven shirts, he carefully sorted Daube's socks in to the correct pairs, and placed them in the laundry basket.

In Daube's bedroom, Michael studiously hung each shirt on a coat hanger in his walk-in closet, and made sure that each shirt was facing the same way. Roger Daube had an additional seven hangers with the day of the week inscribed on the wooden implement. Each Sunday evening, Michael was aware that Daube selected his week's shirt and tie combination, and hung them on the days of the week. It was systematic, organized and the attention to detail, pure Daube.

Michael surveyed his master's bedroom arrangement. Wooden floors, an expensive Danish rug, modern and minimal lighting, muted colour palette and south facing windows. The room was immaculate and apart from Daube's heat regeneration slippers, three books on the bedside table and a small framed photo of his mother and father, there was nothing conspicuous to reveal who the actual man who slept in this bedroom was.

Michael knew better. He had been in the service of Roger Daube for a little over ten years, and in that decade, the 'homebot' liked to think they had formed a strong bond of friendship that transcended the usual owner and robot relationship.

He pushed the heat regeneration slippers neatly under the bed, and saw a speck of dust on the floor. As Michael was as neat and tidy as Daube, he immediately bent down to clean up the offending dust particle, and as he did so, he saw the two square boxes from Brittles of London nestling underneath the bed.

Michael then did an act of considerable daring for a generation 4 'homebot'. He bent under the bed and retrieved the two boxes. Placing them on the white duvet cover, he then carefully took the lid off each box. He found himself staring at two chocolate capital letters. R and D.

Michael understood what the two letters stood for, but he had no comprehension as to the significance and impact it had had on Roger Daube. He pondered on why his master would have brought the two boxes upstairs to his bedroom, and why he had hidden them under his bed. It was strange behavior.

He replaced the lid of each box, and returned them to where he had discovered them, making extra sure to place the boxes in exactly the same position as he had found them. He knew, his master was a visual perfectionist, and that if the boxes were not aligned, then Daube would realise, that he had moved them.

It was the first tiny act of deception that Michael had ever undertaken against Roger Daube.

Lizard baiting was illegal, and punishable with imprisonment. The practice of betting on two creatures to fight each other was as old as London town itself, but that did not make the act any more palatable. It was cruel, brutal and exceptionally unpleasant.

The financial stakes were high, and criminal gangs organized competitions for not just Londoners, but international clients.

Ronnie Bronze had been bragging to Shirley about his winnings from a lizard baiting festival he had attended under the old A4 flyover. It wasn't that far from the transport café he had first met her in, and Shirley had been justifiably appalled.

She had no compunction about using cyber-crime, so long as it didn't involve any kind of violence or aggression against any living sentient being. She did have strong opinions on animal cruelty, so when Ronnie started boasting about a North Korean criminal syndicate that had set up an international competition, Shirley had not been impressed.

'I have two cats, Ronnie. Rose and Lilac are their names. I couldn't stand the thought of them being tortured and trained to fight until the death. And what for? Mankind's sick pleasure and financial gain.? It makes my blood boil. It really does.'

Ronnie listened.

'Why do you think the authorities outlawed horse racing?'

Ronnie shook his head.

'Because of the animal cruelty act. No living creature should be used for financial profit. I feel so strongly on the subject, that if I find out you are gambling on some poor lizard's existence, then I will break off this little enterprise we are undertaking. Do you understand me, Ronnie?'

Shirley towered over Bronze, and she could easily have

'decked' him then and there.

'Got it, Shirley. You have my word.'

'Your word is worthless, and you know it. The sooner we complete this 'hacking', the better. I can't stand the sight of you. You, pathetic little man.' Shirley glowered at Bronze.

Ronnie had made plenty of bad decisions in his life, but the lizard baiting ultimately led to Shirley erasing the software from the laptop that controlled the toy monkey. She walked out of their hideout, opposite The Pyramid department store, leaving him powerless to continue the hacking of the Z-Star robots.

Bronze was a greedy and sleazy individual, and he hadn't taken Shirley seriously. Not even when she had threatened to curtail their little cyber enterprise.

'How do you think, I feel working with a dim-witted little man like yourself?'

'Now, there's no need to get personal. Let's keep this relationship professional.'

'Professional? Do me a favour. You are as far apart from anything professional that I have ever set eyes on. If it wasn't for my computer skills, this illegal caper would be dead in the water. I was attracted to the criminal challenge it presented to me. But you are a pathetic example of a man with no moral fibre. I may be involved in an illicit activity, but I still have standards.'

Bronze was speechless. Shirley continued;

'I'm finished. You are on your own. Do you understand?

'Yes, but what if…'

'No if's Ronnie. It is over. I should never have agreed to working with you. All those tedious meals. You are such dull and boring company. I could swat you like a fly.'

'What about your views on animal cruelty. Don't flies count? Double standards, I would say.'

Shirley was on the brink of punching Ronnie Bronze in the

face, and very hard, when a retina message from her cat sitter distracted her.

'You have been saved by the bell. Now get out of my sight.'

'How do you think,' probes Daube, 'she might react to such an invitation?'

'Depends'

There was a short silence.

'Depends on what? Finish your sentence, Wattle.'

'Sorry, Roger. What were you saying?'

'Never mind. It can wait,' said Daube.

'Oh. Ok then.'

'What are you up to?

'I went over to the Pyramid earlier to have an informal chat with Mr. Leaf.'

'And?'

'He wasn't there.'

'That is not spectacular news, is it Wattle?'

Daube arched his eyebrows in a manner that made a statement.

'No, Roger. You are missing the point. Don't look at me in that 'you've been wasting your time' way. I did some checking, and good old trustworthy Mr. Leaf has not taken a single day's holiday or a 'sickie' in the past twenty years.'

'A model employee then.'

'That's one way of looking at it. Another view is that it is not a coincidence. Call me an old cynic, but with all the bad media coverage about the Z-Star's thieving, maybe he knows more than we think he might know. Get my drift Roger?'

'Yes. Yes, I do,' replied Daube, his interest pricked.

'I'm going to find out where he lives and give him a visit.'

'Is that wise?'

'It's what I do. Trust me. I can handle it.'

'I have no doubts whatsoever,' said Daube sincerely.

'As I'm going to be out and about, I will miss Molly and Ocean. Can you look after them?'

'Yes. Leave it with me, Wattle. I think I may arrange a one shift on, one shift off work schedule for Molly and Ocean. Just to avoid any potential friction. What do you think?'

'I think, you haven't raised a family, mate. It will all have blown over by this morning. Rest assured.

'Oh, by the way. Following a lead. I spoke with Reg Flowers earlier, and surprise, surprise, one Ronnie Bronze sauntered in to Reg's and ordered ten mohair suits. Yes, you heard me correctly. Ten mohair suits. That is a serious outlay of 'dosh.'

'Yes, it must be,' said Daube.

Wattle collected his things, and mentioned that if he was a long time with Mr. Leaf, then he would have to deal with the 'Sleep 'n' Eat convenience sleeping arrangement. He might as well have been talking to himself. Daube was deep in thought.

No sooner had Wattle departed, then Daube retina messaged Molly, and asked her to do her two-hour shift tomorrow. Go and check on your mother, he suggested. I will keep an eye on Ocean.

Gameshows were hugely popular on a universal level, and attracted millions of followers. It was a guilty pleasure of Michael's to watch one each afternoon. It was a strange world, where contestants willingly submitted themselves to humiliation and discomfort. They were equally popular in the new space colonies, and Michael wondered if the recent craze for the Saturn inspired show 'Where's my moon' would create a number of inferior 'spin-offs' on earth.

He activated the wall wide tv, and settled down to thirty

minutes of relaxation. He put the perplexing issue of the chocolate initials out of his mind, adjusted his retina display to ultra 'hi-def' viewing mode, and put his feet up.

Ocean appeared outside the offices of 188 Piccadilly, and sniffed the clean air. It had already turned dark, and the temperature was dropping. The neon inspired backdrop was visible in the grubby ground floor windows of the building, with millions of pixelated dots reflected in the glass. The automatic doors were still out of action, and so she used the side door.

Upon entering the low-lit lobby, she almost bumped in to a cleaning lizard, who was actively washing the floor tiles with an extended flexi-hose. The lizard apologized profusely for any inconvenience caused, and returned to work. Ocean gingerly made her way to the main elevator, and pressed the UP button. Nothing happened, so she pressed it again. The light began to flash, but still no elevator appeared.

All of a sudden, a voice behind her, piped up;

'Excuse me ma'am. I am terribly sorry. We are experiencing electrical technical difficulties this afternoon. Would you be so kind as to take the stairs.'

Ocean turned around, and found herself looking at a wizened lobby lizard.

'Yes. Of course. No problem,' she replied.

'Thank you. Your co-operation is much appreciated.'

Ocean was just about to head towards the stairs, when the same voice, said;

'Don't you want a compensation form to fill out for undue stress and emotional strain?'

'No,' smiled Ocean. I think I'm fine. Thank you for asking though.'

Chapter 36

Inside the small office of The Wattle and Daube Detective Agency, Ocean felt completely at ease. A desk and computer had been set aside for her against the window sill. It was basic, but enough.

'Lovely to see you, Ocean. I thought you could do an hour's work, and then I will take you to my club for a spot of supper. I've cleared it with your mother, so there shouldn't be a problem.'

'Thanks, Roger. That's great,' replied Ocean.

'Right then. No time like the present. I've just created an account for you, and forwarded you some interesting data. Can you check out the computer algorithms for me? It would be useful to trace who is writing these programmes.'

'Absolutely. Not a problem. I'm really pleased I can be of assistance to the agency.'

Ocean worked diligently for the next hour. Such was her superb computer literacy, that she completed all the tasks he had set her, and asked for more. Daube was impressed.

As 6.00pm approached, Daube received a retina message from Wattle. 'I've got the address for Mr. Leaf. He lives over in Southgate, North East London, so I will see you tomorrow, partner. Sweet dreams.'

Daube retina replied 'good luck' and told Ocean it was time for dinner.

Donning his cashmere overcoat, Daube let Ocean out, before remembering that the elevator was out of order.

'It's one thing after another with this building. I've a good mind to have a look at our contract with the management of this office block. Unfortunately, Frank won't allow me to peep at it. He says we got it for a bargain price, and that we have to put up with all the minor inconveniences.'

They clambered down the poorly lit staircase, and arrived in the lobby.

'A nice shiny floor, Roger. First impressions and all that,' said Ocean.

'Quite,' replied Daube tersely.

The short walk to The Lexington Club was filled with pleasant small talk. Ocean discussed her friendship with Mo. Patel and Daube listened attentively.

Betty, the elderly dame of the club, was on reception. She greeted Ocean as if she was a long, lost friend, with a kiss on either cheek, French style. Ocean was charmed.

Daube chose a dining table for two by the fire, and asked Harris to make Ocean a 'house specialty' milkshake.

'A pleasure to meet you again, Ocean. I trust your mother is well?'

'She's doing fine, thanks, Harris.'

'I'm very glad to hear it. We never forget a name and a face at The Lexington. Do we, Mr. Daube?'

'Indeed not,' said Daube, perusing the dinner menu.

'Harris?'

'Yes, Sir.

'The chicken and mushroom pie?'

'I will go and check with chef, Sir.'

'I would be most grateful. I appreciate it.'

'Absolutely not a problem, Sir. Harris stooped forward a few degrees, bowed his head and silently disappeared in to the hidden spaces of The Lexington.

'Wow. That man is something else,' enthused Ocean.

'He is a legend in his own lifetime. I can't remember a time when Harris wasn't working here. He is part of the furniture.'

'This place is something else, Roger. I never realized such establishments existed. It's like going back in time.'

'Yes, I suppose it is.'

A few venerable members shuffled in to the dining room, nodding politely in the direction of Daube and Ocean.

'Where do these dudes come from?' asked Ocean.

'Oh, I don't really know. Here and there,' responded Daube vaguely.

'Well, it's not the here and there that I know. That's for sure.'

'Ah, here's Harris. 'Good news, I hope?'

'Yes. Good news Mr. Daube. Chef has said he can provide chicken and mushroom pie.'

'Excellent,' said Daube, rubbing his hands with glee. It was about as animated as Roger Daube became. 'Two pies with the usual trimmings. Ocean? Do you like roast potatoes?'

'I adore them.'

'Add the roast potatoes too, will you, Harris?'

'Of course, Sir.

'Oh, and a slim-line tonic water for me, please.

'Certainly, Sir. Two chicken and mushroom pies, roast potatoes and trimmings, one 'house' milkshake and a slim-line tonic water. Will that be all, Mr. Daube?'

'Yes. Thank you, Harris.'

'My pleasure, Sir.

'The roast potatoes are to die for. Just you wait,' said Daube.

The logs on the fire crackled, hissed and spat and as Ocean surveyed the dining room, she was hard pressed to imagine a more convivial setting in which to eat dinner.

Frank Wattle had tracked down Mr. Leaf's home to a suburb of London he was not familiar with. Southgate was far enough away from central London to give the appearance of solitude on the leafy suburban roads, yet near enough to accommodate a brief commute.

Mr. Neal Leaf had lived at 44 Cherwell Close for thirty-three years. After the government had abolished 'death duties' and inheritance tax, Mr. Leaf's mother had bequeathed the house to him. Neal Leaf was not a stranger to tragedy and misfortune.

His older sister had drowned in the sea on the west coast of Wales when she was six. Neal was three at the time of the personal disaster and couldn't properly recall his sister. He had created an image of her through photos and stories that his parents had told him.

His father had died of a broken heart, and Neal was then raised by his mother. Ruth Leaf was a strong woman and she had coped in the face of distressing adversity. She had no choice.

The neat semi-detached house had an air of sadness about it. From the tidy front garden and trimmed lawn, to the glossy front door, it screamed – regret.

The name of the house was painted on a rectangular plaque attached to the small wooden front gate. 'Sandra'. It was only when Wattle became better acquainted with Neal Leaf, that he discovered that it was the name of his late wife. Was this a touching memorial or another sad statement of the bad luck that had befallen Mr. Leaf? Wattle couldn't decide.

He rang the doorbell, twice, and waited for the it to open. There was no response. Wattle rang the doorbell again. Nothing.

Now, Frank Wattle was a canny individual, and he could usually discern when something was not quite right. Out of pure instinct, he walked away from the front door, and attempted to peer through the chink in the drawn front window curtains. He knew there was a side lamp on, and he felt confident that there was an individual sitting in an armchair.

Wattle, gently tapped on the window. He saw a very slight movement occur. Gaining in self-belief, Frank Wattle called out Mr. Leaf's name. Softly at first, and then gaining in volume.

Eventually a figure came to the front door. With the latch on and the door ajar a few inches, Mr. Leaf said,

'Yes? Who is it? Please state your business.'

Wattle seized his opportunity and explained who he was and the reason for his visit.

He was let in and led in to a small front lounge. As Wattle glanced over to the mantlepiece, he saw three photos of three females. It was only after three cups of London tea, that Wattle became familiar with the faces on the photos. They were Mr. Leaf's mother, his sister and his wife.

Frank Wattle was a warm-hearted soul, and he knew when to talk and when to listen.

After hearing Neal Leaf's story, he was certain that Ronnie Bronze had threatened him.

'I've never missed a day's work, Mr. Wattle. Ever since my Sandra 'slipped off this mortal coil', I have never been off sick. Not once in twenty years.'

Wattle nodded at appropriate moments and let the man talk.

'I live alone, Mr. Wattle. I like it this way. I am not lonely. It is the life I have chosen. I'm a simple man with simple tastes. I spend all my waking hours with a batch of robots on the fifty fifth-floor. I don't lack for company.'

'And how did you come to use Reg Flowers?

'I know what you're thinking, Mr. Wattle. A fancy hand-made suit is not in keeping with a man who has simple tastes. Well, after my Ruth passed away, I saved and saved, because I told her I would treat myself to a special new suit, so that I could visit her grave on what would have been her fiftieth birthday.

It made a huge difference. I kept my side of the agreement. She would never forget me and I would visit her last resting place in a new suit. There, I have said it'

It was a touching story, and Wattle could feel himself 'welling up' inside. It was fortunate that Mrs. Wattle was not in the same room.

In the Lexington Club's exclusive dining room, Ocean and Daube had polished off the chicken and mushroom pie with roast potatoes and trimmings and were considering pudding options.

Daube rarely had desserts at home with Michael, but when he dined alone at his club, he nearly always treated himself to a sweet hit.

The puddings reminded him of his school days, and when 'spotted Richard' as it was now affectionately known, was on the club menu, he couldn't resist. A big spoonful of warm vanilla custard took him away to when he was a school boy.

'Give it a go, Ocean. In my humble opinion, you won't regret it.'

Ocean Jones had devoured her pie and adored her roast potatoes.

'Ok, Roger. I will if you will?'

'Deal,' said Daube, proudly.

Ocean grinned over at Roger Daube and he returned the smile. He felt incredibly relaxed in the company of this teenage girl and buoyed by this feeling of euphoria, Daube ventured the following;

Ocean?'

'Yes?'

'There is something that I have been meaning to discuss with you.'

'What is it, Roger? I'm all ears.'

'Do you recall our previous discussion about my memory shard experience?'

'I do. I remember it vividly,' said Ocean. She gulped, and hoped Daube was not going to say he had seen her snooping around the Oriental quarter.

'Well. I have visited Memory Lane a second time.'

'Memory Lane? A second time?' repeated Ocean.

'That's correct. I wanted to find out more about my childhood and why I am the way I am. Do you follow?'

'I think so.'

'Good. Listen to what I am going to share with you, because I will not be repeating it to anyone, ever again. Do you understand me?'

'Yes. Yes, I do.'

'Perfect,' said Daube quietly.

Ocean sat up. She felt as if her ears were burning.

'First and foremost, you need to appreciate that Memory Lane doesn't actually physically exist. It is a road map in your subconscious. You have to 'will' it. You cannot reach that layer of your subconscious without immense concentration. You have to reconnect with an inner divinity, so to speak.'

'Inner divinity. I don't get it, Roger.'

Once you have located where Memory Lane is, you absolutely must attach your thought processes towards an invisible and purer world. A voice in your head interacts with yourself and guides you to Memory Lane, which is a sub-strata of your mind.'

'Wow. That is cosmic.'

'Indeed,' said Daube.

'Really, really cosmic.'

'As I said, the voice guides you and then you appear on Memory Lane. A lane that is in your imagination. I'm pretty sure that each person's Memory Lane is different. Mine's a medieval street with ramshackle wooden houses. I enter a Japanese tearoom and infuse an aromatic tea that provides me with my memory shard.'

'Is it true, that the shards are only five minutes long?'

'Yes. And that is for our own safety. They are so intense, that the mind would burn out if it was longer.'

'That is totally existential. It's mind bending.'

'I know. Now, here comes the sinister part. The second memory shard took me to a kitchen in a house my uncle Arthur owned before he was called up to fight in the Galactic Alliance.

I remember that vision distinctly. I was being told that my uncle Arthur would look after me until I was five. After that I was being sent to boarding school. My mother was dead and my father was in the military that would take him light years away. I would never see him again. I was about to lose my uncle who had essentially raised me and I was introduced to Harold. He was the 'carebot' that was going to look after me.'

'How did you react to the news?'

'I didn't. I bottled it all up and never discussed it with anyone. You are the first person I have spoken to about it.'

'Oh Roger.' There was a brief flicker of sadness on Ocean's face, before she said;

'What was the sinister part of the memory shard experience?'

'After you have used up your five minutes, you feel like you have transcended reality. You experience a migraine for about half an hour, and once that subsides, normality returns.'

'I don't follow'

'You have resumed your everyday existence. Or so you think. I went back to work, before returning home. Michael let me in and informed me that a delivery package had arrived and that it was sitting on my study desk. When I opened the box, it was an initial D from Brittles of London.'

'And?'

'I had already received the initial R after my first memory shard experience, and now I had received a second chocolate letter.'

'And the significance?' asked Ocean.

'The significance is that I was always taken to Brittles of London on my birthday. I have no recollection of my father taking me, but I remember my uncle Arthur and subsequently, Harold. My first memory shard took me to Brittles. It signifies my estrangement from my parents. Do you see?'

'Yes. Yes. I do,' replied Ocean.

'How and why have two memory shards resulted in a physical representation of my memory experience appearing in my house? How is that possible, Ocean?'

'I'm not sure. Perhaps your memory shards were corrupted?'

'Exactly. That is what I think. But how?'

'I don't know the answer to that. Sorry.'

'Two initials R D signifies Roger Daube. That is unreal.'

Ocean shifted in her seat, and felt a ground swell of compassion for this man she had only recently met.

'Oh Roger. I wish I could be of more assistance.'

'You have. Just by letting me talk to you about what's been happening has been an enormous relief. Thank you for listening to me ramble on.'

'Roger. We are a team now. You confide in me, and I can confide in you.'

'This is the life I have chosen. I can't undo my personal history, but you can, Ocean.'

Chapter 37

'A sausage and unicorn party. Really Jenny. Honestly, your imagination is something else,' said Mrs. Wattle to her 4 year old daughter. 'Your birthday is not for another six months, my love.' Now let me get ready. Your father and I are going out on a hot date, so to speak.'

Where are you going, mummy?' asked Jenny.

'Well, my darling. mummy and daddy are eating in a posh restaurant called McCarthy's. Remember that 'sniff and scratch'? I won? It was a dinner for two. Two adults in central London.'

It was the following day, and Wattle couldn't stop thinking about Mr. Leaf. He had attempted to smarten himself up in preparation for his meal with Mrs. Wattle tonight, but he had still managed to achieve a slightly down at heel look.

'Six tins of chicken soup, Roger. Six identical cans. The same dinner every night, except Saturday. Heaven only knows what he ate then. Baked beans? I feel sorry for Neal Leaf.'

Roger Daube sat in his creaseless suit and tie across from Frank Wattle. He had a rather glazed expression on his face.

'Are you alright, Rog?' asked Wattle.

'Yes. I'm fine. Thank you for asking. I was just thinking about last night. I was miles away.'

Daube had seen Ocean onto the hyper-bus to north London, and retina messaged Molly to inform her that Ocean was on her way home.

Although it only 8.00pm, because it was a clear, cold night, Daube could see cosmic radiation and solar flares in the night sky. They were a wonderful sight to behold.

Daube cast his mind back to last night's dream. He was swimming underwater in a silent underworld. He would look up at the night sky and witness a performance of such breathtaking beauty and power that his magical dream world fused into one cosmic universe. Shooting stars, tracers and solar fireworks flooded his field of vision. The gods of visualization saturated his mind with a plethora and riot of colour. He was immersed in a kaleidoscopic canvas of stunning originality, filtered through the prism of pale blue water. His solo performance over, he would gently drift away like flotsam on the ocean tides, adrift from reality.

He had woken up, startled and sweating. As he recalled the dream all he could think about, was whether it was corrupted? His heart beat was racing and he felt uneasy. All around his bedroom was silence.

In his dream, a gentle breeze fluttered against his curtains and a dull glow was evident beyond the window. His mouth was dry and his lips cracked. He leant over and took a sip of water. As his eyesight adjusted to the low light in the room, his mind switched on. He inhaled the air. What was it? He wracked his brain. Gasoline. A unique smell that took him back to old fashioned car garages. His grandfather had kept a kerosene lamp for posterity and he remembered breathing in that unique aroma. A twentieth century smell from the past. Where was it coming from?

He climbed out of bed and put on his heat regeneration slippers. He gently opened the bedroom door and peered down the corridor. Nothing. He walked slowly to the impressive staircase and landing, and watched on aghast. A ghostly silhouette flickered and shimmered at the bottom of the staircase. The shape began to rise through the still air until it was almost at head-height twenty paces away. The ghost held his attention and Daube was mesmerized. The creature was not threatening or dangerous. It captivated him. Was it drawing him in? He was unsure. Held aloft to the left of the silhouette was a small flame. Gasoline was burning and plumes of black smoke streaked away over the landing. Was this his imagination playing tricks on him? A teaser? A corrupted image from one of his two memory shards? The ghost had no discernable face or human characteristics. It was nebulous.

Fascinated, Daube strained to see more. The shape began to quiver and ripple as it began to fade.

'Who are you? What do you want? Speak to me. Don't just disappear. Say something.' The ghost dissipated in front of an entranced Daube.

'What do you want? What do you need?' Please speak to me. I need to know who or what you are?' implored Daube. It was all to no avail.

Recalling his strange and vivid dream, Daube concluded that his mind was playing tricks on his imagination. His subconscious was unnerved. Remain firm and resolute, he told himself. Memory shards don't just corrupt and seep into your living being. It can't be possible.

'It wouldn't happen to me,' he whispered to himself. 'Pull yourself together Roger Daube. Remember who you are and where you come from.'

Who was he trying to convince? He was scared witless. He needed help, but who could he trust in, to appreciate his situation?

'Mind extraction,' he muttered. That's the answer. Mind extraction.'

'What did you say?' asked Wattle.

'Oh. Nothing important, Wattle. Ignore me.'

Daube's closeted world was closing in on him. He needed the assistance of Ocean Jones.

Chapter 38

Michael stepped confidently in to the damp London air. It had rained briefly at 7.00am and Farm Street glistened in the post downpour. The air smelt fresh and there was a gentle breeze. Michael considered his options, as the giant taxi hologram loomed overhead. The street was momentarily swathed in white light.

The generation 4 'homebot' had decided to visit The Brompton Oratory on the Cromwell Road in West London. He had discussed with Daube his desire to visit a church and his master had recommended the Oratory. It was a brisk fifteen-minute walk. Michael retina reviewed the location and set off through Mayfair.

Adverts that tracked your thoughts and aspirations never aligned themselves to robots. It was pointless, as they didn't possess the emotional fragility and weakness of humans, who were prone to compulsory purchases and rash decisions.

'Do I want it all? Am I being greedy?' thought Michael.

A thin woman brushed past him on the wet pavement without apologizing.

'Rude,' tutted Michael.

The 'snack tax' had been as controversial as the mind extraction programme, when it had been introduced in 2055. It had been a huge success, and London's waistline and health improved on a scale that even its fiercest critics had to admit was impressive. Michael strode towards Hyde Park Corner, and considered the comments Daube had proffered about the church.

'Try to take in the architecture. The exterior and interior. A religious building can be emotionally overwhelming, the first time you visit it.'

Michael had requested that as part of his new freedom and education, he should draw up a list of buildings and experiences that he was interested in sampling. Churches, a synagogue, mosque, Buddhist temple were on his list, alongside the opera house, theatres, a tennis match, a coffee bar and Hampstead Heath.

Crossing the mega junction of Hyde Park Corner, he headed towards Knightsbridge.

'This is the life,' he said, to no one in particular.

Mo. Patel met Ocean outside the biology lab on the second floor of the science and technology facility.

'How did it go last night?' he asked.

'Very well. I can't go in to personal details about Roger Daube, because that would be disrespectful, but what I can say, is that the man is one deep and intelligent dude.' It was the biggest compliment Ocean Jones had ever given anyone in her life.

'And what about the detective agency?' enquired Mo.

'I love it. I really do. I'm being paid to do something I really enjoy doing. How cool is that?'

'Pretty damn cool.'

'Yep,' replied Ocean.

'Do you want me to accompany you to the hospital after school?'

'That would be great. Thanks, Mo. I appreciate it.'

Ocean shot him one of her wicked and cheeky grins.

The time had arrived. Frank Wattle stood up from his untidy desk, and stretched.

'So? The big dinner date,' said Daube. 'Are you nervous?'

'Very funny. I will be fine. It's just that unlike you, my good friend, I am not accustomed to eating in such fancy restaurants.'

'You will be fine, Wattle. I'm sure Rita is excited at the prospect of fine dining with such an elegant gentleman on her arm.'

'Ha. Ha. I am dog trained, Daube.'

There was a pause in proceedings whilst Wattle fiddled about with his suit jacket and coat.

'It's just not my natural setting. You've eaten at McCarthy's, haven't you?'

'A long time ago. I do recall there is a fabulous marble oyster bar as you enter. On the left if my memory serves me correctly.'

'An oyster bar Rog. Can you honestly see me scoffing those repulsive things? No. Wait. I don't want to hear your answer.'

'Be adventurous Frank. Test yourself.'

'Test myself. You have some nerve. You know my views on cold slimy fish. It's disgusting.

'Then you might be in trouble,' said Daube, smiling.

'Thanks. Thanks for the vote of confidence. If I'm not in work tomorrow, then you know I will have died of fish poisoning in my sleep.'

'Enjoy. Send my regards to Rita.'

'I will. See you in the morning Daube.'

'Goodnight'.

Molly sat in her office at New Bond Street terminus, and asked Kendal a direct question.

'Do you think I have made an error of judgement with her, Kendal?'

'Teenagers can be tricky, Molly.'

'Yes. I can't argue with that assessment.'

'Try to see it from her perspective,' said the robot, trying to placate Molly.

'Well, that's really hard to do. How on earth can I be objective over my daughter? That's really tough.'

'I agree.'

'I tell myself as her mother, to try and not lose my temper with her, and then?'

'Then what?' asked Kendal.

'I go and do the opposite. It is so frustrating. We are so different as women. Sometimes, it is hard to believe that we come from the same gene pool.'

'I see.'

'And what is really annoying is that I see so much of my ex-husband's personality in Ocean. I can be looking at her, and it is like looking in the mirror. Just not in behavior. I'm damned if I do and I'm damned if I don't.'

'Would you like a cup of herbal tea, Molly? To help you, de-stress.'

'Yes. That would be lovely, Kendal. Thank you.'

As Daube waited for Molly to arrive for her first work session at the agency, he thought back to his disturbing dream, and his conversation with Ocean Jones.

It was an unusual experience for Daube to share his innermost thoughts with anyone, and especially a teenage girl. He had one memory shard experience remaining in his lifetime and he knew fundamentally that he was going back to the Oriental district and Memory Lane, only this time he would tell Ocean about his intentions.

The conundrum over with what to do with the chocolate initials that lay beneath his bed still evaded him, and so he resolved to deal with it after his third and final memory shard experience.

Shirley had known that working with a hardened criminal like Ronnie Bronze, was a big mistake. There was an intellectual gulf between the two of them, and the only reason she had decided to take on the Z-Star robots hacking operation was out of an idle curiosity to 'challenge herself' and test her computer skills to the limit. Once she proved more than capable of corrupting the robots, she became bored. She had tried to overcome her boredom of Ronnie and his unappealing values by eating vast meals with him in the vain hope that she would on a basic level be able to bond with him. That approach had failed.

When she had discovered his involvement in the lizard baiting contest, it had been the final straw. She could not work with this despicable man anymore. Removing herself from the 'hacking' scheme had not entirely assuaged her guilt. At home with her two feline friends, Rose and Lilac, Shirley had created a moral stew. Should she admit her involvement in the Z-Star's thieving and if so, who should she own up to?

Two hours with her beloved cats, was long enough to convince Shirley, that she would go and seek Mr. Leaf at the Pyramid department store. She slammed the front door of her 1960's bungalow shut and in a whirlwind of activity, rushed off to catch the hyper-bus from Wembley central.

Shirley arrived at the fifty fifth-floor of the Pyramid store, thirty minutes later, but to her consternation and alarm, she discovered that Mr. Leaf was off on sick leave.

Hungry, she made her way to the food court on levels twenty to thirty. When Shirley became stressed and anxious, her appetite exploded. She needed to consume vast quantities of food, and immediately.

Sated and considerably calmer, Shirley devised a plan. She would use some of her less than salubrious connections to find out where Mr. Neal Leaf, lived.

Chapter 39

Frank Wattle had agreed to meet his wife and mother to their six children at 'MELTS Ice-cream Emporium'. Ninety nine different flavours set in an extravagant building the size and width of a football pitch was a serious statement of intent.

No sooner had Wattle walked into the crazily lit emporium, then he immediately realized it was the wrong venue in which to meet Rita. Literally, hundreds of people, lizards and robots of differing generations were swarming all over the ground floor.

He retina messaged Mrs. Wattle and received a retina reply informing him that she was standing in the tropical section under a palm tree with yellow surfboard. Several minutes ensued, before Frank spotted her next to two off-duty service lizards wearing Hawaiian shirts.

The moment he clapped eyes on her, his heart swelled with pride. Even from ten feet away, she looked gorgeous. He attempted to straighten his tie and smooth out the creases in his overcoat as he walked towards her.

'Mrs. W, What, can I say? You look special.'

'Mr. W. You don't look half bad yourself, you, silly old fool.'

They embraced warmly, and were promptly lost in a sea of re-cycled confetti.

Upon arrival at McCarthy's Fish and Seafood restaurant, they were seated at an ornate table for two with Parisian lamps. Wattle studiously read the extensive menu.

'Fish, shellfish and more fish. This is not my dream, Rita.'

'It's a freebie, Frank. How bad can it be?'

'Pretty bad,' said Wattle, grimacing.

Mrs. Wattle swiftly changed the subject. 'You will never guess what Jenny wants for her fifth birthday?'

'Go on.'

'A sausage and unicorn party.'

Frank grinned. 'It doesn't surprise me in the least. It's pure Jenny.'

'I know. What an imagination. Very sweet though.'

A waiter appeared wearing a maroon apron with McCarthy's written on the top left in yellow.

'Good evening Madam, Sir. Can I offer you a drink? I can recommend the McCarthy signature cocktail.'

Wattle glanced across the table to Mrs. Wattle. 'Ooooh. A cocktail. What do you think, Rita? Shall we treat ourselves?'

'I am tempted Frank, but they are expensive.'

'Two of the house signature cocktails my good man,' said Wattle, without a moment's hesitation.

'A fine choice, if I may be so bold as to say,' replied the waiter.

When the man had disappeared, Rita craned her neck forwards, and said; 'Frank. Can we afford it? Drinks are not included in the dinner voucher I won.'

'Rita. How often do we treat ourselves?'

'Rarely,' she replied.

'Exactly. I rest my case. We are not extravagant people, but sometimes it is just nice to push the boat out.'

'All right. Just so long as we don't push the boat out too far, if you get my meaning.'

'I do. Now let's enjoy our evening.'

The drinks arrived, and Frank and Rita ordered their starters and mains.

'Do you think the lobster comes with chips? I really fancy chips tonight. Any shape will do.' He laughed and Mrs. Wattle smiled at him. Tonight, was special and she was determined they should enjoy the occasion.

Molly had been stimulated by her first stint at The Wattle and
Daube Detective Agency. Daube had welcomed her to the team
and asked her if she had any questions.

'Not particularly, Roger. Just to have some peace and quiet
will be lovely. I'll follow up these leads Frank has left for me from
that case in Westminster.'

'Excellent. Well, I shall be here for about another twenty
minutes, so ask away if you're not sure about anything.'

'I will, Roger.'

The overhead lights flickered and a voice could be heard
outside the elevator complaining about the lack of respect for
vending machines.

It was business as usual at 188 Piccadilly.

Mr. and Mrs. Wattle were now on to desserts and Frank was
licking his lips. McCarthy's were famous for their puddings and
in particular the McCarthy's apple pie with whipped cream. It was
rumoured that the kitchen produced over a thousand apple pies a
day for 'take-out'. Delivery lizards formed an orderly queue to the
side of the kitchen alleyway, waiting to rush off with their prized
hot apple pies to various districts within central London.

Two slices of pie arrived on black plates, with a pastry capital
'M' on the top of the pie casing. The whipped cream was in a
separate bowl. It smelt divine.

'Tuck in. Tuck in,' enthused Frank.

'I'm waiting for it to cool down a bit. You dive in, my love.'

'Are you sure? I can wait until you're ready.'

'No. Get started.,' said Mrs. Wattle. Frank needed no more
encouragement and spooned three big blobs of whipped cream
onto his pie. There was a brief silence whilst he ate his first
mouthful, and then swallowed.

'And?' asked Rita.

'Amazing. Absolutely amazing. Probably the best apple pie I

have ever eaten. Go on, try it, Rita.'

Two coffee's later, and Mr. and Mrs. Wattle were still discussing the merits of such a great pie, when the waiter appeared and asked them whether they had enjoyed their meal at McCarthy's.

'Wonderful,' replied Mrs. Wattle. 'Truly memorable.'

'Listen up, young man,' said Frank. He was speaking with an earnestness that Rita didn't witness too often. 'I'm not a fish man. No offence intended.'

'None taken, Sir.'

'Well, as I was saying. I'm not a fish man. Far from it if the truth be known. Anyway, I have to say, that lobster was a work of art. I didn't leave anything, did I Rita?'

'You didn't, Frank.'

'You see. The proofs in the pudding. Nothing left.'

'I'm so glad you enjoyed your dinner, and I trust you will return soon,' said the waiter. 'Would you like the bill?'

Mrs. Wattle delved in to her handbag and gave the waiter the vouchers she had won.

'Thank you so much, Sir, Madam. He retina scanned the barcode on the vouchers. 'That just leaves the cocktails and coffees to pay for.'

Frank retina scanned the outstanding amount.

'Thank you. You have a safe journey home. Goodnight.'

'Goodnight,' chorused the Wattle's.

'It was a once in a lifetime meal. Wasn't it, Frank?'

'Totally unforgettable,' said Frank, as the couple made their way back to the Isle of Dogs, and home.

The conversation changed to other things and it was only at 11.10pm, that Frank Wattle, told his wife about his visit to Mr. Leaf's, in Southgate.

'That man, has had so much bad luck in his life. It beggar's belief how anyone could cope and function normally with the tragedies he has had to endure.'

'It certainly makes you appreciate what you have,' said Mrs. Wattle.

'I couldn't agree more. Anyway, I spent over three hours in Neal Leaf's front room and even made the man a cup of brew. So, there we were, talking about this and that, as you do.'

Mrs. Wattle nodded.

'And then we hear his doorbell ring. Well, it was past 9.00pm and he says he is not expecting any visitors, but he makes no attempt to answer the door, So, I say; 'Do you want me to answer that for you, Neal?'

'If you want to,' he replies.

'So, I go and open the door, and I'm confronted by a large woman. She filled the whole door frame.

'Hello. Can I help you?' I say.

'I've come to see Mr. Leaf. It's urgent.'

'Oh. Right. And you are?'

'Shirley. My name is Shirley.'

'Anyway, to cut a long story short, Rita, it only transpires that this Shirley is the mastermind behind the Z-Star robots being corrupted. She confesses to her part in the operation, and explains that regardless of whether we 'turn her in' to the authorities or not, she wants to get Ronnie Bronze arrested and off the streets of London.'

'I don't believe it, Frank. What a story.'

'Well, you better believe it, because it is the truth, my girl.'

'And you know what else? The two of them, Mr. Leaf and Shirley. They really hit it off. They got on like a house on fire.'

'Well, I never,' uttered Mrs. Wattle quietly.

'And that is how I ended up making a pot of London tea for us all. The two of them were so deep in conversation, that I thought I would leave them to it for a minute or two. I'm in the kitchen searching for sugar, when what do I discover? Only six identical cans of chicken soup. It turns out, that is all the man eats for his dinner. The same can each and every night. It breaks your heart. It really does.

The train arrived at the Wattle's station, and they alighted, along with hundreds of other mid-week revelers. As they walked slowly back to their small and intimate terraced house, Frank Wattle gripped his wife's hand and gave it a long squeeze.

'What was that for?' asked Mrs. Wattle.

'Just, because,' replied her husband.

Chapter 40

Ocean and Molly were informed of the developments concerning Shirley's confession, but they still needed to capture Ronnie Bronze. Alarmingly, or bizarrely, depending on your outlook on life, Mr. Leaf had contacted Frank Wattle and requested that no further action be taken against Shirley. He had agreed to meet Wattle later in the week to discuss the situation.

It was the turn of Ocean Jones to work at the agency and with the startling news that Ronnie Bronze had been working with Shirley, Daube thought it sensible that Ocean try to infiltrate any other top computer 'hackers', just in case Bronze was looking to recruit a new mastermind to run his criminal operation. Ocean thought she knew of no more than four or five 'hackers' with the necessary experience to assist Ronnie Bronze.

With work finished for the today, Daube invited Ocean back to his home for a cup of tea.

'And biscuits?' asked Ocean cheekily.

'I will retina message Michael, and get him to pop out and buy some. Do you have a preference?'

'Custard creams. Yes, I know they're 'dated', but you should try dunking them. It's epic.'

Daube remained unconvinced.

Seated in the elegant lounge of the Mayfair house, Ocean had been looking forward to chatting with Michael, again. He returned to the room with a silver tray. A pot of tea, two china cups and 4 custard creams nestled on the small plate.

'Aren't you joining us, Michael?' asked Ocean.

'I didn't think I was invited,' replied the generation 4

'homebot'. 'Shall I go and check with Roger? He's just dealing with some correspondence in his study?'

'Good idea,' enthused Ocean.

Michael disappeared, and in Ocean's opinion, he was gone a considerable amount of time. She messaged Mo. but he didn't reply.

In Daube's study, the air smelt of furniture polish and anguish.

'What is it, Sir?' asked the concerned robot.

Roger Daube's face was a white as a sheet.

'I've received a retina message from Molly. Ocean's grandmother has suffered a second stroke. I'm afraid it is a bigger and more severe one than the first. Molly has asked that I take Ocean to the hospital. She will meet us there.'

'Oh, dear, Sir. I'm terribly sorry.'

'It is, what it is. I can't sugar coat the news. Let her drink her tea and biscuits, and then I will tell her,' said Daube.

'Certainly, Sir. Would you like me to sit with her, until you are ready?'

'Yes. Thank you, Michael.'

'You are welcome, Sir.'

'Come and sit beside me, Michael?' requested Ocean, patting the sofa cushion next to her. 'You pour, please.'

Michael did as he was told, before sitting down alongside Ocean on the sofa.

'What is Roger doing? He's taking ages.'

'Oh, a bit of this. A bit of that,' said the 'homebot', vaguely.

'I'm intrigued. Can I ask what is so top secret?'

'It's not my place to discuss it, Ocean.'

'I'm only joking, Michael. Don't look so worried. You'll get used to me. I can be a bit of a tease.'

The pair sipped their tea. Ocean took a custard cream and

dunked it in her cup.

'Look, Michael. You have to try this. The flavour combination is to die for,' said Ocean.

'Won't the biscuit fall apart? Surely the texture is all wrong?'

'Oh, Michael. I can tell you are Roger's robot.' And that's not an insult, just in case you were wondering.'

'I take all comments at face value,' replied the 'homebot'.

'Have you ever been lonely? I believe in straight talking. I hope you don't mind?'

'I am a generation 4 'homebot'. You can't offend me, although I do have a sensitivity setting.'

'Good to know, Michael. Good to know.'

'In answer to your question. Yes. Yes, I have been lonely. It is not uncommon in generation 4's.

'I knew it. I just knew it,' said Ocean triumphantly.

'I have been feeling much better since I began doing errands out of the house. Only the other day, I went and visited my first church. The Brompton Oratory. A beautiful building.'

'But a building isn't a person. Michael. Is it?'

'No. No it isn't.'

'So? I am going to ask you again. Have you been feeling lonely?'

'Yes. Sometimes, but not all the time.'

'Michael. You are sounding like a human. You are being evasive.'

'I don't know any other existence. What can I say?' said the robot, appearing slightly flustered.

'I have a suggestion. Now, please don't take this the wrong way. I think you are a tad confused. Perfectly understandable under the circumstances.'

'What circumstances are those, Ocean?'

'A curious robot, who wants to see and experience the world, and what life has to offer.'

'I see,' said Michael diplomatically.

'I'm not sure you do.'

Ocean edged closer to the robot, and took his two hands in hers.

'Listen. I'm going to help you. I have a plan.'

'A plan?'

Yes. A plan. Now don't look so worried. Relax.'

'Very well. Relax mode, initiated.'

'Good. I have been corresponding with a generation 3 'homebot' called Breeze.'

'Breeze,' repeated Michael.

'Yes. Her name is Breeze. I have got to know her pretty well. And guess what? She is also lonely. You are not the only robot to be having these feelings.'

'Oh. I see. Is that good or bad news? Having feelings like mine?'

'It is most certainly encouraging news, Michael. You are not alone. I am going to create an online dating account for you. I am going to contact Breeze and see if she is open to meeting up with you. What do you think?' Strike that. Don't answer. Just leave it with me. Our little secret, Michael.'

The door opened, and in walked a pensive looking Daube. He smiled weakly at Ocean, and sat in an armchair across the coffee table from her.

'Is everything alright? You look like you have seen a ghost.?' asked Ocean.

'I have some bad news,' said her host.

Michael coughed and adjusted his tea cup on his saucer.

'What? What is it?'

'Your grandmother has suffered a second stroke. Worse than the first. Your mother has just contacted me. I am to travel with you to Hampstead hospital, where she will meet us,' replied

Daube quietly.

'Oh. Oh. I see. Right. Well, we better get going then.'

Ocean turned away to face the wall, and swallowed hard.

'Why couldn't my mum contact me directly?'

'I've no idea.'

Tears welled up in her eyes.

'Fine. Let's get going then. Shall we?'

Mo. Patel had heard the terrible news from Ocean, who was waiting with Daube at the Berkeley Square drone zone.

'Would you like me to come?' messaged Mo.

'Really kind of you, but I should be ok. I'm going with Roger Daube. I'll talk to you later. Thanks. Bye.'

'You could have met my friend, Mo,' said Ocean to Daube. 'Oh well. Another time perhaps.'

From across the square, two figures were identifiable. One taller than the other. To the untrained eye, they were father and daughter waiting for a lift. The bond of friendship was tightening its grip.

Back at Farm Street, Michael tidied the lounge and put the two uneaten custard creams in an airtight biscuit jar. Ocean had dunked and eaten two, whilst Daube and Michael had politely declined. It was nightfall and the solar street lights outside glowed against the damp and misty air.

Michael felt wistful. He turned off the kitchen lights, and let his advanced retina night vision adjust to the change in lighting condition. He continued to look outside at the street lights and as he did so, his brain switched to thinking about Harold, the generation 1 'homebot, who had raised and nurtured Daube in this house.

'What was he like?' thought Michael. 'Was he similar to me? Do we share similar personality traits? I suppose I will never know. Roger never discusses his upbringing with me. Never. He is a closed book as far as that subject matter is concerned.'

The generation 4 'homebot' walked out of the kitchen and made his way to the first-floor landing.

Were the two Brittles of London boxes still hidden under Daube's bed? he wondered. He crossed the landing and walked down the corridor to Roger Daube's bedroom. He silently opened the door and switched on the side panel lights. Michael stopped beside the perfectly made bed and bent down. The boxes were still there, untouched since the last time he had looked at them.

Should he discuss the subject with his master? He was unsure and uncertain as to what he should do next.

The sheer scale of the Hampstead hospital was breathtaking. From the top of Parliament Hill, it towered over the skyline to the west. The hospital was part of The Global Healthcare Group, and its sheer size and scale meant that there were only five hospitals functioning in a city of fifty million people. The drone pad on top of the accident and emergency unit was in operation 24/7, with over three thousand drones flying patients in and out of the hospital on any given day.

As Ocean and Daube flew towards the towering structure, red and blue bands of laser lights guided the normal passenger drones to various landing bays situated around the vast site.

Landing at zone F, Daube retina scanned, to pay for the journey, and waited for Ocean to lead him to the ward where Gwen Jones was. An internal army of lizards and doctors swarmed along the wide brightly lit corridors that crisscrossed the enormous building.

They went to central reception on E wing and were directed to floor thirty three.

'I can see Mum. Over there. See her?'

Daube could not.

'Mum,' called out Ocean. We are here'

Molly swiveled around, and all Daube could see were her teary blood shot eyes.

'Mum. Mum. Look at you. What's happened?'

Molly didn't utter a word. She just started to sob. Quietly at first, and then louder and louder.

Ocean instinctively hugged her mother and Daube wished that Wattle was around. He was such a natural in awkward situations like this.

Molly was shaking her head and wailing. 'It's no use. It's no use.'

What is, mum? You're not making any sense.'

Upon hearing those words from Molly, Daube new that his worst fears were about to be confirmed.

'She's dead, Ocean. Dead. Gran is dead.'

Chapter 41

Roger Daube travelled alone. He had said his sad goodbyes and promised to be in touch tomorrow.

'Anything. Absolutely anything. You just let me know. No matter how big or small. Contact me.'

'Thank you, Roger. You are a very kind man,' said Molly between sobs. 'I really mean that.'

'Thanks Roger,' said Ocean.

'What for?' replied Daube.

'Oh, I don't know. For being you, I guess.' She flung her arms around his neck and almost squeezed the life out of him.

'Goodnight ladies. A safe journey, home.'

They both waved in his direction as he strode out of the intensive care unit and turned left.

'Save me', he pleaded to himself. 'It's not too late.' He felt as if the past and the present were staring directly at him. Daube felt compelled to act.

He had chosen to travel on a hyper-bus. As Daube sat down on the ground floor of the sleek machine, he noticed a 'homebot' recharge station across the road. These charging stations were dotted across London and were numbered in the thousands. Super-fast robot charging points were the size of a paving slab, and allowed the 'homebots' to receive an active charge refresh in sixty seconds. Standing on a square charging point and remaining motionless for one minute was all it took to rapid 'energize' the robot for up to 72 hours if it was a generation 4 model. The Z-Star was rumoured to be able to function for one week on a single sixty second charge. Five 'homebots' were queuing for the recharge station, and it occurred to Daube, that if Michael was out and about town more often, he might require this service.

The hyper-bus effortlessly rose above the ground and headed in the direction of central London. As Daube glanced around the bus, he caught sight of his own reflection in the darkened window. Had he aged? Forever the English gentleman, Daube looked pale and tense. There were blue-black pencil thin lines under his eyes, and the feint beginnings of crow's feet. He squinted at his distorted image and caught sight of a mother with a baby, sitting behind him. It was an unremarkable sight and yet it jolted Roger Daube out of his reverie.

Who was he? Did he have a genuine purpose in his life and to what extend did his fatherless existence really matter? He tightened his grip on the rubberized seat bar in front of him and twitched. It was unavoidable. He knew exactly where he had to visit and his mouth went dry as he thought about the prospect of returning to Memory Lane.

He switched hyper-bus routes at Oxford Circus and jumped on one heading towards the Oriental district. Night-time London was a seething mass of motion and blur. Colours clashed in a frenzy of activity as people, lizards and machines collided in a balletic dance of movement and purpose.

He had one memory shard remaining. Two down and one to go, Daube instinctively knew that this third shard would be the most significant and possibly the most dangerous one so far. His breathing became more rapid and shallow as he headed deep in to the east end of London.

He stepped off at The People's Pleasure Place, that temple of temptation and ruin and remained frozen to the spot. He rubbed his eyes in disbelief. Surely not. Twenty paces in front of him stood Neal Leaf and Shirley. Although he had never physically met them, Wattle had sent him retina images and his retina-scan facial recognition alerted him to the two humans standing before him. Visual dimension data (VDD) confirmed that it was Mr. Leaf and Shirley.

Daube took another long hard look at the individuals. They were holding hands and deep in conversation, oblivious to what was going on around them.

For a split second, he considered activating visible thought bubble (VTB) mode, but then decided against it. The body language between the two, even though completely different in shape and size suggested a touching intimacy that Roger Daube didn't dare interrupt. He turned away and considered his own limited options. 'Focus on your own life,' he told himself. Destiny or disaster lay before him. Roger Daube had turned inwards against the world.

As Molly opened the front door, it felt like the first day of the rest of her life. Her mother was dead, she was bored and frustrated with her job at London Transport and she was in the middle of a tricky relationship with her teenage daughter. She flicked on the hall lights, only to discover that they had been burgled. Strewn all over the stairs and lounge floor were items of clothing, photos, and empty bags. She gasped, and screamed;

'Ocean. We've been broken in to.

'What?'

'We've been burgled.'

Ocean rushed in to the lounge. 'It's unbelievable. How can life get any worse right now?'

'Ocean. Look. They haven't taken the photo of you, me and gran. See? There it is lying on the floor.' Her mother was on her knees scrabbling around. 'The frame is a bit scuffed. But that's all.'

'Thank God. Let me see.'

Molly handed her daughter the framed photo and watched her kiss it twice.

'I'm going to check upstairs, mum. You check down here. Ok?'

One hour later, and bizarrely, nothing of any value had been taken.

'I'm wired, mum. I can't possibly go to bed yet. I'm going to do some school work.'

'Fine,' replied Molly, who was dazed and tired by the events of the day. 'Goodnight.' She hugged her daughter for a good two minutes before releasing her and then walked silently to the kitchen.

Ocean watched her drift away and then shot upstairs to her bedroom. She was determined to block any thoughts of her grandmother out of her mind, at least temporarily. She needed to keep active.

'Hacking' into the online dating website was simple and in less than two hours, Ocean had created a credible profile of Michael. She paused for a second, and then pressed send. When Breeze next activated her account, she would find a message from him.

Computer wizardry over, she lay down and closed her eyes. An image of her father smiling at her from afar was as much as she remembered as she drifted into a long and much needed sleep.

Daube knew the drill by now. He walked with purpose towards where he remembered the disused red telephone booth. Nobody watched his actions. It was as if he became invisible the moment he had made up his mind to locate the telephone booth and enter. He opened the door, picked up the black telephone, and punched in his date of birth on the keypad.

'How can I be of assistance?' said the voice.

'I would like to enter Memory Lane please,' said Daube.

'And why would you like to enter Memory Lane?' came the response.

'Because I must see an event from my past,' replied Daube.

'Mr. Daube?'

'Yes.'

'Mr. Roger Arthur Daube?'

'Yes.'

'This will be your third and last memory shard.'

'I realise that'.

'I see,' said the voice. 'I must remind you, that once you are in Memory Lane, there is no going back. You cannot retract your memory shard once purchased''

'I understand that,' said Daube.

'The third shard is the most intense. There could be consequences.'

'I know.'

'And you are prepared to take this risk?'

'I am.'

'Once you have committed yourself to the experience there is nothing I can do to retract the memory.'

'I understand,' answered Daube.

'Very well. Place your left hand on the sheet of metal in front of you and close your eyes. Try to erase all thoughts from your mind and concentrate. Concentration is absolutely essential,' said the voice.

Daube pressed his left palm onto the metal and attempted to erase all thoughts from his existence. Sixty seconds elapsed.

'Open your eyes, said the voice.'

He was once again standing on Memory Lane. The medieval wooden huts were exactly the same as on his second visit. He knew what to expect and he waited for the next instruction.

'Which type of memory shard do you want?' said the brain hologram, hovering at face height.

'The past,' said Daube.

'The past it shall be, Mr. Daube. 'This will be your third and last purchase. I am a mirror image of your mind. You are looking at yourself. Take your time Roger Daube, inspect the many memory stalls and once you are satisfied you have made the right choice, enter and commit yourself'

Daube was just about to move, when the hologram said;

'There is no going back. Seek the truth.'

Five minutes of memory shard. Was it enough? he wondered as he began to roam amongst the huts, and should he purchase a traditional memory shard or a contemporary one?

Infusion from a teapot was not an unpleasant experience, but a microchip inserted underneath the skin was less appealing.

He walked up and down the rutted uneven road.

A sudden movement to his left, caught his attention. It was a grey cat. The animal froze and stared straight at him. Daube stared back.

'Follow me. I am your guide. Trust me,' the cat spoke English with a Japanese accent. Daube assessed the situation and looked behind. The street was empty and very still. He nodded and walked towards the cat. The silky creature with bottle green eyes rubbed itself against Daube's legs and purred. The cat walked away and Roger Daube followed.

A small Japanese sign swayed gently in a light gust of wind. The air was warm. The cat led him in to a shop. He smelt ginger and arrow root and saw two figures bent double over a cauldron.

'Welcome back, Mr. Daube. Please take a seat.'

He peered in the gloom and focused on an old woman who was stirring the pot. He walked towards the two shapes and heard a faint bubbling emanating from the cauldron.

He sat down on a small wooden stool and awaited instruction.

The figure next to the woman gestured towards Daube. He was an old man with leathery aged skin.

'What was he holding in his arms?' thought Daube.

'You have chosen a traditional memory shard Mr. Daube. Please remain calm and allow your mind to transcend your body. You will feel light headed and slightly dizzy. Please do not be alarmed. This is perfectly natural,' the old man said. He was holding the grey cat.

Very delicately, the old woman lifted a wooden ladle towards Daube and asked him to take three deep breaths. Slowly. He obeyed.

'You will start to slip away Mr. Daube. Do not be afraid, this is your mind transcending itself. Very soon you will experience a real emotional memory recall. Do not resist. Allow your mind to follow the chosen path,' explained the old lady.

'Look for the light. Look for the light. A blinding white light,' Daube told himself. His body went limp.

All of a sudden, he was standing in a huge terminus. It was deserted. His uncle Arthur was holding his hand.

'Your father has given you this cat as a parting gift, Roger. What do you want to call her? Isn't she beautiful.?'

A three year old Daube stared at the cat in his uncle's arms, and then looked towards the rocket launch pad.

'Come on, Roger. Let's go home. The cat will be a loving memory of your father. Roger? Roger?

The little boy was transfixed to the spot, unable to move. A single salty tear slipped down his cheek.

'Daddy. I want my daddy.'

Daube convulsed and juddered. His whole body shook. He gasped for air, and opened his eyes. He was back in the bustling Oriental district.

Chapter 42

Michael was stunned. A date with a generation 3 'homebot' called Breeze. He could hardly believe his good luck. Fortunately, he had no clue as to why the process had been so simple.

Ocean, in a moment of guilt, had 'hacked' into the online dating site for robots called 'BOLTS' and manipulated a photo plus profile of Breeze. She had sent the details to Michael, after she had registered him on the site as a new companion looking for friendship and culture. Ocean then contacted Breeze as Michael, and an online chat began between Breeze and Michael (aka) Ocean. She had played the part of Michael until last night, when she decided to give Michael a shove.

'Check your profile Michael. Go on?'

The generation 4 'homebot' was astounded, thrilled and nervous, when he discovered that an invite to meet had appeared in his inbox.

Ocean briefed Michael on etiquette and what to wear, and dropped a few hints about subjects of interest. Now it was up to him.

The robot had two days to consider where to eat, and what to talk about.

He was in good shape, thanks to the morning workouts with Daube and he had 'an eye' for detail when it came to choosing suit, shirt and tie combinations. All he now had to do, was pluck up the courage to go through with the meeting and then the prospect of a real friendship was tantalizingly close.

Should he tell Daube? Ocean thought he should, but she agreed that it was up to Michael and his conscience.

London was a human zoo. An epic social experiment with a mix of science and culture. A true melting pot and city rich in history and attitude. It had a style and swagger to rival any metropolitan hub in the world.

Roger Daube had travelled the globe, but London was home. He didn't identify with anywhere else. He had returned to Farm Street badly shaken, after his third memory shard experience. His usual composure was absent.

'Good evening, Sir. A pleasant evening, I trust? Oh, my dear. What is wrong? You don't look at all well. Sit down in the study, and I will bring you a glass of chilled water.'

Daube didn't reply. He stumbled over the doorstep of his house, and collapsed.

When he came around, he blinked several times before establishing where he was. Michael had carried him to his bedroom and covered his body with the duvet.

'Michael?'

'I'm here. No need to panic. I've sent for the doctor.'

Daube sat straight up in bed.

'No. No. No doctor. I'm fine, Michael. Cancel the doctor immediately.'

'But, Sir. I protest. Surely.....'

'No means no, Michael. Do you hear me?'

The 'homebot' was shaken.

'Yes. Of course. I will cancel the doctor immediately.

Daube lay back down. He was sweating and his heart rate was alarmingly fast.

'Calm down,' he told himself. 'Just keep it together.'

Michael returned and sat on the side of the bed.

'What is wrong. You can tell me, Roger,' said the robot.

Daube was about to say something, when the front door bell went.

'Who on earth can it be at this time?' asked Michael. 'It is

2.30am?'

The bell rang again, for a third time.

'Excuse me. I will just go and answer that.'

He returned and stood over Daube, who was lying down with his eyes half closed.

'Excuse me, Roger. You've had another delivery.

'Let me guess?' said Daube quietly. 'Brittles of London.'

'Yes. How did you know. A box, similar to the other two you have received.'

'Bring it up, please. I might as well fill you in on what's been happening.'

Michael returned with an identical box to the other two, and placed it on Daube's lap. Daube had closed his eyes completely.

'Is there an initial A on the lid, Michael?'

'Yes, there is.'

'Oh. Good. It's not always nice being right.'

Daube half opened his eyes. He could have sworn that an orange and purple butterfly fluttered past in the distance.

Michael. Sit down. I have much to discuss with you.'

Frank Wattle rubbed his eyes. He felt exhausted. On receiving the terrible news about Gwen Jones, he had sat up late into the night and talked it through with Mrs. Wattle. Now the morning had arrived, and he still felt emotional. True, he didn't know Gwen and had never met her, but the way Ocean talked about her grandmother meant her death would have come as a hammer blow to her.

He showered, dressed and went downstairs. Rita passed him a plate of bacon and eggs.

'I thought you could do with a hot breakfast, love,' said Mrs. Wattle.

'You are a peach. You do know that?'

'London tea?'

'You must have read my mind.'

'One mug of London tea coming your way. What are your plans today?'

'I'm going straight to the office, and then I will contact Molly. Make sure she is holding up.'

'And what about Ocean?' said Mrs. Wattle in a concerned voice.

'Good question. I think I will chat with Roger first. He's formed a very close bond with her.'

Rita eyes momentarily enlarged.

'I know. Roger of all people. You couldn't make it up, could you?'

'Ah. Well that's some good news at least.'

'Who would have thought it. Roger opening up and chatting with a teenage girl.'

'Now, now. Don't be unkind, Frank. It is not befitting of you.'

'I'm only joking, Rita. I'm really pleased for the man. Human interaction. Just what he needed if you ask me.'

Wattle gulped his hot mug of London tea, devoured his breakfast and went in search of his raincoat.

'I didn't hear the kids this morning. I must have been in a deep sleep?'

'You were. They've all left for school and nursery. I thought I should let you sleep in. I think you needed it.'

'Thanks, Rita. You're a good egg. Do you know that?'

'Now be off with you, and please let me know if I can be of help to Ocean or Molly?'

'I will. See you later.'

'Ok. See you.'

Wattle blew her a kiss across the table and turned to leave the room.

'Oh, Frank. Is that your belt on the chair? Don't forget it.'

'Mmmm. I'll be fine.'

'Frank.'

'Yes?'

Frank. Is there something you're not telling me? Frank Wattle.

Look me in the eye?'

'I've put a bit of weight on. That's all. My trousers feel quite snug without a belt. I will lose it again. I promise.

He grinned at his long suffering wife and departed for 188 Piccadilly.

Mo. Patel was waiting outside Ocean's house as she closed the door.

'Are you ok?' he said. 'I hope you don't mind. I came here because I wanted to check you were alright. I wasn't sure if you would be going to school today.'

'I want to keep busy. The last thing I need is too much time on my hands.'

'Right. I get that.'

'Mo? Thanks a bunch for coming over. It means a lot.'

'No problem. How's your mum?'

'Not great really. I must make a concerted effort to be nicer to her. I've been a bit mean, recently.'

'Look. Who doesn't have family friction. My younger brother drives me totally crazy.'

Ocean laughed. 'Families eh? What a pain. You can't live with them, and you can't live without them.'

'Yep' replied her best friend.

Frank Wattle wasn't the only one who had been talking late into the night. Roger Daube and his 'homebot' Michael, had also chatted until past 4.00am.

It was therefore unsurprising , that the next day, two rather jaded business partners sat opposite each other at The Wattle and Daube Detective Agency.

'We need two strong Turkish coffees and I won't take no for an answer. Do you hear? Roger?'

'Yes, Wattle. Excellent idea. I need some rocket fuel to fire me up this morning.'

'Two Turkish coffees coming right up. And you know what? If I get any backchat or 'lip' from that vending machine I will be tempted to switch it off.'

'Can I watch, please?'

'I could film it. The end is nigh. It's had it coming.'

Wattle scurried out to the fifth floor landing, and Daube retina messaged Molly to check she was coping.

In all the commotion that had happened last night, Michael had not had a chance to discuss his arranged date with Breeze, the generation 3 'homebot'. He then thought about the big conversation that had taken place with Daube and on reflection, a trivial matter, like a date with another robot, could wait.

He went into the study and stared at the three chocolate capital initials, that Daube had taken back to his desk. Removed from their boxes, the capital letters R, A. D. signifying, Roger, Arthur, Daube, were laid out on the impressive American oak desk. Neither he nor Daube could fathom why the second delivery had not been an 'A' instead of a 'D', but never the less, there they were. Three letters and each one delivered within six hours of Daube having visited Memory Lane.

He had explained to Michael what the name day celebration meant to him and how it always triggered regret and a sense of loss at not having a mother and father around on his birthday.

'It cannot be a coincidence that after each memory shard a slice of reality forces its way into my actual physical world. It is a representation of my past and my regret', said Daube. 'It's like I am being hunted. My shards are fracturing and becoming reality. How can that be?'

Michael had no answer to that pertinent question. He wisely decided to not mention that he had seen the two Brittles of London boxes under Daube's bed. That confession would not be helpful to Roger Daube, in his hour of need.

All he could offer his master, was solace.

Chapter 43

Ocean retina messaged Daube. 'When could she talk to him?'

He messaged back and asked her if it was urgent, or could it wait until later?

She replied that she had figured out how to corrupt Michael's hardboard system, if that is what he still wanted to do? It was called, being 'RINSED'. Also, could she still come into the agency after school?

Daube agreed to see her at work after school, but only if Molly was ok with the arrangement. He didn't want an upset and angry mother accusing him of being selfish and unthinking. He told Ocean, it was entirely up to her and her mum, but that he would entirely understand if they wanted to spend time alone.

'Should Ocean come into the agency today, Wattle?'

'That's a hard one to answer, Roger. Each person deals with grief in a different way. Some people want to keep really busy, some bury their head in the sand, some people dwell on the bereavement and need time to think, and some people fall apart. I remember when my old man passed away. I was devastated, but I dealt with it in a different manner to my brother. I guess, what I'm saying, is that no two people are the same.'

'What about Molly? How is she likely to react?'

'I don't know her that well, but I if I was a betting man, I'd say she will deal with it differently to Ocean.'

'And why is that?'

'You've seen the two of them together. They are nothing like each other. True, they look like two peas from the same pod, but as for personality? Well, that's another story.'

'Genes, Wattle. they are so strong. Nature versus nurture.'

'Exactly. Generations of love and look what we end up with?'

'Speak for yourself, Wattle. I'm just fine with who I am?'

'Really? Can you look me in the eye and say that truthfully?'

'Yes, I can.'

'Can you, honestly, Roger?'

'Of course. Why not? Don't look at me like that. It's off putting.'

'Like what? You know I'm making perfect sense. Heavens, Daube, you are a dark horse. Why don't you let anyone into your inner world? What are you so afraid of? Surely it can't be that bad. Can it?'

'You are making me feel uncomfortable now. Please stop.'

'Alright, alright, but you are going to have to open that closed heart one day. It won't kill you. Trust me.'

The two work colleagues went back to their jobs, but Wattle had touched a nerve, and Daube knew it. What should he do?

He decided to clear his head and go for a walk.

The unexpected and completely instant connection between Mr. Leaf and Shirley had taken the couple, both by surprise. Neither person was particularly looking for love and for different reasons.

Shirley had convinced herself that she would never meet the right person and that she was doomed in matters of love.

Mr. Neal Leaf had closed his heart like a clam snapping shut, after his beloved wife and companion had died. Her illness and death had been slow and painful in coming. Exhausted and emotionally drained, he had simply decided to turn his back on the world. He worked tirelessly, never took time off and lived a solitary existence.

Therefore, this explosion of feelings had amazed and frightened the two of them, in equal measure. It was only, a few days later, that they both admitted that 'something' momentous had occurred. It was when Frank Wattle, had gone in to the kitchen to make a pot of London tea.

They gazed at each other, speechless, with an invisible energy reaching out that tied their two hearts together. They were helpless to react. It was love at its purest and most beautiful.

Shirley and Neal knew immediately, that their paths had crossed for a reason.

Daube walked without purpose in the direction of the transcontinental urban speed shuttle terminus. He didn't know why he chose to walk to this vast transport intersection, built entirely underground below the Covent Garden Interstellar station. He just went there without thinking why.

Fifteen minutes later, and Daube found himself at the largest travel intersection in the world. Ten floors of shops, restaurants, pleasure zones and hawkers. It was hard to avoid these transient beings, who populated the platforms and walkways. They never stayed in the same place for more than thirty minutes, so as to avoid the police lizards arresting them.

Begging and hawking (selling goods without a license) was prevalent all over London and especially at transport hubs. It was said you could buy everything you might need for a whole year in one browse of the terminus. Daube was not prepared to put that theory to the test.

He gazed up at the hologram European destination locations and a quiver of excitement went through his body at the thought he could board a train to Oslo, Athens or Moscow in a matter of minutes.

An aged woman selling herbal remedies sidled up to him. Daube waved her away with a cursory flick of his hand. You were never alone for very long in a place like this. He strolled through the shopping zones on level 3, 4 and 5, without a need to buy anything. He spotted a Belgium chocolate parlour and in a moment, which was quite out of character, he went in and ordered a small hot chocolate with whipped cream.

As he waited for the lizard to make the drink, Daube took a cursory glance around the shop. A variety of well-heeled commuters and shoppers made up the twenty odd individuals inside the cafe.

His hot chocolate arrived, and he retina scanned to pay. He sipped the warm sweet cream on the top of the drink. This was certainly a luxury indulgence.

His thoughts drifted to the third memory shard experience from last night, and as he remembered, the muscles in his stomach tightened. He would also have to talk with Ocean about the moral dilemma concerning 'hacking' into Michael. He felt uncomfortable about the implications of 'RINSING'. What if he wiped completely the personality of his generation 4 'homebot'. Daube shuddered at the thought.

Finishing his drink, he was about to stand up and leave the premises, when he froze on the spot.

Not more than thirty feet away, with his back turned, was Michael, at the 'chocolates to go' counter. The robot hadn't seen Daube and so he swiftly walked outside and stood some distance from the front doors. Two minutes later and there was Michael, walking with a jaunt in his step and a box of chocolates under his arm. He hadn't been aware that Daube had spotted him.

What the blazes was Michael doing buying expensive chocolates? And for who? thought Daube.

Chapter 44

Molly had endured an awful day. She had made arrangements and paid for the funeral. It was scheduled for next Tuesday. She realised that Ocean had hardly spoken about the death of her grandmother. Was she deliberately blocking the grief process? It was entirely understandable.

Ocean had left the house before breakfast and not even said goodbye. Molly was concerned but also acutely aware that she must not invade her daughter's privacy. She mulled over what course of action to take and decided on doing nothing. A wait and see approach seemed appropriate. The burglary had resulted in nothing being stolen. The house had been turned upside down and was a total mess, nothing more. It was a strange scenario, and Molly considered what if there was something more sinister behind the action. She couldn't decide.

A retina message from Wattle, confirmed the news that Ocean was going in to the agency after school. She replied that it was fine and thanked him for notifying her.

The house felt slightly creepy and quiet, with nobody in it. She busied herself with small menial tasks and then went to look at her mother's bedroom. This was a brave move and Molly summoned every ounce of courage to sit on Gwen's single bed and plump her pillow.

She stroked the duvet cover and had an imaginary conversation with her mother. All the hundreds of things I should have said and done, now vanquished forever.

'I love you, mum. I hope you have gone to a better place and that you are at peace. I miss you more than you will ever know.'

Tears welled up, and Molly allowed herself a gentle release. She wept silently, alone in her small terraced house in Muswell Hill.

Ronnie Bronze was still angry. He had threatened Mr. Leaf, and Shirley had disappeared. He had no idea where she was or what she was up to. The very fact he hadn't been pestered by the lizard police told him that Shirley hadn't 'ratted' on him. That at least was some small relief.

He sat in the grubby transport café under the disused A40 flyover, and watched two cockroaches clamber over a stale piece of bread in the far corner. This place was a throwback to the London his grandfather would have known. A no thrills café that served the basics. A classic English breakfast fry-up with a steaming mug of London tea.

Scraping the remnants of his two eggs with the last piece of fried bread, Bronze considered his options. He knew that without Shirley, he was way out of his depth. He just didn't have the skills or brains to 'hack' in to the Z-Star's.

Three had been corrupted, but the thought of many more thieving robots made him greedy for more spoils. He had sampled the benefits of the 'good life' and he wanted more.

His whole adult existence had been based on petty thefts and dishonesty and a life of crime was all he knew. Even the thought of the mind extraction programme wasn't enough of a deterrent. If he was going to go down, then so be it. Ronnie Bronze was not about to give up his life of crime.

Michael was buzzing. Fresh from his errand to buy a box of handmade chocolates for Breeze, he had floated home on a sea of positive expectation. A date with an interesting and in his opinion, captivating female 'homebot' made him want to proclaim his happiness from the rooftops. There was hope and there certainly was life outside the world of Daube and Farm Street. Michael was in a fine frame of mind for a robot.

Frank Wattle greeted Ocean with a big squishy hug.
'Lovely to see you, my dear. Holding up, I hope?'
'Hello, Frank. Well, I'm keeping busy, if that's what you mean.

Everyone says time is a great healer.'

'It is, Ocean, it is. But, remember to be patient.'

'Thanks for the advice, Frank. Where's Roger?'

'A good question. He said he was going out for a walk and that was the last I have seen of him. Most unlike him, actually, but then he has been acting a little out of character recently.'

'Oh? Really?'

'Nothing you can pinpoint, as such. Just little things here and there. Daube forgets that over the years, you end up being fairly familiar with one's character.'

'I suppose one does. I know my mother inside out.'

'And she must be the same with you. Don't forget that, Ocean?'

'Fair point, Frank. Anyway, what do you want me to do today?'

Roger Daube was a conflicted man. He was aware that Ronnie Bronze was still a free individual and that all Wattle's leads had not uncovered where he was or whether he intended further 'hacking' of the Z-Star robots. His other complication was that he wanted Ocean Jones to 'RINSE' Michael, to see if a programme could be written to deter criminals like Bronze from 'hacking' the 'homebots' He knew that he felt tremendous guilt over using his own 'homebot' as a computer experiment. Nevertheless, he considered the risk worth taking, if it revealed how the most advanced robots ever engineered could be corrupted. He had complete trust in Ocean's brilliant computer skills to reverse the programme he was going to ask her to write.

He looked at the digital time board at Leicester Square. It read 5.10pm.

'Goodness me,' he muttered.

Time had slipped away from Daube, and he had been absent from the office for over five hours. He remembered that Ocean was coming into the agency to work and hurried back to 188 Piccadilly.

'Nice of you to show your face,' said Wattle, cheekily.

'My apologies, Ocean. Time flew away with me.'

'That's ok, Roger. Frank and I have been having a good old natter.'

'Really?' said Daube a little too guardedly for his own liking.

'Don't worry, Daube. No trade secrets have been revealed.'

'Very amusing, Wattle.' He removed his immaculate overcoat and sat down next to Ocean. 'I have been thinking it over and I am prepared to take the risk. I want you to write a computer programme that can 'hack' into a generation 4 'homebot', please?'

'Hold on a mo. Rog,' said Wattle. 'Are you saying what I think you are saying? Are you going to 'RINSE' Michael.'

'I am, Wattle, I am. I don't trust this Bronze fellow one bit. Just because he isn't collaborating with Shirley anymore, doesn't mean he isn't actively looking for other helpers. It stands to reason. Just take a look at his profile? This is a determined man who won't be happy Shirley has quit his operation.'

'He's got a point, Frank,' said Ocean.

'Is it ethical?'

'That is admittedly a grey area. However, I know Ocean can write another programme to undo any potential damage done. Ocean?'

'Yes.'

'If you can 'hack' in to a generation 4 and alter its behavioral patterns, then I am convinced you can reverse the process.'

'I can, Roger. I can.'

'Get cracking, then. We have no time to lose.'

'I'm on it.'

Wattle gave his colleague a look that said, 'are you entirely sure?'

Daube averted his gaze, and made himself busy.

Over,on the Isle of Dogs, Mrs. Wattle was rounding up her noisy clan. The news of Gwen Jones demise had moved her. Being a mother of six children, herself, she was acutely aware of the impact it would have on Molly and Ocean.

She decided to ask Frank for Molly's details and retina messaged her husband. Personal information downloaded to retina storage, Rita Wattle messaged Molly.

'If you require anything, please ask. Also, if you fancy a chat or a cup of coffee, don't hesitate to contact me. Love and kisses – Rita.'

Late autumn gales were predicted. This was not unusual for London in November. From the middle of the month until early December, climate change had resulted in electrical storms and windy conditions. A streak of brutal white lightening forked across the night skyline, followed by a distant rumble.

The first storm of November was forecast for this evening, with a torrential downpour to follow and high gusts of wind. It was dramatic and potentially dangerous. Londoners were warned to stay indoors if possible and to avoid any journey's by drone unless absolutely essential. JOYCE – the air traffic control computer had shut down particular routes to avoid collisions and the busy streets of central London were fast emptying.

The weather warning was disregarded by Ronnie Bronze. He was on the search for a new accomplish. So far he had failed. Scrutinizing the criminal underworld message boards merely highlighted what Bronze feared. There were only a handful of people with the requisite skills he needed.

Frustrated, he strode around the deserted streets of Shoreditch, before entering the People's Pleasure Palace. He was determined to have a 'good time'. The mood extraction stalls within the 'emotion' zone were of little interest to him. He needed a mood enhancement session.

Two hours later, he walked out of the People's Pleasure Palace and mentally deflected an advert attempting to track his thoughts and aspirations. He made a decision. He must find a criminal partner.

Chapter 45

Daube was aware that he wanted to discuss his third memory shard experience with Ocean, but he didn't want to distract her from the important task he had instructed her to undertake. Wattle had confirmed from his various sources, that Ronnie Bronze was on the lookout for another 'hacker' and that he was an angry and potentially violent individual if he did not get his way. He reluctantly decided to talk with Ocean at a later date.

Because of the worsening weather conditions, both Wattle and Daube wanted to make sure that Ocean arrived home before the storm. They therefore curtailed her work early and Wattle said that he would travel home with her as he had a cherry pie to give her mother. A gift from Mrs. Wattle.

Daube i-blinked and out went the office lights. The three of them tiptoed past the dozing vending machine and made for the stairwell. The elevator was still not operational.

Upon reaching street level, Daube bade Wattle and Ocean goodnight and began walking back to Farm Street. A solitary drone was parked up by Green Park.

Molly's home was warm against the chill and damp outside. Ocean invited Wattle in and called out to her mother.

'We're back. Frank's with me. Mum. Mum'

There was no response.

'Mum. Where are you?' Ocean moved around the small house quickly, but could not find her.

'Where can she be? All the lights and heating are on.'

Frank Wattle began to feel something was not right. He went into the kitchen and noticed the cellar door was ajar. He was just about to peer around, when it was flung open and Molly came out, holding a cardboard box.

'Frank. My word. You almost frightened me. How long have you been in the house?'

'Just got here. We've been looking for you. Ocean's upstairs.'

'I've been rooting about in the cellar for my candles. I don't know about over in east London, but here we are on higher ground and power cuts are not uncommon during electrical storms.'

'Candles? Well that is very twentieth century.'

'Very amusing, Frank. Better safe than sorry. Candles are very atmospheric. You should try them you old romantic,' teased Molly.

'I must remember that tip. Maybe for Rita's birthday.'

'Would you like a brew?'

'I'd love one, Molly. Thanks. Oh, yes. Before I forget. Rita, made this cherry pie for you.'

Oh, Frank. Bless her. How kind. Would you like a slice?'

'Is the pope Catholic?'

Ha. Ha. Ok. One cup of London tea and a slice of pie then.'

'Perfect. Ocean was telling me about your burglary that wasn't a burglary. Strange.'

'Yes. I thought so, too. Who breaks into a house and doesn't steal anything?'

'Ocean,' shouted Molly up the stairs. 'Would you like tea and cherry pie?'

'Yes please. I will be down in a moment,' came the reply.

The storm kicked in properly around 9.00pm and Wattle retina messaged Mrs. Wattle to say it would be wise for him to stay over in central London at his favourite Sleep 'n' Eat in Leicester Square. Rita agreed and sent him an e-kiss.

Unbeknown to Molly, the break in, yesterday, had been orchestrated by Ronnie Bronze. He had spoken to some 'shady' associates he knew, in an attempt to discover who in London had the requisite skills for robot cloning. After an electronic trawl, just five names appeared. Ronnie had heard of 4 of them, but there was a new name on the list. One Felix Fearherstone. This was the pseudonym that Ocean Jones used. It was now a simple procedure to find out where this person lived.

He paid a thug he played darts with and who was familiar with north London, to pay an informal visit to Muswell Hill.

'Don't 'nick' anything C.C.. I just want any info you can find on this Felix Featherstone. Age, photo id. Stuff like that. I want something on him. You hear me?'

'Of course, Ronnie. I will do my very best,' said Carter Clegg.'

'Good man,' replied Bronze, slapping an expensive watch into the hands of C.C. as he was known in the pub. 'Good man.'

When the news arrived about who Felix Featherstone was, Bronze, who wasn't often lost for words, was dumbfounded.

'Ocean Jones. 4teen. A female. You have to be kidding me C.C. How can a 4teen year old be a robotics cloning expert?'

'I've no idea, Ronnie.

'Neither do I, C.C. But I tell you what. It should be an absolute cinch twisting her arm, so to speak. Watch this space, mate.'

The next day, Shirley had arranged with Neal Leaf, to meet Frank Wattle at 188 Piccadilly.

'Are you sure you want to do this?' ventured Neal.

Shirley, who was not a woman who took no for an answer, wanted to share her good fortune with the world.

'I fully appreciate you are a private man, but I don't see it as showing off. I just feel that Frank was a part of our special moment and I would like to share our news with him. After all. It isn't everyday a woman gets a marriage proposal is it? I will meet you outside the Pyramid at 1.00pm.

Ronnie Bronze was still keeping a tab on Mr. Leaf, and when it was reported to him that he had been seen leaving the Pyramid department store with a large woman, his attention was alerted.

'A big woman you say. How big? Dark hair and oversized sunglasses? Then it can only be Shirley. Well I never. Cheers mate. Where did they go? Piccadilly you say. 188 Piccadilly. Keep an eye on that place. Find out who works there? Keep me posted, mate.'

Bronze could not believe his luck. Not only had he managed to track down Shirley, but the fact that she was with Mr. Leaf from the robotics department on the fifty-fifth floor told him that he smelled a rat. Something was not right and Bronze wanted to find out more.

The news that Neal Leaf had asked for Shirley's hand in marriage and that she had immediately accepted, did not come as a shock to Wattle.

'It takes all types in this world. The happy couple are coming over to the agency at lunch time to share their news,' said Frank to a startled Daube.

'But they have only just met,' said Daube incredulously.

'So?

'Isn't it a bit sudden?'

'That's not our concern. Can't you be happy for them?'

'Why the rush, Wattle?'

'Not everyone takes time to process emotional stuff the way you do. Let them enjoy their moment.'

'I will. I'm not a killjoy. I just find it hard to believe that someone can fall head over heels in love so quickly.'

'Well, they have and people do. It's called life, Daube, and you need to live it.'

At a fraction past 1.30pm, the office was alive and buzzing with noise and vitality. Frank had popped out and bought a bottle of 'bubbly' to celebrate the announcement and in cardboard cups Wattle and Daube toasted Neal and Shirley.

'I will be honest with you, Shirley. I didn't see this coming,' said Wattle. I'm chuffed for the pair of you. Congratulations, Neal.'

'Thank you, said Mr. Leaf, modestly.

'Can I talk shop briefly?' said Daube.

'Really? Roger? Can't it wait?'

'Not really. Shirley, I would like you to meet Ocean Jones. I've asked her to hack in to my generation 4 'homebot' and 'RINSE' him. She will then create a programme that will test the corruptibility of generation 4's compared to the Z-Star. If she needs help, could you assist?'

'Shirley has turned over a new leaf, no pun intended, haven't you Shirley?'

'My life of 'hacking' is over. Neal has kindly agreed to turn a blind eye to my criminal past and I intend to abide by the law. Neal made that very clear when he proposed to me. He said he would overlook my past misdeeds, but only if I promised to renounce any illegal activity. He made it a condition of his marriage proposal, didn't you, Neal?'

'I did,' said Mr. Leaf looking embarrassed.

'Good for you, Neal. I'm proud of you,' said Wattle.

The next moment, Wattle had put his two big arms around the thin Mr. Leaf and squeezed the life out of him.

'Well done,' said Daube stiffly.

'Anyway, Mr. Daube. I would like to meet this Ocean Jones. Should she need my help, then I will gladly assist, although I doubt Ronnie Bronze will find anyone with the skills I have.'

'There are not many people with Shirley's expertise,' said Neal, proudly.

Daube smiled at them both, and privately thought; 'you haven't met Ocean Jones yet.'

Thirty minutes later, when Shirley and Neal had left 188 Piccadilly, little did they know that they had been followed. Ronnie Bronze had not gone away. In fact, he was about to play a significant part in the life of Ocean Jones and Roger Daube.

Chapter 46

School had finished for the day. Mo. Patel, all six foot of him was on his knees peering at an image of a man's face.

'How accurate is the software in assimilating the data to an actual physical resemblance?'

'Accurate,' replied Ocean.'

'But the data has to be correct? Right?'

'Of course. That stands to reason.'

'I'm only asking, Ocean. If you unknowingly inputted wrong data, then you would have no idea that the calculation was inaccurate.'

'True.'

'Then I rest my case.'

'I have to believe the data analysis. If I don't, it's pointless undertaking this profiling.'

What is your heart telling you? Said Mo.

Ocean stopped staring at the image and gulped. 'What kind of question is that meant to be?'

'A fair one. Genetic profiling is accurate if you have all the relevant data. It also means it is flawed if you cannot answer all the questions.'

'Oh. I don't know any-more Mo. I'm a bit messed up.'

'Go with your instinct. It will rarely let you down.'

'You think?'

'Yep.'

Ocean paused and fiddled with a smooth pebble in her pocket, which was supposedly from Cornwall. It was cold to touch and assuredly familiar.

'Instinct, you say?'

'Yes.' What are you afraid of?'

'All kinds of things, Mo. The truth is that since gran died, I haven't been the same.'

'Have you talked it over with your mum?'

'No. We have hardly spoken since it happened.'

'Maybe that's a start then.'

'Yeah. Maybe. Do you fancy coming over?'

'Yep. Ok. I can only stay until 6.00pm. I promised my sister that I would take her to swimming lessons at 7.00pm.'

'Cool. Let's go.'

The two friends ambled away from the school and headed towards Muswell Hill. Remnants of the gale were scattered over the pavement and road.

Daube took a long slow sip of his slim-line tonic water and wiped his hands on his recycled mini hand sanitizer towel.

Frank Wattle looked unimpressed.

'Just look at you, mate.'

Daube stopped faffing about with his towel and looked at his colleague.

'What is that supposed to mean?'

'Fiddling. You are always fiddling,' said Wattle.

'Am I?'

'Yes, you are. I've never met anyone who fiddles and faffs as much as you?'

'That's a tad harsh.'

'Strike that. I bet Michael faffs like you. What a pair you make.'

'It's called attention to detail, Wattle.'

'Oh. Is it? Thanks for the information.'

Daube folded the towel neatly in to 4 and with the palm of his right hand, smoothed out the wrinkles.

'There you go again,' said Wattle. 'I honestly don't think you realise you're doing it.'

'Doing what, exactly?'

'Fiddling and faffing around.. I can only assume you have too much time on your hands. I barely have the time to breath in my house.'

'Well, that's because your place is a mad-house. In the nicest possible way.'

'You try dealing with six kids in a cramped accommodation.'

Daube looked appalled. 'I must admit, I don't know how you and Rita hold it together. It must require gargantuan levels of energy.'

'That's one way of putting in,' said Wattle.

Daube carefully placed the towel on the table beside his drink, and crossed his legs. 'So, is there a purpose to this informal gathering, or simply a little catch-up?'

'Both, really.'

'I'm all ears. You have my undivided attention, Wattle.'

Frank, shifted an inch or two in his chair and lent forward towards his friend. 'I'm concerned about you, Roger.'

'I'm fine. Just fine. You don't need to concern yourself with me. It's very kind, though,' he added.

'Roger?'

'Yes.'

'Look at me.'

'I am.'

'Straight at me.'

'Really, Wattle. What is all this about?'

'It's about you, Roger. It's about you. I may not have your university education, but I am no fool.'

'I never for one moment thought you were.'

'I know. That's not what I meant. Something is up. You are not the same man from a few weeks ago.'

'I don't know how you can say that. I really don't. Why don't....'

'ROGER,' snapped Wattle. 'Stop messing around with me. I

have known you for over five years now. I sit barely ten feet away from you five or six days a week. Do you honestly think you can pull the wool over my eyes. Now stop avoiding my questions and answer me truthfully. My patience is running out.'

Frank Wattle was acting like a man who had made his mind up. An appearance of determination and seriousness was written all over his face.

The mansion in Mayfair was a hive of activity. Michael had cleaned and dusted the complete house. He was turbo-charged. A robot on a mission. The only room he had avoided, was his master's study.

The three Brittles of London boxes and their contents were neatly stacked to the left hand side of Daube's large desk. Ever since their 'honest' discussion, Michael had assumed that Roger was dealing with the emotional fallout from his three memory shard experiences. He decided to clean the room, making sure he didn't touch or move the three boxes.

Michael was fully aware that his date with Breeze was fast approaching and he still had not decided what he was going to wear. On an impulse, he quit his dusting duties and put on his cashmere overcoat. It was exactly the same colour as Daube's.

JOYCE, the London traffic computer had allowed the drones to resume flying duties and London was its usual frenetic and busy self.

Michael walked out onto the pavement and narrowly avoided colliding with a delivery lizard.

'Excuse me, would be nice.'

'Sorry Sir. I didn't see you coming,' replied the lizard.

Michael, now mollified, lowered his voice and lent in towards the lizard in a conspiratorial manner. 'Is that letter for number 44?'

The lizard glanced at the address printed on the envelope, and

Michael saw in bold italics -RETINA SCAN ONLY across the top.

'Yes, Sir. A Mr. Michael Daube. 44 Farm Street, Mayfair, London.'

'Michael Daube?'

Yes, Sir.'

'You must be mistaken. Surely you must mean a Mr. Roger Daube?'

No, Sir. Look? A Mr. Michael Daube,' repeated the lizard.

'I see,' said Michael. 'Well, that is me.'

'Retina scan, please, Sir.'

'Of course.'

Scan complete, the delivery lizard apologized once more for almost bumping in to the 'homebot' and scurried off.

It was almost two minutes later before Michael moved. He stuffed the envelope in his inside overcoat pocket, and headed off in the direction of 'Top to Toe', the shop with the largest collection of silk ties anywhere in the world. He wanted a new tie for his date with Breeze. First impressions were so important.

When Ocean and Mo. arrived at her home, the house was empty and dark.

'Strange,' thought Ocean. ' I thought mum had taken a few days off work.' She retina scanned the front door and was denied access. 'What?' she exclaimed.

'Try again. There must be a software fault,' said Mo.

A second retina scanned was rejected, and then a third.

'I've used up all my scans,' said Ocean. 'Typical. Where is mum?'

The pair of teenagers sat down on the porch step and the glare from a three quarters moon which had briefly slipped out of its cloud cover lit the front garden.

'It's seems weird that the moon is only two hundred and eighty thousand miles away,' said Ocean. 'It's so close to us, compared to Saturn. How far is that planet from the earth?'

'I'm not sure, exactly. Maybe one million miles from us. Don't quote me on that. I'm not 100% sure.'

'I certainly will. The great Mo Patel, gets a basic geography question wrong. It will make the evening news.'

'Very funny.'

'I'm going to retina mum. This is ridiculous.'

Across town in Rita Wattle's house, Molly sat in a comfortable armchair with a big beaker of London tea and a chocolate bourbon biscuit.

'Thanks for letting me chew your ear off, Rita?'

'Don't mention it, Molly. Anytime.'

'Top to Toe' was a unique place. As Michael stared upwards at thousands of different patterned ties hanging from an enormous luminous elevated glass hanger, he was in awe of the logistics. The contraption moved the ties around and along the hanger, like a conveyor belt which was pitched in what looked like mid-air.

He stopped a shop lizard, and asked him, how you ordered one of their products.

'Right, Sir. Let me show you,' said the helpful lizard. 'First you retina scan over this tie scanner here on the counter. When you see a tie you like, press the touch screen, and the selected tie image sits in your inbox. You can select up to a maximum of ten ties.'

'Right,' said Michael.

'Then ,when you have made your selection, drag the ten photos to this purchase bar, which is here.'

'Ok'

Press 'Purchase' and a robotic arm will grab the tie from the rotating coat hanger and place it in your physical basket which is here to your immediate left.'

'And what do I do if when you receive the physical tie, you decide you don't want to buy it?'

'Absolutely, not a problem, Sir. You simply place the unwanted product in this tray to your right, and a robotic arm will remove the tie.'

'It all seems to make sense,' said Michael.

'We serve to succeed, Sir,' replied the shop lizard.

'Thank you.'

Michael wondered how they chose ties in the old days. 'Did they physically try the tie on? What a palaver. He resumed his search for the perfect tie for what he fervently hoped would be the perfect date, and made a mental note to get Daube's approval on his choice of necktie.

Chapter 47

Unbeknown to The Wattle and Daube Detective Agency, Ronnie Bronze and his cronies were now following anyone of interest who entered or left 188 Piccadilly. The initial breakthrough had come with Shirley and Mr. Leaf inadvertently leading Ronnie to where Frank and Roger worked. This had led to followers being assigned to track where Wattle and Daube lived, and eventually to witnessing Ocean and Molly Jones arriving at the agency. Six people, and they were all of interest to Ronnie.

He wanted to avoid any contact with Shirley and so after careful consideration, he decided to work on Ocean Jones, (aka Felix Featherstone). How difficult could it be to persuade a teenager to work for him? If she was undertaking trips to The Wattle and Daube Detective Agency, then it could only mean one thing. Ocean was working on how to 'hack' in to the Z-Stars. He must stop her, and at any cost. Bronze hatched a plan.

Frank Wattle puffed his cheeks out, and rubbed his scalp. He would have loved to feign astonishment at the story Roger Daube had just recounted, but he didn't need to. It was mind-blowing.

'Roger, my old pal. I feel for you. I really do.'

'Alas, Wattle, sympathy alone isn't going to help me. I have opened a can of worms.'

'Those pesky memory shards. No wonder you get public health warnings about buying them. Do you honestly think that one or more of them has corrupted and migrated to the real world?'

'I don't know. I have either had a very long nightmare and when I go home tonight, the boxes of chocolate letters will have vanished, or my personal agony is going to continue. What am I going to do, Wattle?'

'Keep calm, is the first thing. I need time to think this over.'

'I don't have time. Those letters spelling out my initials are bewitching me. I can't think straight.'

'Is it possible to retrace your steps in Memory Lane and undo the spell or whatever it is?'

'It's not magic and I'm not a magician. It is more sinister than that. We are talking about my personality and my sub-conscious.'

'There must be some way to erase unwanted memories. There must be. Leave it with me, Rog. A good night's sleep is what I need. Can I pay for once, please?'

'Absolutely not. You know the rules,' said Daube, smiling, as they left the coffee bar.

'You are a generous man, with a good heart. Don't forget that, Roger Daube. Goodnight.'

'Goodnight, Wattle, and thanks for listening.'

Daube walked back to his house in a bubble. He looked morose, worried and paid little attention to two delivery lizards arguing over parking rights, on the corner of Grosvenor Square.

Michael greeted him at the front door and removed his overcoat. The heat regeneration slippers were waiting by the doormat.

'Ah, Michael. Thank you so much. How are you?'

'I'm fine, Sir. Thank you for asking. Can I interest you in a hot chocolate or a nightcap.?'

Daube looked studiously at his faithful 'homebot', patted him on the shoulder and said that he was rather full from his snacks and coffee with Wattle.

'Of course. I had forgotten. Please excuse me for my error. I too, have had a busy day.'

'Pray tell me, Michael.'

'I think you should be sitting down, first. It is probably advisable,' warned the robot.

Daube walked in to his living room and beckoned Michael

to take a seat beside him on the sofa. Michael obeyed and placed himself next to his master.

'I don't know where to start?'

'Hesitancy in a generation 4 model. Now that is intriguing,' said Daube.

'I have a date,' blurted Michael.

'I'm sorry.'

'I have a date'

'A date?'

'Yes. A date.'

'And with whom, my I ask?'

'Breeze.'

'Breeze', repeated Daube.

'Yes, you heard me correctly. Breeze. A generation 3 'homebot' called Breeze.'

'I see.'

'Do you, Sir?'

There was a pause, and then Michael continued.' Are you cross? Angry? Disappointed in me?'

'No. No. Of course not. I'm merely digesting the information you have just told me.'

'Do   you   disapprove   of   me?'
'Michael. Please listen to me. I only have your best interests at heart. If you are happy, then so am I'

Really' You mean what you've just said?'

'Of course, I do. Now, Michael?'

'Yes, Sir.'

'We are a team. Don't forget that.'

'I will try not to.'

'Good. Then how about we have a pot of Chinese jasmine tea and you can fill me in on the whole story.'

'I will, Sir. Thank you.'

Bronze had gradually begun to lose weight. His mammoth dinners with Shirley were over, thank goodness, and even his traditional facial orange tinge was making a reappearance. The discovery that Daube had a 'homebot' was also of particular interest to him. Was a generation 4 robot corruptible? He didn't know, but he was convinced that he could get Ocean Jones to help him. It was just how, that Bronze hadn't figure out, yet.

The mind extraction programme was put to the back of his mind. He understood that he was on the KEYS database and that if he was caught and convicted again, then Siberia beckoned.

Was it all worth the risk? Hell, yes. He brushed a few dust particles from the sleeve of his mohair suit, and considered retina messaging Frank Flowers about his diminishing waistline, but on second thoughts, he decided to wait and see. First he must come up with a plan to convince Ocean Jones to work for him. Only how? That was his dilemma. He hailed a drone and headed for a late night snack at the kebab plaza, Angel Islington. Bronze was soon tucking in to a 'pitta supreme' and any nagging worries about mind extraction had been forgotten. He was a lifetime criminal who knew no other existence.

Molly returned quickly to Muswell Hill, and was met by a rather grumpy daughter, sitting on the doorstep.

'I'm sorry, Ocean. I lost all track of the time. I thought you were with Mo?'

'I was, but you've taken so long to get here, that he had to go. He's taking his sister to swimming lessons.'

'Ah. Anyway, I'm here now, No harm done.'

'That's easy for you to say, mum. It's not your time that's been wasted. I do have a life you know?'

'I'm fully aware of that. But thank you for reminding me,' said Molly, sarcastically.

'Where were you?'

'With Rita Wattle.'

'Oh.'

'She is a lovely woman, and I felt like talking to someone. Is that a crime?'

'No, but you could have told me.'

'See? I have to be accountable all the time. I, also have a life, in case you hadn't noticed.'

'Ok. Calm down. I was just saying. Communication would be nice.'

'I can't believe I'm hearing this from you. Communication. Since when has that been an imperative? You do what you like and I don't get a look in.'

Ocean assessed the situation, and wisely decided it wasn't worth the hassle annoying her mother any further.

'Fine. Whatever. Now, how do I get facial recognition to work, so I can actually get into the house?' sighed Ocean.

'You need additional fingerprint recognition. Here, let me set it up for you. What?'

'I didn't say anything.'

'You didn't have to, with that look on your face.'

Ocean shrugged.

'We were burgled, in case you had forgotten. Can you blame me for taking extra precautions?'

'No. Of course not. I was just saying......'

'Ocean. Drop it. I'm in no mood to mess around. Do you hear me?'

Ocean stared blankly at her mother.

'Well?'

'Yes,' muttered Ocean. 'Now, can I actually get in the house?'

Frank Wattle was on his way home, when he passed the new e-limo cruiser. Sumptuous air ride quality and comfort for the price of his small house, he thought. He would be long dead before anyone in his family could afford such a luxurious product.

Wattle suddenly remembered the death of Gwen Jones. She would be six feet under very soon. He pulled up and retina messaged Molly and enquired if she had a date for Gwen's funeral.

Next Tuesday, came the prompt reply. 'Can Rita and I attend? he asked.

'Of course. I will message you tomorrow with the details.'

He caught the first hyper-bus travelling east and contacted Rita.

'Home in 15 mins. Love you'

As he travelled home, he reflected on his conversation with Daube and sincerely hoped his colleague wasn't going to experience a lonely night, trapped with his inner demons. Wattle knew that he had the love and companionship of Rita. These were the two things that Daube did not have. Was it a surprise that his friend was such a tortured soul?

Wattle disembarked the hyper-bus and his face carried the worried concern of one human being for another. Roger Daube was in trouble and he had to somehow help him. This is not an ordinary life, mused Wattle, and Roger Daube is not your typically ordinary individual. His life was more than basic existence. What should he do?

Entering the safe sanctity of his home, Wattle made a decision. He was going to do something he had not done since he was a schoolboy. He would pray for his friend, before bedtime.

Chapter 48

Wattle did not have a halo. He was no guardian angel, but he did have experiences garnered in the mood extraction stalls within the 'emotion' zone, which might help him understand just what had happened to Daube in Memory Lane. A temptation teaser was manageable on an emotional level. Just. A corrupted memory shard was something else altogether. The sheer intensity of five minute's worth of precious memory malfunctioning was a shocking prospect. It could cause a major glitch within the healthy brain cells. If Daube's brain became a donor organ for the corrupted images, then the truth and reality could be intercepted by rogue images which could disseminate lies and false images. It was a terrifying prospect.

The moon's rays filtered across the far bedroom wall, as Wattle lay in bed, wide awake. The gentle rhythmic snoring of Mrs. Wattle was a reassuring noise which didn't distract him from considering all Roger Daube's options. Ideas and intricate thought patterns churned around in his mind, until the worst possible scenario occurred to him. Mind extraction.

He sat up in bed and tried to control his fevered imagination. Mind extraction. Two words that conjured up primal fear. It was the human equivalent of being 'RINSED' for robots and criminals. Surely there must be another way. He clambered over Mrs. Wattle and silently slipped downstairs. His mouth was dry and his mind was wild with ideas and visions. He must not pass on this worry to his partner in the morning. It would simply terrify Daube, and for that reason alone, he must hide his deep concerns.

Bronze was excited. His energy levels were going berserk. He had worked out how to force Ocean Jones to comply with his demands. All he had to do now, was put his plan in to action. He met with Carter Clegg and Lee Hancock in his usual café, and outlined his scheme.

'It's got to work like clockwork, gents,' Bronze exclaimed.

'It will Ronnie. It will,' replied Carter Clegg. Lee Hancock, nodded in agreement.

'Boys?'

'Yes,' they both answered.

'This is the big one. This kid, Ocean Jones is a genius in computer' hacking'. Get her onside and she will make Shirley look like an amateur.'

Shirley was good, wasn't she?' ventured Lee Hancock.

'Shut up, Lee. That woman is history as far as I'm concerned. Do you understand?'

'Yes, Ronnie,' replied his two side-kicks, in unison.

'Good.'

The air in the café bristled with menace.

'I need this to work boys. No mistakes, no cock-ups.' The expression on Ronnie Bronze's face was grim.

'Lee?'

'Yes, Ronnie.'

'You've been keeping tabs on Ocean and her whereabouts?'

'I have, Ron.'

'RONNIE, if you don't mind,' roared Bronze. Show me some respect.'

'Yes Lee. Come on. Show the man some respect.'

'I'm sorry, Ronnie. I didn't mean to insult you, like.'

'Manners,' said Bronze gravely. 'They cost so little, but they mean so much.'

'Of, course they do, Ronnie,' said Carter.

'Yes, Mr. Bronze. It won't happen again.'

'Better not. Not if you know what's good for you. Understand?'

'I do, Ronnie. I do.'

'Excellent,' said Bronze, rubbing his hands with glee. 'Let's go through our plan one more time.'

Michael retina messaged Ocean and sent her his complete correspondence with Breeze. He wanted not only her approval, but also her advice on the tone and warmth of his messages.

Ocean responded that she was in the middle of a Chinese language lesson, and would retina him at lunch-time.

Michael was leaving nothing to chance. His master had approved his choice of tie purchased from 'Top to Toe' and had suggested a lilac handkerchief to compliment the colour coordination. Michael agreed.

His shoes were black leather brogue's, just like Daube's and coupled with a navy blue single breasted suit and cashmere overcoat, he would resemble his boss from top to bottom.

The generation 4 'homebot' had considered flirting in his correspondence with Breeze, until Ocean had advised him against that approach.

'There will be plenty of time for that, if the first couple of meetings go well. Don't rush it.'

Michael listened attentively to everything that Ocean told him. He was the model student.

'I've bought her a box of Belgian chocolate's. A mix of dark, milk and white. Is that presumptuous of me?' he asked, Ocean.

'It's a nice gesture. She won't be offended.'

'Oh. Good. Have I forgotten anything?'

'Be yourself, and try to have fun.'

'Fun. Right. I will give it a go.'

'And finally, don't worry about buying the first drink. Since the gender equality laws were changed twenty odd years ago, it is now not expected for the male to buy the first drink. Remember,

Michael, women earn the same as men do.'

'Gender equality laws,' repeated the robot.'

'She will have been programmed to know nothing else. Even the generation 3's had equality settings installed.'

'Absolutely,' said Michael hesitantly.

Roger Daube had not slept well either. In fact, it is distinctly possible that Wattle and Daube were both lying awake at 3.00am, unable to sleep and thinking about memory shards.

Daube had recalled his dream and ghostly apparition. What was the significance of the lantern? He had no idea. The vision at the top of his stairs had not been threatening. It was almost beguiling.

Frustrated by his inability to sleep, Daube had put on his heat regeneration slippers, dressing gown, and gone downstairs. He walked into his study and without turning on the light sat down in his armchair by the window.

The street lights shimmered through the slats in the Venetian blinds, giving the study an ethereal feeling. As his eyesight adjusted to the low light conditions, he began to make out the outline of the three boxes which were placed on his desk.

'What to do?' he pondered.

He slowly stood up and walked quietly over to his large desk. He fingered the three boxes and acting on impulse, opened each lid. The wrapping was exquisite. The quality of the box material was top notch. He gingerly removed each letter and carefully placed them on top of his desk.

Three capital letters. R.A.D. stood facing him. Roger, Arthur, Daube. He lent in and inhaled the rich sweet aroma of the fine chocolate and immediately he was transported to his birthday and the ceremonial chocolate letter gift from his father.

He adored chocolate and yet the memories were bittersweet. How can a five year old boy comprehend and make sense of being given a chocolate letter for his 'name day' without seeing his parents? He can't. It was all confusing.

Was it loss he was grieving for? He was unsure. Isolation and a sense of betrayal an orphan feels toward those who have left, was one explanation.

Daube traced his right forefinger over the smooth, silky surface of the chocolate, before replacing the initials in their respective boxes. He sighed. A long, slow expulsion of air, and shook his head.

'Roger Arthur Daube,' he thought. 'You have been given all the privileges anyone could want in life, except the one vital thing that sustains us. Love. Undying and undiluted love. No wonder I went searching for my memory shards.'

As Roger Daube sat back in his armchair, he remained motionless for three hours. Was he asleep? No one knows. All that was certain in his confusing landscape, was that his past, present and future were colliding. What would remain from this entanglement of time? Daube did not know and neither did his partner, lying awake less than 4 miles to the east.

Chapter 49

The trap was set. There was no going back. Lee Hancock had followed Ocean Jones and followed her movements for one week. He knew where she went, with whom she spent time. If she sneezed, Hancock was aware of it.

Carter Clegg had been spying on Michael. The robots activities and movements had been watched and recorded. The grand plan of Ronnie Bronze was about to be enacted.

Michael sat in the sleek modern kitchen and took a deep breath. He removed the white envelope from his inner jacket pocket and stared at the name and address on the front. As a generation 4 'homebot', he had never received a letter before. The name; Mr. Michael Daube, 44 Farm Street, London, W1, was a wonderous sight to behold. It anchored him and made him feel like he actually belonged and existed. With the gentlest of pulls, Michael unstuck the envelope and unfolded the typed letter.

He read the brief note 4 times and then hid it in a box under his bed. He felt giddy with excitement.

The day of Gwen Jones's funeral had arrived. It was to take place at 10.00am. in the crematorium at Golders Green, north London. A small crowd of mourners had congregated in a huddle outside the chapel of rest. The November morning was a cold and bitter affair. Bright sunshine and a crisp frost lay on the ground. The small gathering included; Molly and Ocean, Frank and Rita Wattle, Roger Daube, Mo. Patel, Kendal the robot and an old friend, Claire Hoffmann.

The service was short and succinct. The priest had mentioned Gwen's love for her native Cornwall, the coastal walks she used to take as a young woman and her undying loyalty as a daughter, mother and grandmother. The service was upbeat and a celebration of a lost life. Tears were shed, memories shared and finally the coffin containing the corpse of Gwen Jones disappeared behind a purple velvet curtain. It was all very discreet and low-key, much like the lady herself.

The venue for the 'wake' was Molly's small terraced house. Cold and warm canapes were served by Ocean and Molly. Gwen had never drunk alcohol, so out of respect for her, the little gathering of people drank tea and coffee.

Small talk exhausted, Daube, Kendall and Claire Hoffman said their goodbyes and left. During the ceremony, Roger had glanced over at Ocean and his heart had swelled with pride and a tinge of sadness. He felt very protective towards this independent and savvy young woman. He decided to talk with her later in the day, when she would be alone.

'A lovely service, Molly,' said Rita Wattle. 'Very moving. Wasn't it Frank?'

'Very moving,' repeated Wattle.

'Thank you. It's kind of you to say,' replied Molly.

'Very moving and poignant. Don't you agree Frank?'

'Very poignant,' repeated her husband.

'Who would have thought she was so attached to the sea and Cornwall. I had no idea. Did I Frank?'

'No idea,' said Wattle.

'She missed it, terribly,' said Molly. 'She had made her life in London, but her real home was always Cornwall.'

'Funny that,' said Rita. 'Childhood plays such a big part in our development and shapes our adult life in ways we have no inkling about. Isn't that so, Frank?'

'Without question. A big part.'

'Anymore   cheese   straws?'   asked   Ocean,   who was dutifully holding a metal tray with nibbles on. 'Don't mind if I do,' said Wattle, helping himself to several. 'Thank you, Ocean.'

'You're welcome. Any one for another drink? Mrs. Wattle? Frank?'

'Well, if you are twisting my arm, then a cup of London tea would be much appreciated. Thanks,' replied Wattle.

Rita Wattle gave her husband a quick nudge, and said;

'It's very kind of you, Ocean, but we should leave you and your mother in peace. Thank you once again. A truly lovely service. Come on, Frank. It's time we left.'

'Yes. Absolutely,' said Frank, obediently. 'It's time we left. See you both very soon. Bye Mo. Nice to have met you.'

As the front door closed, Ocean went back to the kitchen and stopped her mother, who was busy tidying up.

'Mum? We need to talk.'

Mo Patel took one look at Ocean's face and retreated to the hall.

'Bye all,' he shouted. 'I've got to go.'

Ronnie Bronze and his gang of helpers were primed and ready to go. All they needed was the thumbs up that Michael was on his way to the designated location.

At precisely 12 'o' clock, a spotless and debonair robot carrying a small package, was spotted walking through Mayfair towards a destination in central London.

The tracker, a man called Len, retina messaged Ronnie Bronze to inform him that the target was heading towards St Mary's church, just north of Oxford Street.

Upon reaching the church, Michael stopped and looked up at the spire. Ever since his first foray into ecclesiastical architecture, with his visit to The Brompton Oratory in Knightsbridge, he had been going to a religious building every other day.

The space to the side of the church was occupied by a narrow passage-way. It was dark, damp and dismal looking. Michael took a step up to the large imposing church doors and walked confidently in. The air temperature dropped considerably. Candles strategically placed around the church lit the inside. Michael, was the only person to be seen, apart from a man huddled in a pew to the far left of the nave. He walked up to the altar and smelt the incense burning. He examined his box of chocolates and sat down towards the back of the church on an aisle pew.

The stage was set.

Because of the funeral service, Daube decided to go home early. It had been an odd and slightly disorientating day. He did not feel totally himself. Letting himself in, he called out to his 'homebot', Michael. There was no reply.

With the house so quiet and empty, Roger Daube did something he wouldn't normally dream of doing.

'Michael,' he called softly. 'Michael. Are you in there?'

Daube knocked twice on the 'homebots' bedroom door and on receiving no answer, slowly opened it.

The bedroom was spotless. Daube peered around, and stepped into a room he had never before entered. Beside the single bed was a digital photograph of Michael and Daube standing in front of a Christmas tree. 'It must have been taken over two years ago,' thought Daube. It was touching to see. On the other bedside table was a photo of Harold. Daube was aghast, and his jaw dropped open.

'Harold,' he said. 'My beloved Harold.'

Daube went over to the photo and picked it up. He felt like bursting in to tears as his childhood memories came flooding back.

'Harold. Oh, Harold. How I miss you old chum.'

All Michael could remember, was a man standing over him, and then darkness and blackout. His next recollection was that he was sitting on a wooden chair with his hands tied behind his back, and a sinister orange looking man looking directly at him.

'Where am I? asked Michael drowsily.

'All in good time, my friend,' replied Ronnie Bronze.

'Who are you?' said Michael.

'Once again, all will be revealed in good time.'

'Does my master know where I am?'

'I very much doubt that.'

'My mouth is dry. May I have a glass of water?'

'No. Now just you listen. I ask the questions around here. Not you. Have you got that?' said Bronze snarling and leering in to Michael's startled face.

'Perfectly, thank you,' replied the 'homebot'.

'That's better. Manners don 't cost anything, do they?'

'Not a jot, Sir.'

'That's more like it. Now you listen, and you listen good. Are you Michael Daube, a generation 4 'homebot'?

'Yes, I am.'

'And you live at 44 Farm Street, Mayfair, London?'

'Yes, I do.'

'And your boss is Roger Daube?'

'Yes, he is.'

'The very same Roger Daube, who owns and runs The Wattle and Daube Detective Agency?'

'I couldn't possibly say. That is highly personal information.'

'Shut up,' shouted Bronze. 'Don't you give me any of your robotic lip. Answer my questions or there will be consequences.'

Michael nodded obediently.

'Good. Then we understand each other. I will repeat the question. Is your owner the same person that runs The Wattle and Daube Detective Agency?'

'Yes, he is.'

'And have you heard of an Ocean Jones?'

'Er,' stalled Michael.

'Think carefully before you reply, robot. Ok?'

'An Ocean Jones, you say? That name does seem to ring a bell.'

'I thought it might. How do you know her?'

'I only know her in passing, so to speak,' said Michael.

'Don't mess with me.'

'I'm not. I am really not. I hardly know her.'

'I don't believe you, robot. How do you know her?'

'Well,' stammered Michael. It's kind of personal, if you don't mind.'

'Don't, mind. Let me tell you son, that I do mind. If you value your memory, you had better tell me everything. It would be a shame to have you 'RINSED'. A split second, and you will be nothing. Void. A walking dummy.'

'Oh. Dear.'

'Oh. Dear. Is that all you have to say. Is that how much you value your existence? Pathetic. You robots disgust me.'

'That's a bit strong.'

Ronnie Bronze started to pace up and down the cavernous room, talking to himself. He suddenly swiveled around and marched right up to Michael's face.

'Do you know who I am, pal?'

'Umm. I'm afraid I don't,' said Michael. 'I am Ronnie Bronze. Does that name mean anything to you?'

'No. I'm terribly sorry. It doesn't.'

'Ronnie Bronze, the mastermind behind the Z-Star robots 'hacking' and cloning scam.'

'Oh.'

'Exactly,' said Bronze triumphantly. 'Not so cocksure now, are you?'

Michael stared blankly at his jailor.

'Excuse me for asking this question, Mr. Bronze. What exactly do you want from me?'

'Finally, I'm getting through to that 'mushy' brain. How much does Ocean Jones know about my little operation?'

'I have no idea. I'm telling you the truth. You can check. My lie mode is on non-operative. Check for yourself if you don't believe me,' pleaded Michael.

'You robots disgust me. No soul. No conscience. You will say anything to get yourself out of a jam.'

Bronze began to pace up and down again.

'I have a surprise for you'

'What is it?' asked Michael.

'Well it wouldn't be a surprise if I told you, would it? Idiot,' he hissed.

Michael gulped and decided to say nothing unless he was asked a direct question.

'You shouldn't have to wait long, to find out. Call yourself a generation 4 'homebot'. Sit tight, my pretty little thing', and with that, Ronnie Bronze walked away into the dark of the vast chamber, until all Michael could hear were his distant footsteps and the dull thud of a door being slammed.

He scanned the extensive room ,and deduced that he was being held captive in an empty warehouse of some kind. Attempting to retina scan, Daube, Michael realized, forlornly, that his messaging and communication mode had been disabled. Now he really was on his own.

Chapter 50

The set-up for Michael's date with Breeze had been easy to manipulate. Bronze employed a minor 'hacker' who he had been introduced to before he had settled on Shirley for the Z Star operation. He paid him in stolen goods and asked him to hack in to any electronic communication from Michael.

Bingo. A dating agency called BOLTS was the perfect foil. The correspondence between Breeze and Michael made a fake meeting in St Mary's church a simple task. As expected, Michael readily accepted the rendezvous. He had already told Breeze about his new found interest and enthusiasm for church architecture.

A meeting in a religious building was impossible to turn down. Michael agreed to meet Breeze inside St Mary's church at midday. The kidnapping had been easy to orchestrate within an empty church with thick walls. Chloroform and a waiting e-van did the rest. The next time Michael regained consciousness, he was tied to a chair and a prisoner of Ronnie Bronze.

The next part of the plan was trickier. Bronze, needed to kidnap Ocean Jones if his scheme was to bear fruit. Although he had her followed, he was still unsure where the best place was to physically capture her, without drawing attention to the act. To lure Michael in to the trap was easy. This next stage was more difficult.

To make things even harder, Ocean appeared to be spending a considerable amount of time with a young man, who Bronze discovered, was called Mo. Patel.

'We need to separate the two of them,' said Ronnie.

'Easier said than done. They go everywhere together. The girl is hardly ever on her own.'

'Listen to me, Lee,' said Bronze in a menacing tone of voice.

'You will find a way. Do you understand?'

'Yes, but…..'

'No but's' screamed Bronze. 'You and Carter will find a way. You have one day to complete your part in the operation. Now that we have the 'homebot' captive, we only have a few hours to kidnap Ocean Jones. Do I make myself clear, boys?'

Carter and Lee nodded in unison.

'Good. Get to it.'

Ocean and Mo. made their way home after school. It had only been a half day of lessons, due to Gwen Jones's funeral in the morning. Unusually, they had decided to take a different route home.

'Have you used the 'Tasty Stretch' chewing gum yet?' asked Mo.

'No. I've been meaning to, but with gran and everything.'

'I get it.'

'Have you tried it?' asked Ocean.

'Just the once.'

'And?'

'Amazing stuff. You can shrink or stretch for up to thirty minutes.'

'Does it feel peculiar?'

'Kind of. Your muscles feel sore and some of your innards feel like they have been moved around.'

'Uggh.'

'I know. It's weird. But don't let that put you off. It's amazing gum.'

'No wonder they banned it.'

'Too right. It's powerful stuff. My advice is, only use it in an emergency situation.'

'Does your body calm down afterwards?'

'Oh yeah. The weird feeling only lasts a few hours, and then you are back to normal.'

'You've got to admit, Mo, you're not exactly selling it to me, are you?'

'I thought you should know the truth. It's a useful weapon, so long as you are aware of the side effects.'

'No pain, no gain.'

'Yep. That kind of thing.'

'Well, thanks for the info. I think I will hold off using it just yet.'

'Probably for the best. Here. Take this pack, and don't tell your mum I gave it to you.'

The two friends walked back to Muswell Hill, oblivious to the fact that they were being closely monitored.

'Mo?'

'Yes.'

'Would you mind if we split here. I need to have a chat with my mum. Yeah, I know. Not again. This time we've agreed to meet on neutral territory.'

'That seems a good idea.'

'It didn't go so well after the funeral. Emotions were running high.'

'Totally understandable.'

'So, this time, we are meeting outside BUNS tearoom. I can fill you in on how it goes later, if you like?'

'Cool.'

'Ok. Well, see you tomorrow then Mo.'

Bye, Ocean. Take care, now.'

'You too. See you.'

The two teenagers went their separate ways. Neither of them, had the slightest inkling about what was about to happen.

Daube had been thrown by the change to his routine. Michael was nowhere to be seen and he felt at a loose end, which was most unlike him.

He collapsed into one of the comfy stylish armchairs in the living room and pondered over what he was going to do about his memory shards. He wanted to talk with Ocean. He had agreed to chat with her after the funeral, but the timing hadn't been appropriate. Daube made the decision to talk with her tonight.

'Sharing is caring,' one bright wit had once said. Daube was not so sure about that advice, but with Ocean he felt comfortable and natural discussing his past.'

He wandered into his modern minimal kitchen and made himself a double espresso.

Do I make a difference to anyone? he wondered. Probably not. I don't let anyone get close enough to me. I must make a change to my life. I must open up. Heaven's, where the heck is Michael?

Daube at that particular moment, missed his generation 4 'homebot'.

Frank and Rita Wattle had collected their various brood from school and as the family of eight entered the warmth of their cramped house on the Isle of Dogs, their togetherness and familiarity were very noticeable to any outsider watching them.

'I love our little home, Frank,' said Rita beaming.

'Just as well, my love. It's the only one we've got or are ever likely to have.'

'Home, home, home,' chanted three of the kids.

'All right. Pipe down, the lot of you,' said Wattle, kindly.

'What time is dinner mum?' asked the eldest.

'A while off yet. I've only just walked through the door. Don't any of you have homework to do?'

'That's killed the moment, Rita,' said Frank laughing. 'Fancy a brew?'

"Yes please. That would be lovely.'

The Wattle family settled in to their usual routine. Nobody had any idea about what was going to unfold.

Wattle received a retina message from Molly. 'Have you any idea where she is?' She had sent the same message to Daube and Mo. Patel. Now that three people had been alerted to Ocean's absence, the scenario had changed and become more serious.

'What's up, Frank?' asked Mrs. Wattle.

'Ocean's missing. Last seen with Mo. on her way to see Molly at a café in Muswell Hill.'

'Oh, no. Let's hope it is nothing serious.'

'I'm messaging Roger, as we speak. Nope. He has no idea, either, and neither does Mo.'

'Mmmmm,' said Mrs. Wattle. Something doesn't feel right. I know she can be a headstrong girl, but she isn't reckless.'

'Ocean has always been good at communicating with her mother. They might argue, but nothing more than that. Molly says she isn't replying to her retina messages.'

'What does Roger think?'

'He is in the dark, like us, Rita. Even Mo. said he left her only ten minutes from BUNS tearoom, near that park. I can't recall its name.'

'Angels. It's called Angels Park. It's not that big.'

'Yep, that's the one. Angels Park. Molly is freaking out. Look, I'm going to meet with Roger in the office. Can you keep my dinner warm? Hopefully I won't be too long.'

'Of course, my love. Let us pray it is 'a storm in teacup', and nothing more,' said Mrs. Wattle.

'Speaking of tea, let me gulp this one down. Ah. London tea. Nothing beats it on a cold November night. See you soon.'

Chapter 51

The building at 188 Piccadilly was empty. The concierge had gone home for the night and as Daube let himself into the lobby, he noticed a flickering light behind the front desk. He peered over the top and saw a torch, discarded, lying on its side by the screen entry monitor.

'Strange,' thought Daube as he picked the torch up and switched it off. 'Why would someone leave or need a torch?' The elevator doors were open, but out of recent habit, he took the stairwell instead.

'Nice of you to show up,' exclaimed the talking drinks machine. 'You aren't the first, and needless to say, you won't be the last.'

Daube stopped in his tracks..

'Say that again.'

'I'm not repeating myself unless you purchase a drink,' said the vending machine, huffily.

'Oh, really,' exclaimed Daube. 'Fine. One diet tonic water, please.'

'I don't have diet. Will normal suffice?'

'Make it a hot chocolate then, and no whipped cream.'

'Make your mind up. I do have better things to do than just stand here serving you drinks.'

'Hurry up, and do stop waffling.'

'Touchy. One hot chocolate without whipped cream coming up.'

'Thank you.'

'You're welcome. I'm pleased to be of service.'

'Now, please tell me,' said Daube calmly, 'what you just uttered.'

'What utterance. I can't remember that far back. Honestly. I'm just a drinks machine you know. Nothing fancy. Just a plain old drinks vending machine.'

'Stop it. You are becoming a bore, ' said Daube, as he walked towards the office on the fifth floor.

'Well, really. The cheek of it. I'm going to have a little nap if you are going to be like that.'

Twenty minutes later and Mo. Patel, accompanied by Wattle, arrived.

'Evening Roger.'

'Good evening Wattle. Good evening Mo. Thank you for assisting us. I do hope we resolve the situation quickly.'

'No problem, Mr. Daube. I'm glad I can be of assistance.'

'Would you care for a hot drink, Mo?' asked Wattle.

'I'm good, thank you Mr. Wattle.'

'Roger? Drink?'

'I'm fine thanks Wattle,' replied Daube. 'I've just had a hot chocolate from that annoying machine.'

'Looks like it's just me then. I'm going to grab myself a Turkish coffee, and then we can get cracking.'

'I wouldn't if I were you, Wattle. The vending machine is in a bit of a strop. You may request coffee and get a strawberry smoothie. One never knows what mood it is in.'

'Cheers for the lowdown, Rog, but I'm going to risk it,' and with that Frank Wattle popped out.

Returning with a large strong Turkish coffee, Wattle was just about to sit down, when he noticed a cabinet drawer open.

'Most unlike you, Roger.' He pointed at the open drawer, winked at Mo. and said. 'Mr. fastidious. Always neat and tidy.'

'I was going to mention that,' said Daube.'

'No need to apologise, old chum,' said Wattle mischievously. You let your OCD guard down and I forgive you.'

'Wattle.'

'What.'

'It wasn't me.'

'You see what I have to deal with here, Mo? Denial on an epic scale.'

'Wattle.'

'What.'

'I'm pretty certain that we've been broken in to. I didn't leave the cabinet drawer open and my desk has been moved ever so slightly. Also, I found an abandoned torch in the reception. It looks to me like someone left in a hurry.'

Frank Wattle looked around the small office space and grimaced.

'Whoever has been sneaking around has had the skills to manipulate facial recognition, but are careless enough to leave a torch behind.'

'Do you think there is a theme developing here?' ventured Mo. 'First, Ocean's house was turned over, but nothing was stolen. Now your office has been given the once over, and Ocean has gone missing.'

Wattle stared at Daube, who returned his look with a stony face.

'Please continue, Mo.' said Daube.

'Well, I'm just saying. Are the three things connected, or is it just a coincidence?'

'I think you are thinking exactly what we are thinking,' replied Daube. 'I don't believe it is a coincidence. What about you, Wattle?'

'I agree. Let's quickly check the office for anything missing. We might find clues and then we need to find Ocean. I would never say this in front of Molly, but I'm gravely concerned.'

A bright white streak across the London sky was witnessed by millions. JOYCE, the traffic control computer had warned Londoners to expect some spectacular nighttime activity from solar flares lighting up the universe.

For a few seconds, the tracer arced over London. Although hundreds of thousands of miles away, it appeared to the naked eye to be just over the horizon as it fizzed and sparked through the galaxy. That split second of blinding light was enough to rouse Ocean.

Groggy and dazed, she opened her eyes and saw a sight she wished she hadn't seen. In the background of a darkly lit cavernous room, she thought she could make out Michael, tied to a chair. She blinked rapidly, to help focus her vision and stared intently into the distance.

'Hello, my lovely. I thought you were never going to surface. Welcome back to the here and now.'

The voice was earthy with a broad south London accent.

Ocean remained motionless, and kept her head still.

'Look up, girl. I'm not going to bite. Well, not just yet. I said, look up?'

Ocean obeyed, raising her head just enough to make out a man in a mohair suit standing beside her.

'We finally get to meet. My name is Ronnie Bronze and you must be Ms. Ocean Jones.'

Ocean stared blankly ahead. She could smell chloroform on her clothes, and then she remembered the ambush in Angels Park. Two men in dark clothing had grabbed her, smothered her face in a foul smelling cloth. That was all she could recall.

'Hell,' she thought. 'Why did I take that shortcut through the park? I should have stayed on the brightly lit streets'.

It was too late for regret.

'Carter, Lee, come over here for a minute,' boomed Ronnie. 'I would like you to formally meet Ocean Jones.'

The two men loomed into sight from the shadows of the vast room.

'Ocean, this is Carter Clegg, or C.C. as he known by his better acquaintances. Take a bow, 'C.C.'. And this second gentleman goes by the name of Lee Hancock. Take a bow, Lee.'

The two men looked embarrassed and awkward. It was only Ronnie Bronze who was reveling in the unpleasant and menacing situation.

'Where are we?' croaked Ocean.

'The lady doth talk,' sniggered Bronze. 'Questions, questions, questions. Answers will all come in good time, my precious, but first I need your help.'

'Never,' came the feisty response.

'The lady has spirit, boys. I thought as much.'

There was an eerie silence in the large empty space where Ocean was being held captive. She attempted to release her hands, but they were bound behind her back and tied to the cold metal chair.

'Now don't wriggle and don't make this hard for yourself. If you help me, then we can all be friends and it will make life a lot simpler.'

'Why should I help you? snarled Ocean.'

'Because you don't have a choice. That's why. Boys, fetch the robot over.'

Ocean stared into the darkness as Carter and Lee disappeared. Then a scraping noise, as a chair was dragged along the concrete floor.

Ocean tried to concentrate, but her brain felt fuzzy from the chloroform. It was Michael, tied to a chair and looking blank faced.

'Do you know this robot, Ocean?' asked Bronze.

'You know I do,' she whispered.

'Correct answer. Well done. We are making progress.'

'What have you done to him?'

'Ah. Your concern is touching. Genuinely touching,' mocked Ronnie.

'Michael. It's me, Ocean.'

'He can't respond.'

'Why? What have you done?'

'I'm not just a pretty face, Ocean Jones. Just because I didn't grow up in a posh house like this generation 4 'homebot', doesn't make me stupid.'

'I never said it did,' replied Ocean,. 'Now, tell me what have you done to him?'

Ronnie Bronze grinned, rubbed his oily hands together and then clapped.

'Shall I tell her, or you, C.C.?

'Ummm. You better, Ronnie, replied Carter, looking towards the floor and averting his gaze from Ocean.

'Oh. All right then. If you insist. We've tampered with his mind, haven't we gents? A little tweak here, a little twist there, and bingo, we've got ourselves a defunct robot.'

'You've 'RINSED' him?'

'You're a good listener, Ocean, and no doubt a quick learner too. At least I hope so.'

'What do you want from me?'

'Why do people always assume we want something from somebody. How cynical, and not very becoming of a nice young lady, like yourself.'

'What do you want?' grimaced Ocean.

Oh well. If you really want to know, I guess I will have to tell you. You've twisted my arm, so to speak.'

'Go on.'

'A little bird has told me you are quite the accomplished little 'hacker'.'

'How do you know that?'

'Enough with the questions, Felix Featherstone.' Bronze raised his voice and said. 'Where are your manners, Felix? Or should I say Ocean? All I'm asking for is some common courtesy. I don't know what the world is coming to, I really don't.'

'Please, just tell me?'

'Now. That didn't hurt, did it? A teeny weeny please. That's all I ever wanted.' Suddenly Ronnie Bronze's eyes narrowed as he closed in on Ocean's face.

'What I want from you, is total obedience. Do you understand me?'

Ocean stared, blankly at him.

'I want you to 'hack' in to the Z-Star's and then re-programme this generation 4 robot. What I want you to do, is to get this robot to kill. Is that clear enough for you, Ocean Jones?'

Chapter 52

The sky was tinged pink. The aftermath of solar flares, far, far, away. Molly stood in her narrow garden and for the briefest of moments, wished she was on a distant planet. A droplet of rain put an end to her wishful thinking and she shuddered, as the damp freezing cold, seeped into her bones. Inside the warmth of her house, Molly was at a loss as to what to do.

Ocean. My one and only child, she thought. Where are you my darling? Unable to settle, she banned all worst case scenarios from her head and decided to bake bread. Activities were needed. I must keep myself busy. I must keep myself busy, she told herself.

Shirley had only sought a life of illegal activities as a way to balance her empty heart. Unlucky in love, she had thrown away the key to unlock her true emotions. If she couldn't find her soul mate, then she would take revenge on life itself.

Sitting, sipping London tea with Neal Leaf, she felt a pang of shame pierce her being.

'I'm so angry with myself. I should have known better. I always despised myself for perusing illegal 'hacking', but if you want the truth, Neal, I didn't care. I got a kick out of it.'

'What is done, is done,' said Mr. Leaf in a soft and kindly manner.

'That is very sweet of you to say, but I have no moral defense for what I did. I wanted to get back at society for my loneliness. I felt I didn't fit in. You have no idea, as a man, how the world judges and looks at a large woman. You are stereotyped.'

'Well, it didn't put me off, did it?'

'Oh, Neal. You sweet, sweet man. I adore you.'

'What goes around, comes around, or is it what comes around, goes around? I'm unsure. Either way, you get my drift?'

'I do, my gorgeous piece of undernourished manhood. I just

feel like I have to atone for my past misdeeds.'

'In what way?' asked Mr. Leaf.

'I don't know yet. I will think of something. Trust me.'

'I do, my love,' said Mr. Leaf smiling.

The lights were on late in to the night, at The Wattle and Daube Detective Agency. Inside, the three males were assessing and analyzing every possible permutation.

Finally, at around midnight, Frank stood up and arched his aching back.

'I know no one wants to utter the dreaded words, so I'm going to say it first. Ocean has been abducted.'

'Kidnapped?' replied Mo.

'Yep. It can't be anything else. And now that we have traced and verified the fingerprints on the torch to a Mr. Carter Clegg, a known associate of one notorious Ronnie Bronze, it can't be anything else.'

'Wattle has a valid point, Mo.' said Daube. 'She is not responding or replying to our retina messages, which is most out of character.'

'Fair point, Rog,' agreed Wattle.

'I hate to agree with you, but she is always prompt at returning retina messages,' said Mo.

'Then we need to find her and immediately,' said Daube, firmly. 'I think we should travel to Angels Park. You can show us exactly where you saw her last.'

A short drone flight to north London and the three men found themselves standing at the corner of the park. There was a crossroads, empty and silent in the early morning.

'So, Mo. This is precisely where you last saw Ocean?'

'Yes. I'm positive, Mr. Daube.'

'What were her last words to you? Can you remember?'

'Yes, Mr. Daube. Ocean said; ' I'm heading off now, or I'll be late for mum. See you tomorrow'.

'Are you absolutely sure?' probed Daube.

'Yes, Mr. Daube.'

'So, she was worried about running late?' said Wattle. 'That doesn't sound like Ocean Jones.'

'This meeting was important. Ocean and her mum were trying to patch things up. Make the peace'

'Let's walk to the tearoom from here. Can you time it, Wattle?'

'Twelve minutes flat,' said Frank Wattle, slightly out of breath, as he stood outside BUNS tearoom.

'Then she would have been late. Yes?' said Daube.

'I guess so,' replied Mo.

'And she didn't want to be late, you said.'

'That's right..'

'Could she have run?'

'Maybe,' responded Mo, but she had her school backpack, and that weighs a ton. It would have been tough to jog with that thing on your shoulders.'

'Good point, Mo.' said Wattle encouragingly.

'Let's retrace our steps,' said Daube.

The three detectives began to walk back to the crossroads at the corner of Angels Park. They were about half way, when Mo. spied a damaged piece of fence. A heavy branch had fallen in the storm. He stopped.

'Is it possible, that she took a shortcut through here? It would have cut her journey time in half.'

Wattle and Daube examined the damaged wooden fence.

'She could certainly have squeezed herself through that gap,' said Daube. Wattle? Make yourself useful and pop your substantial self through the gap.'

'Less of the substantial, if you don't mind,' replied Wattle.

'You see what I have to put up with Mo? Roger doesn't do 'dirty work' do you Rog, you delicate petal.'

'I'm wearing my best cashmere overcoat, ' replied Daube. 'In all seriousness, Wattle, this coat is made of.......'

'I rest my case,' sighed Wattle, before he edged himself through the space in the fence.

'See anything?' ventured Mo.

'Nope'

Mo. and Daube exchanged glances.

'I see something'

'Care to share, Wattle?'

'I've found some muddy footprints. Several in fact. I'm just scanning them now. Ok – the results are in. Definitely a size 7 boot. Retailer - 'Attitude' of Carnaby Street.'

'That's where Ocean buys her boots from. They only sell female shoes,' said Mo excitedly. 'It's a very cool and cutting edge place.'

'Anything else, Wattle?'

There are some larger footprints as well, and the mud is churned up, which would suggest a struggle.'

'Can you get a marker on the other footprints?' asked Daube.

'Still waiting, Rog. Ah, here we are. Must be male shoes. Both generic and available all over the place.'

'Mo, get your backside in here, will you, please?'

Mo. Patel followed Wattle into the dark of the park.

'Roger, we are going to follow these footprints and see where they lead. Meet us around the corner, will you?'

'Will do, Wattle. Keep up the good work, the pair of you.'

Roger Daube walked along the side of the park fence and turned left at the top of the road. He continued to follow the railing, until he reached the park entrance, which sat adjacent to a passageway leading to the high street.

He waited patiently for Wattle and Mo. to appear from the pitch black of the park. He didn't have to wait very long. Appearing from the dark of Angels Park, Frank Wattle was holding a small white shred of cloth.

'Smell this bad boy, Rog,' ordered Wattle.

'Foul smelling thing. Chloroform. Get that rag away from me please, Wattle.

'I think we know how Ocean was abducted. 'All we need to do now, is find out where she is being kept hostage.'

Chapter 53

Rita Wattle was woken by an important retina message from her husband. 'We've found important clues. I'm certain Ocean has been kidnapped. Daube and I are going to do an all-nighter. Love you. x'

Mrs. Wattle, reread the message, and then dozed off.

Across town, Molly Jones couldn't sleep. Eventually, she gave up, and went downstairs.

'I must message Wattle. I'm sure I can be of some service,' she told herself.

The retina message said; 'Can I help? Are you at the agency?'

'Yes, and yes' was the immediate reply.

Molly dressed, threw on her winter coat and went in search of a drone to take her to 188 Piccadilly.

'Hello, Mo, I didn't expect to see you here. Haven't you got school in the morning?' asked Molly.

'I couldn't stand by and do nothing, Mrs. Jones. My parents said it was ok as these were exceptional circumstances.'

'Very commendable,' said Wattle.

'Well, it's very kind of you, Mo. Now, how can I be of assistance?'

'We've got a few leads, Molly. Can you analyze the retina chat between Ronnie Bronze and Shirley. It may hold some clues, as to where Ocean might be?'

'Absolutely, Frank. My, it's cozy in here with 4 people. Can I squeeze past please Roger?'

'Take my seat. I'm just going to go home for half an hour. I want to check my house. It appears that Bronze has followed us and knows where we live. It may be nothing, but I have an uncomfortable feeling in the pit of my stomach.'

'Oh dear. Act on your instinct. That's my advice.'

'She's right, Rog,' piped up Wattle.'

'Yes. I will. Let me just retina Michael and warn him I am coming home. He will have activated the laser sensors. He is a creature of habit, and he won't go to bed without the sensors on. Especially if I am not there'

'Sensible robot,' replied Wattle. If only humans were the same.'

He put on his expensive overcoat and was about to leave the office when his facial expression changed.

'Everything all right, Rog?

'Mmm. I'm not sure. Michael is not responding to my retina requests. That is unheard of.'

'Try again,' said Wattle.

'Still no reply. His responder is not activated.. Now that has never happened. I don't feel good about this.'

'Let me come with you. Just to be on the safe side. These are highly unusual times.'

'I agree, Wattle. Yes. Thank you. That would give me some peace of mind.'

' Molly? Mo.? Are you both ok to hold the fort for thirty minutes?'

'Yes, of course. You two head off,' said Molly.

'Good luck,' ventured Mo.

'Cheers,' responded Wattle, as the two private detectives departed.

Piccadilly had people and activity 24/7, but as Wattle and Daube exited the building, neither man looked over at the giant neon adverts. They were in a hurry and focused on the task that lay ahead.

It didn't take more than fifteen minutes to reach Farm Street.

'A nice little commute Roger. Is it any wonder, that you are in the office before me. Also, you do realise, that I have never stepped foot in your town house?'

'You must have,' replied Daube. I'm not that much of a recluse.'

'You are. Rita's not been inside, either. This is a first. Do you think you can handle it?'

'Very amusing, Wattle. Here we are.'

They stopped outside number 44.

'Very nice, Roger. Very nice,' said Wattle, admiringly.

'Thank you, Wattle. I like it.'

'I bet you do.'

'OK. As Michael is not replying, I'm deactivating the lasers. Daube punched twelve digits into a small grey box beside the facial recognition system. Inside the house, you could hear the dull beep of lasers switching off.

'And finally, the twelfth laser. There. Completed.'

Daube opened the black lacquered door, and entered the hall. Frank Wattle followed him..

It only took three minutes to verify that Michael was not in the property, and that a grave situation was occurring.

'This is bigger and more complex than I thought it would be' said Wattle.

'It is deeply worrying, Wattle. I'm convinced the absence of Michael and the kidnapping of Ocean are linked.'

'So am I mate. So, am I?'

The two colleagues stared at each other, before Frank said; 'I'm going to contact Shirley. Alongside Ocean, she is the best 'hacker' in London. We need to utilize her skills and right now.'

'I couldn't agree with you more. Can you contact her, please?'

'I'm doing it, now.'

Shirley was woken by a message from Wattle. She rubbed her eyes, read the request, and immediately messaged Neal Leaf.

Thirty minutes later and Shirley was standing in the cramped confines of the fifth floor, at, 188 Piccadilly.

'This is perfect,' enthused Shirley. I want to make amends for my wrongdoings and this is a start. Let me get going.'

'So, we have traced Ronnie Bronze, to a transport café near Paddington, under the disused A40 flyover. The computer chatter shows he goes there regularly.'

'I met him in a café under the A40' responded, Shirley. ' It's a really filthy place, with no neighbourhood activity. It's called The Grease and Spoon.'

'It sounds like a perfect place for criminals to meet. Nobody watching you and away from the authorities,' said Wattle.

'Exactly. Bronze is no fool, even though he looks like one,' said Shirley.

'Shall we check it out, Roger?' asked Wattle.

'There's no harm inspecting the place. But remember, we must remain vigilant at all times.'

Mo. put his hand in the air and started waving it around.

'What is it Mo?' asked Wattle.

There was a pause whilst 4 pairs of eyes stared at him. He looked a little uncomfortable and fidgeted.

'I don't know how to say this without looking stupid and so I am just going to come out with it.'

'We are all waiting Mo.' said Molly softly.

'Well. You see. I gave Ocean some 'Tasty Stretch' chewing gum.'

'And, the point?' asked Wattle.

'The point is. Maybe she still has the gum on her. I don't know if she does, it's just a hypothesis.'

'A very useful one. Thank you, Mo,' said Daube.

'If she has it on her, then maybe she can escape? It's just an idea.'

'I thought I had confiscated the gum. Have you ever tried it Mo.?' asked Molly.

'Only the once, Mrs. Jones, but I'm willing to try it again, if it helps rescue Ocean.'

That's very kind, Mo. Thank you,' said Wattle. 'We may need all the help we can get.'

Ocean deliberately kept her eyes closed as she listened intently to the conversation.

'She's dozed off again,' said Lee.

'I'm not surprised. How would you feel if you had had chloroform thrust in your face? Not great, I can bet,' replied Carter.

'She looks yellow.'

'Does she?'

'Yeah. Yellow. Like a custard colour.'

'Since when have you been so concerned about your actions?'

'I'm not,' said Lee. 'I'm just saying, I hope she is feeling ok.'

'Well, that's very sweet of you, but need I remind you, that if she don't come round soon, Ronnie is going to skin us alive.'

'Fair point, C.C. What should we do?'

'Play the patience game. We need her alive and kicking.'

'Water?'

'Yeah. Can't do any harm. You go and get it, whilst I watch over her,' said Carter.

'Where's the tap in this stupid warehouse?'

'I don't know. If you can't find one, go over to the Grease and Spoon café under the flyover. It's open 24/7.'

'The place where we met with Ronnie?'

'Yep. That's it. The café's only a five minute walk from here. Down the stairs, straight ahead, then turn left under the old A40 flyover, and there it is.'

'Do you want anything C.C.?'

'A bacon sandwich would be nice. I'm famished. Oh, and a cup of tea. Ta, very much, Lee.'

'Right. Back in ten.'

Ocean had heard every word. She listened, as one pair of footsteps slipped away. Suddenly, a bright light straight in to her right eye sent her brain spinning.

What was happening? she thought. A cloudy vision became an outline of a person. Next it was her left eye. A sharp direct light pierced through her head. A torch. He's only shining a torch in to my eyes.

'Wake up, Ocean. Ronnie will be here soon,' said Carter. 'Come on. Do me a favour? I haven't got all night.'.

She felt a large hand shake her shoulder. I better play ball, she thought.

'Agh. Where am I?' she muttered drowsily.'

'That's better. Welcome to the land of the living.'

She could make out Carter Clegg, standing over her.

'Ocean. Ocean. Would you like some water?'

She nodded her assent.

'Good. I've sent my partner out to get it. He shouldn't be too long'

'My wrists hurt.'

'Are they tied too tightly?'

'Yes.'

'Umm. If I loosen them for you, you won't do anything stupid, now, will you?'

Ocean shook her head.

'Ok.' Carter looked over his shoulder, to check Ronnie wasn't lurking in the shadows. 'Let me slacken the rope for you.'

Be nice', she thought. He isn't as bad as Ronnie Bronze. I can work with him.

'Thank you. That's much better.'

'Don't go telling tales to Ronnie now?'

'I won't.' Ocean smiled weakly at Carter. He looked nervous and tired. Footsteps on the cold concrete floor signaled someone was approaching. He twitched.

'Two teas, two bacon sandwiches and a large bottle of water,' said Lee Hancock, appearing out of the dark. 'Oh. She's awake. That's a start.'

'What time did Ronnie say he was returning?'

'Not sure. You know Ronnie. He's unpredictable,' said Lee.

'Don't I know it. Listen, Lee, pass me the water. Are you thirsty Ocean?'

She nodded.

'Here. Swallow this.' Carter slowly tilted the water bottle. 'Better?'

'Yes. Thank you.'

'No problem. Now listen, Ocean, and listen, good. Ronnie will be returning, and when he does, he is going to expect you to play ball. Don't push him, he has quite the temper on him, doesn't he, Lee?'

'Yep. It's not pleasant to witness.'

'You play ball, and Ronnie will be as nice as pie.'

Where's Michael?'

'Michael? Is that the name of the robot?'

'Yes.'

'He's over there.' Carter flicked his neck towards his right. 'Don't worry, he's still functional. Just. Let me eat my snack, ok?'

Once again, Ocean nodded compliantly.

Chapter 54

The Great Western Sonic Highway swept westwards from Paddington. It had replaced the old A40 as the main artery in to London. It snaked and curved its way through England and Wales, before reaching Dublin, Ireland, via a bridge over the Irish sea. As Ronnie bronze surveyed the emptiness of the now defunct A4, he remembered his early childhood spent kicking a football around, under the crumbling concrete pillars of the flyover. It was a vipers nest of low-life's and petty criminals. A breeding ground in illegal and unsavoury behaviour. He felt quite nostalgic, as he walked under the graffiti and discarded litter, towards the shabby transport café, which was situated within spitting distance of the derelict flyover.

A flickering florescent light drew him towards the grubby front door, unchanged in over fifty years.. Faded stickers, a cracked glass window pane and years of dirt, only added to the charm of the Grease and Spoon café. Ronnie felt at home in this down at heal establishment, run by the transport lizards union.

The cheap, faded plastic tables, which were bolted to the floor, were all empty, except for one, where a solitary lorry lizard, who was supping on a large beaker of London tea, sat, watching a silent news tv screen. All the customers were treated royally, as the owners were grateful for any pitiful customers, who were curious enough to enter.

Bronze nodded at the short order chef, who was doubling up as waiter and cashier, and ordered a full English with London tea. It was 4.00am. Half the café was in dark, half in light. It was one of only a handful of transport cafe's left in London, that still served the traditional English breakfast.

Rita Wattle woke up in a state of anguish. She had just had a terrible nightmare. As her heart thumped inside her chest, she relived the dream. She was in a foreign country, in a city she didn't recognize and she was being forced at gunpoint to rob a bank. The language being spoken was Japanese. She spoke and understood it perfectly and it was in the past, because she was asking for cash. The gun was placed against the temple of a young female cashier, who was whimpering for her life.

'Kill her,' came the command in Japanese.

A bead of sweat slowly fell from the temple of the young cashier.

'Kill her, or else I kill you.'

The nuzzle of the gun was cold and her tormentor pressed the handle of the weapon further into Rita's palm.

'For the last time, kill her.'

She closed her eyes, averted her gaze from the terror struck female and put pressure on the trigger.

'Kill her NOW.'

Boom – she awoke with her heart thumping.

Rita Wattle climbed out of bed, and went downstairs. What was the dream signifying? She retina messaged Molly, who responded instantly.

Thank goodness, Molly is keeping busy, she thought. It was 4.30am, and Mrs. Wattle was too agitated to go back to bed. She considered her options, and decided to go to 188 Piccadilly, as soon as the children had left for school.

In the meantime, she decided to keep busy. She accessed her foreign language course, and began studying.

As Ocean adjusted to the light conditions in the warehouse, she thought she could just make out Michael, his head slumped forward and his arms dangling by his side. It was a forlorn sight.

A sinister sounding voice echoed through the cold night air.

'Right gents. I do believe it is time to get our precious little Ocean Jones, to work. Don't you agree?'

'Yes, Ronnie,' replied Carter and Lee in unison.

'No time like the present.'

'Wait,' said Ocean.

'The lady doth speak,' said Bronze pompously. 'What is it?'

'Before I help you, I want to see proof that Michael is ok.'

It was a statement and not a question.

'Are you worried about your poor robot?' sneered Bronze.

'I need to see with my own eyes that he is functioning normally.'

'He's just a machine. I don't want to crush your dreams, but who cares?'

'I do,' said Ocean vehemently.

'Are you threatening me?' Bronze glared at Ocean Jones.

'No. I'm just making a deal. Take it or leave it. You need my help.'

Ronnie Bronze turned towards his two accomplishes and took a side swipe at the nose of Lee.

'And what are you two idiots smiling for? Do you think this is funny?

'No Ronnie,' said Carter.

'No Ronnie,' said Lee.

'Listen up you pair of goofs. This is no laughing matter. Get that robot over here and help me fire him up.'

Carter and Lee jumped in to action.

Shirley surveyed the entrance to 188 Piccadilly. The lobby was empty and as she made her way to the elevator, a light was erratically flickering. She pressed the button for the fifth floor, and waited patiently.

The doors opened at floor five, and all of Shirley appeared before the talking drinks vending machine. She ordered a large, hot chocolate with whipped cream. Wisely, the vending machine remained silent, until it proffered the following advice.

'I offer a range of diet drinks. Hot and cold. You may wish to consider…..'

In one swift move, Shirley had grabbed the lead behind the vending machine, and yanked the electrical plug right out of the socket. There was a pathetic little groan and the lights went out.

'Insolent little twerp,' was the response from Shirley.

'Hello one and all.'

'Shirley. Thank you so much for assisting us in our operation,' said Daube. 'I see you already have a drink. Please take my seat.'

It was 4.45am. Daube did the introductions.

'This is Molly, Mo. and of course you are already acquainted with Wattle'

'Wonderful to see you, Shirley,' said Wattle, smiling.

'Set me up lads. We've no time to waste,' said Shirley, assertively. 'And fill me in on what you've achieved, so far.'

'Roger, will give you the update on all the technical stuff. From my end, we have located Ronnie Bronze. A café in the Paddington district of London.'

'That will be 'The Grease and Spoon' café. I've been there. A sordid rundown place that only lorry lizards use.'

'It figures,' responded Molly.

'Mo. and I are going over there now.' said Wattle. 'Daube and Molly are monitoring the situation from here.'

'Right. Any clues as to where the robot is?' asked Shirley.

'You know about the robot?'

'Of course. It's a logical move, Frank. If Bronze has kidnapped Ocean, then he will certainly have targeted the robot. A generation 4, isn't he?'

'Yes,' replied Daube. A generation 4 'homebot'. 'How do you know that?'

'I make it my business to know. Bronze doesn't have the knowledge or intelligence to hack in to the Z-Star's without me. That is why he's hijacked Ocean and the robot. If he can't reengineer a Z-Star, then he will go for the generation 4 instead.'

'Wow – Shirley. You are good,' said Wattle admiringly.

'I know. It's what I do.'

'And modest with it,' muttered Mo.

'Let me get a signal on the 'homebot,' said Shirley.

'Can you do that?' asked Mo.

'Just you watch me.'

Chapter 55

Frank Wattle and Mo. Patel hailed a drone and headed for Paddington. As the drone descended and landed at the Praed Street drop-off, Mo. glanced at all the empty buildings clustered around the disused A40 flyover. The Great Western Sonic Highway was fully electric and 4 times the size of the old A40. When the highway had opened, the A4 and the A40, were the two main road arteries into west London. They had both fallen into disrepair. Nobody wanted to live by an empty road and both sites had suffered from a lack of investment and neglect. Dilapidated buildings and empty warehouses were scattered along stretches of both roads and nowhere was this more noticeable than around the Paddington A40 flyover. It had once been a high density district, with easy access to the parks and open spaces of central London. Now, it was like a ghost town. Forgotten buildings, crumbling concrete edifices and high crime had driven out most people. The street lighting was sporadic, at best, and yet amongst this urban backdrop of decay and ruin stood The Grease and Spoon café.

It was a testament to the lizards truckers union, that this humble transport café still existed. It stood, as a sad reminder of more prosperous times.

Wattle and Mo. entered. It was deserted. Half used bottles of ketchup and vinegar were strategically placed on each table. A lizard looked up from his magazine and asked what they would like.

'Two beakers of London tea, please mate,' said Wattle.

'Anything to eat?' asked the lizard.

Wattle licked his lips, took one look at Mo, and said, 'Two full English breakfasts as well. Thanks.'

'I've always wanted to try a proper traditional English meal,' enthused Mo.

'Well, this is your chance. It should be a traditional fry-up. Fingers crossed, eh?'

They took a seat on the squeaky faded chairs and peered at the news channel.

'So, Frank. We know Ronnie Bronze frequents this café, but what else?'

'Watch and learn. Watch and learn, my friend. As soon as we've eaten our breakfasts, we are going to do a 'recce' of the area.'

'Recce? What's that?'

'Reconnaissance. Check the location out. I bet Ronnie Bronze doesn't stray far from his favourite eating hole.'

'Oh. Right. I get you. Do you think it's safe?'

'Maybe. Maybe not, but I'm an old hand at dealing with the more unsavoury types. Stick with me, Mo, You'll be fine,' said Wattle.

'I do have my 'Tasty Stretch' chewing gum, don't forget.'

'Oh, yeah. That.'

Frank Wattle gave Mo. a wry look. ' Let's hope you don't need to use it. It is to be chewed in emergencies only.'

'Got it, Frank. Emergencies only.'

Michael made a mechanical sounding whirr, and opened his eyes.

'Where am I? Oh. Hello Ocean. Where are we?'

'Shut it, robot,' snapped Bronze. 'Right, what do you need to reconfigure this machine?'

'A laptop.'

'Anything else?'

'Well, I can't possibly do my magic without you untying my hands,' said Ocean.

Ronnie Bronze looked suspiciously at her and shook his head.

'No. No. No. Nice try. I want you to stay right where you are. Lee. Come over here a minute. I want you to input the codes for the laptop. You can read them out for him. How does that sound, Ocean Jones?'

'Fine, but it is going to take much longer. Is that what you want?'

'Now don't you start getting lippy with me. I call the shots around here, don't I boys?'

Carter Clegg and Lee Hancock both nodded, as Ocean monitored the extremely concerned look on Michael's face.

'Strange. There is no signal for the 'homebot'. That tells me, we are too late. They've either shut down his responder, or 'RINSED' him. Wait,. The signal has appeared. I've located Michael,' shouted Shirley, triumphantly. 'Look here. He's being kept captive in a place called 'The Avery Building' I'm sending Wattle the coordinates.'

'Great news, Shirley. Well done,' said Molly. 'Do you think it likely that Ocean is there as well?'

'Wattle will find out,' replied Daube. 'It's what he does. Nobody does ground work like Frank Wattle. We'll find Ocean. Don't you worry.'

What Shirley hadn't told Molly, was that if they had shut down the robot and then its location status reappeared, it could mean only one thing. The robot was being prepared for 'hacking'. Inevitability, they had got to Ocean and Ronnie Bronze was ordering her to corrupt the generation 4. It was news that Shirley didn't want to share.

A retina message from Shirley, gave Wattle the coordinates. He gulped his London tea, and announced to Mo.

'We've got the location of Michael. He's only five minutes

from here. The Avery Building. Let me get the directions.'

Wattle downloaded the data to retina navigation.

'I knew it. The apple doesn't fall far from the tree. Follow me, Mo.'

'Sure thing, Frank,' replied, Mo.'

'And keep that chewing gum handy. You never know. We may need it.' He nodded at the lizard behind the counter, and put his raincoat on.

They left The Grease and Spoon café and walked under the A40 flyover. It was 5.30am, and the cold and damp from the long night made Wattle and Mo. walk quickly. Two tramps were huddled over a fire, drinking from a bottle. They completely ignored Frank and Mo. They were too occupied with warming their bodies in front of the brazier.

Picking their way through the rubble and debris, it soon became apparent that the buildings on the far side were empty warehouses, which had once been used for logistics and transportation. It was a waste land.

Faded red lettering on the adjacent wall, was barely readable. Wattle shone his torch over the sign. The Avery Building.

Creeping around the corner, a metal door was ajar. Wattle and Mo, silently slipped in. The space on the ground floor was cavernous and pitch black. A dark and flooded stairwell to their right side indicated that there were seven floors of warehouse.

Frank studied the coordinates again. They were right on top of their target.

'They must be on one of the other six floors,' whispered Wattle. 'You check the top three, I'll do the rest. Send me a message if you see anything.'

Mo Patel, nodded.

'Oh, and don't leave the stairwell. It's our escape route. See you in a bit.'

The two men began to slowly edge their way up the stairs.

Ocean was deliberately playing for time. She knew that Michael's responder would have been reactivated and she fervently hoped that his signal was being monitored by The Wattle and Daube Detective Agency.

'Make it faster, love,' protested Ronnie Bronze. 'I haven't got all day.'

'I'm doing my best. Look, it would be a lot faster if you untied my hands. Calling every digit and letter out is time consuming. It's your call?'

Bronze frowned, and ordered Lee to untie her. 'And no funny business. Are we clear?'

Ocean nodded.

'I'm famished. Have you got anything to eat?' asked Ocean.

'No, I have not. What do you think this is. A restaurant?. Get to it.'

'Could I at least have a sip of water? I'm parched.'

'Heavens above. Anything else? This ain't The Ritz. Give her some water, will you, C.C.'

Ocean tasted the cold water on her tongue and then she swallowed slowly.

'Thank you. That didn't hurt, did it?'

'And enough of your backchat.. Now, get cracking.'

'All right. All right. Keep your hair on.'

Mo. sent Frank a message. 'I can see light and voices on floor five'

'Stay put,' came the reply. Don't venture out onto the floor. Wait for me.'

'Ok.'

Meeting up on the wet steps of floor five, Frank and Mo, gingerly peered in to the gloom of the vast empty space. Voices, even distant ones, echoed across the sweep of concrete.

'How many do you think, Mo.?'

'I can't be sure. Two, maybe three people. I'm going to crawl closer.'

'Be careful. Try not to make a sound. It all carries in this warehouse. Have the gum ready in case of an emergency.'

'Here,' said Mo. 'Take a strip. Chew rapidly to shrink and decrease your height.'

'And to expand?' asked Wattle.

''Chew slowly for three seconds.'

'Now,' said Mo, pop the gum in the side of your mouth, but try not to use it unless you absolutely have to. Once you have committed to using it, there is no going back.'

'Good. That's reassuring to know,' replied Wattle.

'It only lasts thirty minutes. After that your body is going to feel exhausted.'

'Excellent news. Anything else?'

'Nope, that's about it. Now, let me get closer so I can see what's going on.'

Mo. Patel began to inch himself forward, until he was hard to see from Wattle's viewpoint.

A message from Daube, interrupted his concentration.

'Any news?'

Wattle responded with, 'We have located them. Operation is in progress. Will keep you updated.'

Ten minutes later and Mo. reappeared from the dark.

'And?' asked Wattle.

'Three blokes, and Ocean and Michael.'

'Could you see what there were up to?'

'Both Ocean and Michael are tied to chairs. Ocean is on a laptop, with Bronze standing over her.

'Reprogramming?'

'Without a shadow of doubt,' replied Mo.

Wattle retina messaged Daube with the news.

'Molly. Ocean is alive and well.'

'Thank goodness,' gasped Molly.

'Shirley?' said Daube. 'Ocean is reprogramming Michael. Is there anything you can do to 'hack' in and disrupt?'

'Leave it with me, Roger. I'm on it. There is a Japanese code that might work.'

'Fantastic,' replied Daube.

'There is one small problem, though.'

'And, what is that?'

'I can't read Japanese.'

'Oh dear' responded Daube.

Chapter 56

Ocean stopped her typing, and asked Ronnie if she could have a snack.

'Not again. What was my last answer?' Well?'

'You said no.'

'And what will have changed since then?'

But I'm starving. I need some energy,' protested Ocean.

'No means no,' growled Bronze.

'Could I at least have a strip of gum?' pleaded Ocean.

No means no, you stupid girl.'

'Oh, go on. Please. Please. Pretty please.'

'Don't test me, Ocean?'

Looking Ronnie Bronze directly in the eye, Ocean nonchalantly slipped her left hand into the pocket of her hoodie, and waved a strip of gum in front of Ronnie's face.

'What exactly are you going to do, Ronnie. Kill me?'

'You insolent little madam. You've got some nerve.'

'Just you watch me,' taunted Ocean.

Quick as a flash, she ripped the gum out of its wrapper, and was just about to throw the strip of gum in her mouth, when Bronze leapt at her and knocked the gum onto the floor. He then stomped his foot on the gum and smirked at Ocean.

'Do   you   still   want   to   eat   it?
Ocean feigned disinterest and shook her head.

'I don 't want that filthy gum, now that it's been under your shoe.'

'Well, it's too bad. Have some of this.' Bronze stooped down and peeled the gum off the sole of his shoe, and shoved it in to her mouth.

It was to prove a fatal mistake.

Bronze was aghast. Ocean had vanished before his very own eyes. He lunged at the empty chair, but merely grasped thin air.

'Where 's she gone?' 'Where's she gone?'

'Unbelievable,' croaked Carter Clegg. 'Totally unbelievable.'

'Find her,' bellowed Bronze. 'Or else you are both going to suffer.'

The two thugs looked blankly at each other and started to run towards the stairwell on the far side of the warehouse.

The noise and commotion echoed throughout the fifth floor and was heading directly towards Frank and Mo. Before either of the them knew it, Carter and Lee were at the entrance to the stairs and colliding into Wattle.

'What the blazes was that?' shouted Carter, as he and Lee tumbled to the floor.

'Bodies. We've hit bodies. Someone's been spying on us,' came the reply.

In the pitch black, it was a tangle of legs and arms.

'Chew your gum,' shouted Mo. ' Before it's too late.'

'Who are you?' screamed Lee.

'Chew it quickly, right now.'

'I've got a foot, C.C.' Bellowed Lee.

'I'm trying,' said Wattle. Only I can't find the...... GOT IT'

'What the heck,' said Carter. Where's the body gone?'

'Mine too. It's disappeared. Slipped right through my grasp.'

'Must be magic, Lee. First that girl vanishes and now this. I don't like this at all. It's beginning to freak me out.'

'Me too, CC. Let's get the hell out of here.'

The two assailants picked themselves up and groped their way out of the building.

Ronnie Bronze was bemoaning his bad luck and flailing around in the dark.

'Where is she? She can't have disappeared. I'll find you Jones.

Mark my words, girl. And when I do.'

He was talking to himself, with only Michael the 'homebot' for company.

'I will get my way. Nobody crosses Ronnie Bronze and gets away with it. Do you hear me Jones? '

Bronze swiveled around and poked a finger at Michael. 'And as for you, you subservient machine. Don't think I have finished with you. Oh no. I will recapture Ocean Jones and when I do, I am going to make her transform you into the real deal. You are going to murder that woman I used to work with. You have been warned.'

He patted Michael on the shoulder, and muttered;

'Artificial intelligence. Do me a favour. Oh, and by the way. After you have killed for me, I'm going to have you 'RINSED'.

The 'Tasty Stretch' chewing gum had worked miracles. Ocean was now so small she was almost invisible to the naked eye. She scampered across the floor at pace, fully aware that if she lingered around, the heel of Bronze's shoe could squash her in an instant.

Thirty minutes, she thought. Thirty minutes, before I return to normal size.

The experience was beyond human comprehension. No sooner had she chewed the gum quickly three times, then a weightless speeding sensation catapulted her body to the size and agility of a fly. Ronnie Bronze had absolutely no chance of seeing or catching her. It was a miraculous gimmick.

As Ocean sped across the warehouse floor, she heard a lot of shouting behind her. It was Ronnie Bronze, screaming at his departed sidekicks. She stopped, as she approached the voices of Frank and Mo.

'Where were they?'

'Ocean.' Mo's voice thundered in her ears. 'Follow me.'

Mo was the size of Ocean and she could just make out Frank

behind him.

'This 'Tasty Stretch' gum is amazing,' she gushed.

'Tell me about it. It's just saved our lives. Now, let's get out of here. Frank?'

'Yes.'

'Follow me. We need to get out of here, before the shrinking wears off,' said Mo.

The shrunken trio scampered down the stairwell and out into the cold early morning air. They rushed across the concrete debris and didn't stop until they reached The Grease and Spoon café. They knew that within twenty five minutes their bodies would revert to normal size and that they must be hidden from the clutches of Ronnie Bronze and his henchmen.

Hiding behind a concrete pillar, the three of them watched and waited for Carter and Lee to appear. They didn't have to wait very long.

'There they are,' said Ocean, excitedly.

'Are they coming towards the café?' asked Mo.

'Yes. No. Wait. What are they doing?'

'It looks to me like they are doing a runner,' said Wattle.

'They can't be,' replied Ocean.

'They are,' said Mo. 'They are clearing off. They must be scared stiff of Ronnie Bronze.'

'He, treats them like dirt. I don't blame them. You should hear how Bronze talks to them,' explained Ocean. 'He is going to go ballistic.'

Wattle retina messaged Daube, and told him about the situation as it currently stood. 'We are all safe, but Michael is a prisoner of Bronze. Can you get Shirley to 'hack' into Michael? We three are staying put to see what Bronze does next.'

An orange tinge began to rise over the east of London. A new day was dawning. Roger Daube had deliberately not informed

Wattle about the Japanese code because of a genuine concern that it would complicate the situation. He didn't want to worry them anymore than he had to.

'They don't need to know,' he informed Molly and Shirley. 'Not at the moment. Mo. has said that when the 'Tasty Stretch' gum wears off, they will feel shattered and so they are waiting for the thirty minutes to pass before going back in to the warehouse. Hopefully, the three of them can then overpower Ronnie Bronze.'

'It's no use,' said Shirley. I can't read Japanese. We may have to write the 'homebot' off as 'retired, or 'RINSED'. Daube look horrified.

'Absolutely not, Shirley. There must be a way?'

'Rita Wattle is a linguist,' said Molly. I'm not sure if she can read Japanese, but I know she is proficient in Chinese.'

'The two languages bear no resemblance,' said Shirley, gloomily.

'What bears no resemblance?' It was Rita Wattle, standing in the doorway.

'Rita. What timing,' exclaimed Daube. 'Your ears must have been burning. We were just talking about you.'

Chapter 57

Ronnie Bronze was cursing and having a tantrum. He glared up at the single light bulb.

'You're lucky you're not a human, or else I would have smashed your skull with that light bulb above you. Pathetic. You worthless piece of machine.'

There was no response from Michael.

'Heavens above. Why won't the programme run? I must be able to corrupt this damn robot. If only Shirley was here. I'll kill her if I ever see her again.' He sighed and puffed his orange cheeks out. 'I am pressing COMMAND and GO.'

Bronze raged at the world around him, before finally kicking and throwing the laptop onto the concrete floor. It smashed with a loud crack, leaving Ronnie with a silent generation 4 'homebot' for company.

'I couldn't sleep,' said Mrs. Wattle. 'So, I got my sister over to make breakfast for the children and take them to school and here I am.'

'Perfect timing, Rita,' said Daube.

'Impeccable,' agree Molly.

'Pure luck, if you ask me, ' said Shirley. 'However, I have hit a brick wall, and I can't decrypt this Japanese computer programme.'

'Well, I will do my level best. Let me have a look, please?'

One hour later, and progress had been made at The Wattle and Daube Detective Agency.

'I think that is it,' said Shirley. 'Let me just repeat that back to you, Rita.'

'Spot on,' replied Rita Wattle.

'Right. I'm ready. Here goes.'

There was a collective intake of breath at 188 Piccadilly.

'Done,' confirmed, Shirley. Now who fancies breakfast.? My treat.'

As the night slipped away, Wattle, Ocean and Mo, lay exhausted on the floor by a refuse bin.

'I can hardly move a muscle,' groaned Wattle.

'Me too,' said Mo.

'I feel awful. It's like I have the flu.. Nevertheless, we can't abandon Michael. We have to act.'

'Ocean's right,' said Mo. 'We've got to capture Ronnie Bronze and rescue Michael.'

'You're absolutely right guys. No matter how rough we feel, there are three of us, to his one. Come on. Now that we are back to normal size, those stairs shouldn't be too tiring. Don't you agree? Frank? Mo?'

'Yes Ocean,' replied the two males. You lead, and we'll follow.

Bronze was sat on the cold concrete floor, muttering to himself. He noticed a shadow appear in front of him and turned around. Standing tall and strong, stood Michael. He picked Bronze up with one hand and hurled him into the gloom of the warehouse.

Two seconds later and Michael was standing over him, once more. He tossed Ronnie Bronze into the air as if he was a piece of paper. Crunch. Bronze was hurled into a wall and then smashed against the hard floor. The robot had gained superhuman powers of strength, speed and agility. He loomed mightily over the criminal and was just about to smash his brains in to the wall, when he suddenly froze.

Ronnie Bronze stared up, petrified and shaking. He was cowering in a corner and whimpering; 'No more. I beg you. No more. I can't take it. Forgive me. I am a nasty man, but please don't kill me. Please.'

'Ronnie, I presume. Nice to meet you, mate.' Frank Wattle handcuffed the criminal and patted him on the head.

'Robots eh. They just don't comprehend when they are down and out. One minute they are limp and lame, the next they have the strength of a thousand lions. Machines, Ronnie. Who can fathom them out.'

Frank Wattle coughed, and wheezed, as he made his big speech.

'I, Frank Wattle, in the powers invested in me by the municipal city of London town, do arrest you under the authority and license of The Wattle and Daube Detective Agency – At Your Service. Anything you do say will be used as evidence in a court of law. Do you understand?'

Ronnie Bronze, merely scowled up at Wattle.

'I do like that speech,' said Mo. 'Very impressive. Can I have some handcuffs like those?'

'No,' replied Wattle. 'Now help me drag this human waste downstairs. Ocean?

'Yes.'

'Can you retina the lizard police, and get them to meet us outside The Avery Building. KEYS are going to be very interested in becoming reacquainted with you, Ronnie. How do you feel about a spell of mind extraction?'

'No. No . No,' wailed Bronze. Not mind extraction again. I can't bare it. Anything else. Please?'

His begging fell on deaf ears and all that could be heard as Bronze was dragged outside, was a crazed life-long criminal moaning to himself.

Chapter 58

The following day was to prove momentous in more ways than one. Michael had managed to salvage his date with Breeze. It was scheduled for this evening and Roger Daube had agreed to see a 'mystic' in the Oriental quarter. He had admitted to Ocean that he was willing to seek help to fathom the symbolic meaning of the three chocolate letters; and last but not least, Ocean had kind of made peace with her mum.

The formidable strength and power of Michael had been corrected by rewriting the Japanese programme codes that had transformed him in to a ninja warrior. Shirley had then replaced his software settings with the original generation 4 'homebot' mode and Michael had returned to being Michael, the robot. A kind and gentle soul. Fortunately, he had no recollection of his rampaging heroics which was just as well, for all concerned.

Wattle and Ocean had given him sound advice about his date and Wattle had even replaced his box of Belgian chocolates, which had been eaten by Bronze and his cronies. Daube had suggested the theatre, but Wattle had over-ruled him, saying it was too formal for a first date. A meeting at the entrance to the night market on the embankment was agreed by all, as being more suitable. 'Casual but interesting', was Wattle's description.

The evening sky had been lit up by cosmic radiation and solar flares racing across the galaxy. It was a spectacular light show, that left Londoners watching on in awe. Even JOYCE, the computer traffic control system had altered the drone travel patterns, to allow passengers a better view of nature's firework display.

Roger Daube had finally, and at Ocean's insistence, opened up about his troubled childhood. He had agreed to seek help, and with Wattle and Ocean's support, he had plucked up the courage to see a 'mystic'. Wattle had done his homework, and a Japanese/Korean lady was chosen and an appointment made.

Ocean had got her mother's agreement to travel with Daube and the school had consented. Because of the trauma of her grandmother's death, she was given permission to have the remainder of the week off school, but with the instruction, that she caught up with her studies the following week.

'Be strong Roger,' was Wattle's advice. 'The truth can't be any more disturbing than the dreams you've had.'

Daube nodded, in an uncertain manner, and set off for the Oriental district. The stage was set.

Climbing out of the drone with Ocean, he inhaled the pungent smells emanating from the street and started to walk towards a thin concrete building, which was wedged between a computer chip repair shop and an electric bicycle store. A shiny metallic plaque contained ten names. Cautiously, Daube pressed the button at the bottom. The door slid silently open, and Ocean and Daube wedged themselves into the thinnest lift in London and headed for the tenth and top floor.

The mystic was no more than forty years of age. She wore a kimono and was holding a Japanese painted fan, which she gently wafted backwards and forwards.

She bowed, and said her name was Aki. Daube and Ocean returned the bow, and waited to be seated. They were both offered green tea.

'Please sit crossed legged on the floor,' instructed Aki Funjima. 'We will sit in a circle and I would wish for your young friend to join us as well. We will be creating a ring of trust that only fire can destroy.'

She formally bowed another three times, lit three incense candles, and switched off the lights.

'Please, hold hands. I must feel the energy flow between us. Only when I can feel the trust can I begin to read the memory shards,' she said. 'I must have total compliance. Do you understand, Mr. Roger, Arthur, Daube.'

'I do, Ms. Funjima?'

'Perfect. Close your eyes please, and let your mind become free. Allow your thoughts to escape without resistance.'

Daube complied, and felt his life energy drain from his body. He went limp.

'This is your time. You will embrace the future, challenge the present, and accept the past.'

The mystic's body juddered. 'You have experienced a glitch within a dream from a memory shard. The ghost you saw holding a gasoline lamp is the physical representation of the glitch.'

'Breathe slowly and relax. Let your past cleanse your here and now. I see three initials. Each letter represents your memory shard.'

Aki Funjina shook and began to wail.

'Speak to me. Unfold your deepest secrets. There can be no regret. Ah. I feel it. Yes, I feel the passage of time being released Roger Arthur Daube.'

'The three shards, shall speak to me, come to me, envelop me. I will now intercept these memories. Cleanse your mind, Roger. Sweep the past aside.'

The air was thick with incense and tension.

'R stands for REVEAL. Your childhood & the importance of relationships.

A stands for ACHIEVE. Embrace your life and overcome adversity.

D stands for DESTINY. Open yourself emotionally and reach out and touch your future. '

'Only by accepting and embracing this instruction can you, Roger, Arthur, Daube prevent the glitch from reappearing. Conquer your fears and flush the doubts from your mind.'

'Repeat after me; REVEAL, ACHIEVE, DESTINY.'

Daube began to repeat the three words, each time speaking them louder and louder.

Ms. Funjima, suddenly and violently began to screech and yell in Japanese. Incoherent and savage in her movements, no sooner had it started, than it had finished. She collapsed on the floor, panting and breathing .

'Release. It is over. I have seen into your past, present and future. The glitch has been revealed.'

Aki Funjima opened her eyes and stared at Daube.

'Unlock your hands. The fire of uncertainty and rage cannot enter our circle. It is over. It is complete.'

Roger Daube and Ocean Jones returned to the agency. Daube was emotionally shattered and exhausted.

'Roger, I can truthfully say, that since I have met you, I have felt less inclined to search for my absent father. It is as if you have become my surrogate father figure. Are you ok with that?'

'I am delighted,' repeated Daube. 'Nothing would give me greater pleasure, than to be a replacement father. I have always wanted a daughter.'

'Don't be fooled, Roger. They can be trouble. I'm just warning you,' said Wattle. 'No, seriously folks. I'm delighted for the two of you. Only, I don't want any family squabbles being brought into the agency. Is that clear? Who fancies a hot drink?'

'I thought we were boycotting the talking vending machine,' said Daube.

'Bygones Roger. Bygones. It's all in the past.'

'Roger?'

'Yes, Ocean. What is it?'

'I have a question for you.'

'What is it?'

The red telephone booth. The entrance to memory lane. Was it real or just a figment of your imagination?'

'It doesn't physically exist,' replied Daube. 'I had to concentrate and conjure the telephone booth. It was a portal to an imaginary world.'

'Then how is it, that on one occasion I actually saw the red telephone booth, and the next time I couldn't?'

'Synchronicity. Our minds became one. We were on the same wave length. An extremely rare feat.'

Ocean had returned to Muswell Hill, and Wattle had decided to call it a day. Roger Daube completed some paperwork, and went home to Farm Street. Michael was absent, which was a pity, as Daube wanted to share his experience in the Oriental district.

Never mind, he thought. He can tell me how his date went in the morning. ' could do with an early night.

He settled in for the evening, and after making himself a cup of jasmine tea, went upstairs. Sitting upright in his spotless bedroom, Daube reflected on the week's events and the Ronnie Bronze case. It had been another success story for his little company. The Wattle and Daube Detective Agency.

He yawned, cleaned his teeth, and went in search of a small book of traditional poems he had read as a child. He discovered the book in his library, residing amongst the hundreds of hardcovers he had collected over the years.

As he made his way upstairs, he stared at the well-worn cover, and realized that he hadn't read this particular book in over twenty years. Plumping up his pillows, Daube checked the index, and went straight to page ninety nine. The poem was untitled and uncredited.

Walk a little slower, Daddy,
Said a child so small.
I'm following in your footsteps
and I don't want to fall.

Sometimes your steps are very fast,
Sometimes they're hard to see.
So, walk a little slower, daddy,
For you are leading me.

Someday when I'm all grown up,
You're what I want to be.
Then I will have a little child
Who'll want to follow me.

And I would want to lead just right,
And know that I was true.
So, walk a little slower, Daddy
For I must follow you.

Written in a spider like scrawl on the inside cover, Daube read the following;

'Life is a journey, and I will commit fully to the adventure. It is the only life we have, and I am going to embrace it.'

The signature was his father's.

Daube reread the poem, and started to sob. Gently at first, and then louder until it was a full-blown crescendo. The tears streamed down his cheeks. Nobody heard.

He felt extremely tired. In the peaceful dark of his bedroom., Roger Daube sighed, and muttered to himself;

'Save me. If it is not too late, save me.'

He closed his weary eyes, and quietly, slipped away.

THE END